Cast of C

Dorothy "Duds" Lethbridge. L: depressed and thinks a Christmas houseparty will lift her spirits. Is she ever wrong.

Tommy Lethbridge. He's back from duty on a minesweeper and recently inherited Old Place, a smallish Buckinghamshire manor house. He's devoted to Duds, whether she knows it all the time or not.

Flo Harnet Pinhorn. One of two 25-year-old twins, cousins to Duds. She's the nice one.

Jo Harnet. The other twin, she's not so nice and ought to know that at Christmas time someone is making a list and checking it twice.

Gordon Pinhorn. Flo's handsome husband. He's a pleasant enough fellow but there's something about him that is just a bit off-putting to Tommy and Lupin.

Sandy Ferguson. Another of Duds' cousins, he spent the war in a German POW camp. He's angry and depressed, perhaps because of unrequited love. He drinks as if he doesn't know gin is rationed.

Henry Dumbleton. He's an old flame of Duds—she was very young at the time—who still appears to be on the prowl, though he's married to a very devoted woman. He thinks he's an expert on everything.

Irene Dumbleton. She's a bore but good-hearted and certainly knows how to stand by her man.

Mr. Veazey. Jo's boss, he's a publisher. He's got a secret.

Olivia Ordemar. Veazey's wife and also one of his authors. She has a proposal that chills Tommy to the core.

Sir John and Lady Holroyd. Relations of Olivia's and neighbors of the Lethbridges.

Mr. Borden. A private detective who occasionally helps Lady Lupin.

Lady Lupin. She married the much older Vicar of Glanville when she was quite young and is absolutely devoted to him and her two children. She may be scatterbrained but somehow she always manages to get at the truth. She's no judge of fresh fish, however.

Plus assorted servants, children, and villagers.

Books by Joan Coggin

The Lady Lupin Quartet

Who Killed the Curate? (1944)
The Mystery of Orchard House (1946)
Why Did She Die? (1947)
(U.S. title: *Penelope Passes or Why Did She Die?*)
Dancing with Death (1947*)
*Note: Some sources give 1949 as the
publication year.

Girls' Books

Betty of Turner House (1935)
Catherine Goes to School (1945)
Jane Runs Away from School (1946)
Catherine, Head of House (1947)
Audrey, a New Girl (1948)
Three New Girls (1949)

Dancing
with
Death

A Lady Lupin Mystery

---

by
Joan Coggin

Rue Morgue Press
Boulder / Lyons

FIRST AMERICAN EDITION

ISBN: 0-915230-62-3

The editors thank William F. Deeck
and Katherine Hall Page
for bringing the Lady Lupin
mysteries to their attention.

PRINTED IN THE UNITED STATES OF AMERICA

About Joan Coggin

In *Who Killed the Curate?* (1944), we were introduced to the lovely Lady Lupin Lorrimer, a 21-year-old earl's daughter who unexpectedly married 43-year-old Andrew Hastings, vicar of St. Mark's parish in Glanville in Sussex. Totally unprepared for the duties incumbent upon a clergyman's wife (she often confused Jews with Jesuits), somehow Lupin managed to soldier on, gladly abandoning her previous life of parties and indolence to be with her soulmate. As scatterbrained as she was, Lupin's tender heart and genuine concern for others won over even those parishioners who thought her too young and too pretty to be a vicar's wife, and her unconventional thought processes still pointed the way to identifying the murderer in this debut mystery.

The Mystery of Orchard House (1946) takes up her story over two years later, again in some indefinite period shortly before World War II. Lupin now has a two-year-old son, Peter, but a recent bout of influenza has forced her to leave him in the care of her husband and her old nanny while she takes a rest cure in the country at the hotel run by her good friend Diana Turner, a children's book writer. There's little rest in store for her, unfortunately, and once again Lupin's peculiar talent for getting at the truth, however circuitous a route she might take, comes in handy when the eccentric guests at Orchard House are plagued by a series of thefts and an attempted murder.

The final two books in the series, *Why Did She Die?* (1947)— published in the U.S. as *Penelope Passes or Why Did She Die?*—and

Dancing with Death (1947, although some sources say 1949) are set just after World War II. *Dancing with Death,* in fact, is a marvelous portrait of the postwar austerity in Britain, in addition to being perhaps the best plotted book in the series. The first and fourth are the more clearly identifiable as traditional detective stories, although all four fit comfortably in the genre. All were originally published by Hurst & Blackett, a relatively obscure and long-since defunct London publishing house, in what must have been fiendishly small print runs, as they are extraordinarily difficult to find on the used-book market. None was ever published in the United States. *Why Did She Die?* appears to have been written and published in a great hurry, since the original book is filled with typos and two of the characters are given more than one name.

In addition to her four mysteries, Coggin, using the pseudonym Joanna Lloyd, wrote six girls' books set at the imaginary Shaftesbury School and based on Coggin's own school years at Wycombe Abbey. These stories are as charmingly told as Coggin's mysteries, and indeed the young Catherine, who figures in several of these books, bears a remarkable resemblance to Lady Lupin, although unlike Lupin, there's no doubt that Catherine has a first-class mind. Both Lupin and Catherine have problems with fish, however, which is a running joke throughout the Lupin series

Born in Lemsford, Hertfordshire, in 1898, Coggin was the granddaughter on her mother's side of Edward Lloyd, founder of *Lloyd's Weekly London Newspaper*, which no doubt is why she used Lloyd as a pseudonym for her schoolgirl books. Her mother died when Coggin was eight and the family moved to Eastbourne, one of the easternmost towns in Britain, where she was to make her home for the rest of her life and which was clearly the model for Glanville.

After she was graduated from Wycombe Abbey in 1916 in the middle of World War I, Coggin worked as a nurse at an Eastbourne hospital. Although she suffered from a mild form of epilepsy, Coggin did not let it inhibit her lifestyle. After the war, she returned to those activities expected of a young woman of her class and upbringing—the social round of bridge, tennis, golf and books. She also worked with the blind.

In the 1930s, she turned to writing, producing her first girls' book, *Betty of Turner House*, in 1935. With the exception of that book Coggin's writing career was limited to a five-year period between 1944 and 1949, during which she produced nine books. For the last thirty years of her life she apparently did no more writing. She died in 1980 at the age of 82.

Her contribution to crime fiction was slight but memorable. Lupin, probably the first clergyman's wife to take up crime-solving as a hobby, may remind readers of Gracie Allen of Burns and Allen. She's certainly the spiritual godmother of the Pauline Collins character in the very funny BBC comedy series *No, Honestly* from a few years ago. The Collins character came many years later, of course, and although Coggin may well have been familiar with Gracie Allen's routines, there is little doubt that Lady Lupin sprang fullblown from Coggin's own imagination. She's that rarity in cozy crime fiction—in spite of her many eccentricities she seems more real than most of the people we encounter in real life. Or maybe that's just wishful thinking.

Tom & Enid Schantz
Boulder, Colorado

Dancing
with
Death

CHAPTER 1

"AM IN GREAT TROUBLE, please come at once. Duds." Lady Lupin Hastings read the telegram through twice, with a puzzled expression on her pretty face, then she handed it back to her maid. "Staines," she said, "can you make head or tail of this?"

Staines had been with Lupin since she was a girl. She had come with her, as lady's maid, when she left Lorrimer Castle for Glanville Vicarage. Now she did nearly all the work of the house and a great deal of the work of the parish. She adjusted her pince-nez and took the flimsy piece of paper. "I fancy, my lady, that this is from Mrs. Lethbridge and that she is in trouble."

"Yes, I know. But how and why?"

Staines read the message once more. "She does not say, my lady."

"It really is most inconvenient," grumbled Lupin. "There is the Sunday school treat tomorrow and the Good Wives' Fellowship in the evening, and the next day it is the Mothers' Union and Nanny's afternoon out."

"I daresay Nurse would kindly change her day to tomorrow, my lady, in which case I could take Master Peter and Miss Jill to the Sunday school treat."

"That's a good idea, but don't let them make themselves sick, and don't let them grab all the best things for themselves, it does look so bad. And for pity's sake don't let Peter fight any of the other children. He always wins and then the mother of the other child won't let it come to

Sunday school any more, and that upsets the vicar. Talking of the vicar, whatever will he think when he comes back tonight and finds that I have gone away?"

"I could tell him that you have gone to Mrs. Lethbridge's, my lady."

"So you could, and you will have to go to the Good Wives' Fellowship tomorrow evening too, not that you are exactly a good wife, but then no more am I, if it comes to that. I always forget that Mr. Hastings can't eat pastry at night, and that he doesn't like one to use his nail scissors for cutting string. I think that they are having a discussion, the wives I mean, about religion or food or something of that sort. I suppose you will have to take the chair."

"Perhaps it would be best, my lady, if I were just to go round and say that you had been called away and would be glad if one of the other ladies would take the chair in your place, my not being a wife, so to speak."

"But if you ask one of them to take the chair, the others will all walk out and there will be no discussion. Not that that would be a bad thing, as discussions so often lead to unpleasantness."

"Should I suggest that they vote themselves a chairman, a secret ballot as they say?"

"Absolutely! Good idea! It must be very secret. Just the thing! With any luck it will keep them quiet and happy for the whole evening. Remember to take down plenty of paper and pencils and India rubbers. Oh, I know what the discussion was: 'What should one do with a disobedient child?' I know what I should do, give it a good smack. Jill, what on earth are you doing?" Five-year-old Jill had just marched into the room in her pajamas, having grown tired of her afternoon rest. "You awful child, don't you realize that it is the coldest day there has ever been, and you will be frozen, and anyway you ought to be asleep—go back to bed at once."

"Want to hear about the free bears."

"Oh bother. I'll just have to run up and tell her the story, Staines, then I'll come down and we'll arrange about the Mothers' Union. You might be looking up some trains."

As Lupin came downstairs she heard voices in the library and found eight-year-old Peter, who was home for the holidays after his first term at school, sitting on the floor assembling the pieces of his model airplane. His father's papers lay all around him, as he had accidentally knocked them off the table while looking for some glue.

"Peter, this is Daddy's zone. What are you doing in it? Take your airplane up to the nursery."

"There is a better landing-ground here. Look, Mummy, do you think that bit goes in there?"

"I shouldn't think so. And there is Daddy's sermon all over the floor, or is it his income tax returns? Anyway, whatever it is, it is all stuck together and will never be any good again. Talk about children trailing clouds of glory! Oh, and about the Mothers' Union, Staines. I think they will run their own party all right. Mrs. Smythe will do the refreshments. I had made out a list of games, but I don't know where it is, and anyway I don't expect they will want any suggestions. Oh, I know where I put it, inside my ration book so that I should know where it was, or was it my prayer book? But don't make any suggestions unless they ask you for them, just hover about helpfully, if you know what I mean. Oh, are those the trains? Glanville, 4:10; Victoria, 5:45 Paddington, 6:20; yes, but how? There won't be any taxis. Fordham, 7:30. I shall be far too exhausted by then to be of any help to anyone, even if I catch the 6:20, which is very doubtful. Oh, there you are, Nanny. Do you think you could get Peter to go up to the nursery? Oh dear, that's the picture of me as a bride," as Peter's airplane suddenly and unexpectedly flew across the room and collided with a framed photograph. "No one will know now that I was ever married and I will have to resign from the Good Wives' Fellowship. I have got to run off into Buckinghamshire immediately to Mrs. Lethbridge. Staines will tell you all about it, not that we know anything, but you will be able to cope between you, won't you? And do you think you could possibly change your afternoon to tomorrow? What is the time? I will have to fly. Staines, will you order a taxi, while I put some things together?"

"I hope Mrs. Lethbridge is not ill, my lady. I will get you a cup of tea while Miss Staines rings up the taxi and packs your case. Go up to the nursery at once, Peter. Don't you worry about anything, my lady. Everything will be all right." And Nanny walked out of the room followed by Peter.

"Well, it is a good thing mine are obedient children," said Lupin. "Obedient to Nanny, I mean," she added, on second thought.

Staines accompanied her mistress to the station and saw her into the train. "You will explain everything to Mr. Hastings, won't you, Staines?" said Lupin, as the porter arranged her case on the rack.

"Yes, my lady," and Staines descended to the platform.

A good many of the citizens of Glanville were seeing off their Christmas visitors by this train and the usually quiet platform was quite crowded.

Lupin leaned out of the window, calling out last-minute instructions. "I am sorry to have landed you with the Sunday school treat, it is sure to be pretty frightful, but you need not take any active part, except in stopping Peter and Jill from getting too rough. And you know about the Good Wives' Fellowship and the Mothers' Union. I don't think there is anything else. Remind Mr. Hastings about the parish council meeting tomorrow. And I believe the Boy Scouts were doing something some time this week and he promised to look in, or was it the Darts Club? And don't let him forget his Eno's each morning, whatever you do. It makes all the difference. And then of course there will be some services in church you know, see that he goes to them."

"I am sure Mr. Hastings will remember them, my lady."

"Let's hope so." By this time the train had started and Staines had to hurry along beside it to hear her mistress's last words.

"Don't let the vicar gobble his food," Lupin called out clearly.

"Very good, my lady," called back Staines.

Lupin sank into her seat and took a letter out of her bag.

Dearest Loops,

Many thanks for the records. My dear, this is the scaliest Christmas I have ever had. I thought it would be fun to have a real old-fashioned Christmas houseparty, so I asked a few friends and relations. Naturally I wanted to ask you and Andrew, but Tommy said you would be having services and confirmations and youth movements. I asked Flo and Jo, you remember them, they were bridesmaids with you at my wedding, and Sandy Ferguson who is a sort of cousin too, and then I had a letter from Henry Dumbleton asking if he might bring his new wife, so I said 'yes, delighted,' and he has turned out too frightful, or was he always like that ? Anyway, Tommy says he will murder him before the week is out, Christmas or no Christmas!

Lupin put down the letter and looked out of the window. Of course she had not taken it seriously when she received it. It was the sort of thing anyone might say, but the telegram had put a different complexion on it. It seemed impossible think of Tommy, good-natured, happy-go-lucky Tommy, committing a murder. From what Lupin remembered of Henry he was just the type that called for a spot of murder. But that did not mean that she wanted him to be murdered and at any rate not by the husband of her best friend.

Lupin and Duds had been friends since their childhood. They had gone to their first parties together. Then Duds had married Tommy and Lupin had enjoyed paying her frequent visits. It had been refreshing to exchange the county society that surrounded Lorrimer Castle for the more free and easy atmosphere of the Lethbridges' circle. She had not hesitated a moment in responding to Dud's telegram, but she could not help wishing that her friends did not so frequently get involved in murder cases. It was a funny thing, she reflected, but since her marriage she had already been involved in three ordeals of this kind. It is true that one had turned out to be an accident and another a suicide, but it had all been very harrowing, especially when two of her friends had actually spent several days in prison.

She wondered if Tommy were in prison. Was there any chance of this turning out to be an accident? She hoped for the best, but she had not much hope. She knew Henry. Surely he and Duds had not restarted their old flirtation. Surely she would not have been so silly, she was devoted to Tommy. But men never understood how difficult it was to resist a flirtation at times, especially with an old flame, although it meant absolutely nothing at all. She was sure Andrew would understand, but then there was no other husband like Andrew. And of course such a thing would not arise in their case, as flirting would not be becoming in a clergyman's wife. She sighed a little at this reflection. Still, being married to Andrew made up for everything.

Her thoughts turned back to Duds and Tommy. Duds had probably just had a twilight touch with Henry—just the eeriest recollection of old times, a squeeze of the hand, a chaste kiss, and in had burst Tommy, all caveman, and had knocked Henry down. Unfortunately Henry had caught his head against the table in falling, or on the curb of the fender, or perhaps he had had a heart attack and conked out that way. Tommy had not meant to kill him. It really was an accident, and that was the line they must take. She did hope he and Duds had not done anything silly, like pretending they had not touched him or faking an alibi, that would look suspicious at once. The truth, the whole truth and nothing but the truth was much the safest card to play unless one had actually committed a murder, which she was sure Tommy hadn't. Of course he might be imprisoned for a bit for manslaughter. It was all very, very sad. Poor Tommy, poor, poor Duds!

Lupin sighed heavily and wished that she were back at Glanville, even though it was the Sunday school treat tomorrow. She would rather be coping with sticky children, weeping children, sick children, or quarrelsome children. She would rather even cope with their parents than with a brokenhearted Duds and a Tommy accused of murder.

CHAPTER 2

"DO LET"S HAVE a real old-fashioned Christmas this year," suggested Duds Lethbridge to her husband.

"Why?" asked Tommy.

"Oh, I don't know, but life is so dreary nowadays,with nothing to eat, nothing to drink, and nothing to wear, and no way of keeping warm."

"And you think you would like to have one of those Christmases we used to have, with blazing yule logs, groaning tables and bowls of punch?"

"Well, it would be rather nice, wouldn't it?"

"It would. You had better write to the Minister of Fuel, the Minister of Food, and the Minister of Drink and see what they can do about it."

"Talking of ministers, we must have Lupin."

"What has she to do with ministers? Is she in with some of them? If you think she will be able to work us some extra rations, contact her by all means."

"I mean she is married to a minister."

"Oh, I see what you mean. I never thought of Andrew as a minister. The word seems to go with muttonchop whiskers and a frock coat. But in any case, though I am not well up in the subject, I don't think ministers or clergymen and their wives go gallivanting about at Christmas-time. They go round their parish singing carols, they hold services, they have Sunday school treats and youth rallies and gatherings of young wives and old spinsters and good mothers and hearty lads and so on."

"Oh dear, I am rather glad I didn't marry a clergyman, though of course Andrew is much better looking than you are. But it must be a very tiring life. It won't be nearly such fun without Lupin," she added sadly.

"No, no more it will. Let's put it off until she can come. I suppose there is a close season in the church some time, isn't there?"

"I wouldn't know. But as far as I remember Lent comes pretty soon and I'm not sure that Septuagesima doesn't come first and then of course there is Easter. Anyway, what I want is a real Christmas party like we used to have before the war."

"But how?"

"We will have to pretend, of course, but surely we can do that. After all in the old days it wasn't just eating and drinking, it was the atmosphere of the thing—that is what we want to get back. We will decorate the house with holly and ivy, and we will play silly games, and we will go to church on Christmas Day and sing 'Hark! the herald angels sing,' and there will be the Hunt Ball, and oh, do let's, Tommy."

"Right you are, of course we will if you like," said her husband. It was nice to see Duds eager and excited again. The war years had told on her. She had had a job at the Admiralty while he had been at sea on a minesweeper, and it was the separation and the anxiety about each other that had got them down. They were a particularly devoted couple. In nineteen thirty-nine they were still in their twenties, living a carefree, hand to mouth existence. Now they were halfway through the thirties and felt themselves older than their years.

An uncle of Tommy's had died during the war and had left him this pleasant old farmhouse and surrounding hundred acres, together with just enough money to live on. They were beginning to settle down at last and were full of plans for the future. Already they had chickens and rabbits and were thinking of pigs and perhaps a cow or two, and Tommy was hoping to make something out of the vegetable garden. They were both liking country life. Although they had enjoyed their years in London as a young married couple, they had both been brought up in the country and were very glad to return to it, now that they were no longer so very young. They had brought their hospitable habits with them, and though happy alone, they both, especially Duds, dearly loved a party. As she looked at the old-fashioned hall and the lovely staircase leading from it, she imagined it full of a happy excited crowd of friends. As she had said, they could pretend about the food and drink; so long as they all laughed and joked the whole time, nothing else would matter. They would recapture the real Christmas atmosphere.

"I tell you what," she said aloud, "we will ask the people for a week, and then they will bring their ration books. The more people and ration books there are, the further the food goes. I suppose we don't know any vegetarians or Jews, do we?"

"Why Jews?"

"They don't eat bacon. But I tell you whom I want to ask most awfully—Flo and Jo."

"What don't they eat?"

"I don't know, but I shouldn't think they have very big appetites. They have got such lovely figures and they are at the age when they will think about their complexions and will refuse gin."

"They are not likely to have an opportunity of doing that."

"Surely you can get a bottle from somewhere, and do stop being such a wet blanket. After all, we don't know how long the peace will last, so let's have a little pleasure while we can. We shall feel pretty sick when the next war breaks out if we have wasted the whole of the time in between. At least it will be something, as we fly asunder, to be able to say to ourselves, 'Well, anyhow, we enjoyed ourselves while we could.' "

"I shouldn't think we will have much time to make a dying speech."

"Oh, do be quiet. I think I know where I can get a turkey, and Mrs. Elphick will let me have a rabbit if ours aren't ready, and Edith's young man has a friend who might be able to lay his hand on a hare, and all being well we shall have our own eggs. I don't see why we shouldn't manage quite well."

"Well, I daresay I could lay my hands on a bottle or two."

"Good! I don't expect anyone will want a lot to drink, but it is nice to have an occasional glass. It gives one the party feeling. I wonder if we could get a Christmas tree."

"Who are we going to ask to this do? There are your two young cousins and their husband, so far."

Duds laughed. "It is Flo's husband. As a matter of fact, it does seem funny to think of one of them being married and not the other. I went to the wedding. You remember, I wrote and told you about it. He looked awfully nice, but I can never think of the twins as grown up, though as a matter of fact they must be twenty-five. The war has used up a lot of time, hasn't it?"

"I remember them at our wedding. Pretty girls, but one couldn't

tell one from t'other. Oh, and we spent a Christmas there just before the war. I kept thinking I'd had one over the eight whenever I
saw them."

"It wouldn't seem like a real Christmas without them. I always
used to stay with them when they were little, and they were such
darlings. I used to help fill their stockings. I know what, we will give
everyone a stocking on Christmas Day—we can find all sorts of little
things."

"Good idea! But who else are we going to have? Just Flo and Jo
and Jo's husband?"

"Flo's husband, darling. I wish we could think of some one exciting for Jo."

"I don't think I know anyone very exciting. Besides, all my friends
are married."

"Nor do I, and if we did they wouldn't fit in very well, would
they?"

"Probably Jo has got plenty of young men of her own already
and will quite enjoy a rest from them. Haven't they just come in for
a pot of money or something?"

"Yes, their grandfather died. The one on the other side, if you
know what I mean—none of my grandfathers ever had any money.
He left rather a funny will."

"How do you mean, funny?"

"He left everything to his eldest grandchild."

"Rather sickening for the others!"

"Yes, I thought it rather unfair. I suppose he didn't want the estate
divided up, but anyhow it didn't matter, because there were only the
twins, at least I've never heard of any others, so naturally they would
divide it between them."

"Did they?"

"I suppose so. It turned out that Flo was actually the older of
the two, so she inherited it, but I am sure she would have divided it
up with Jo. They always shared everything. Oh, by the way, talking
of cousins, do let's ask Sandy. He always used to be there in the old
days and it will seem just like old times to have him too. They were
all three such great friends. He was a prisoner of war in Germany,
poor old thing, and I haven't seen him since he came back. He'll
love a real old Christmas party and I'll love to have him. He is
always so cheerful and amusing."

"I remember him, a decent chap. He is another cousin of yours, isn't he?"

"Once removed or something. His cousin was a cousin of our mothers, the twins and mine, I mean."

"Well, that will be four. So long as they bring their ration books with them, I don't see any snag. What about the housework and all that?"

"Mrs. Elphick will come in and give a hand and the twins will help. It will be rather a picnic, but that will be all the more fun."

Duds wrote off to the twins and Sandy, visited Mrs. Elphick and secured her services for Christmas week. She also got into touch with all those who might have access to chickens, rabbits, hares or any other form of unrationed food. When she got in the second post had just arrived and she found a letter awaiting her, addressed in a familiar handwriting.

She looked at the envelope for a minute or two, recalling old sensations. Once her heart would have leapt at the sight of that writing. She had been very much in love with Henry Dumbleton when she was a girl. How long ago was it? Ten years, fifteen years? And was it really love? No, she knew now that it wasn't. But it had passed for love then. She was only twenty and Henry had been thirty and a married man. She was used to boys being in love with her, but this was thing different, more exciting. To be sought by a man of the world, a married man and a man of experience, was an irresistible compliment.

She had been thrilled by him. She remembered the evening that he had first kissed her. It had been in a garden during a dance, and it had been June. The air had been full of night-scented stock and tobacco plant. The moon had shone down on them, and beyond them was the sea. What a night for romance! Even now she remembered that evening as the most romantic of her life. It had been a hectic period after that, full of surreptitious meetings. It had not been a happy time; it was exciting and restless and unsatisfying. She had realized by degrees that Henry was not one to whom the world would be well lost for love. He enjoyed his respectability. He was a well-known lawyer and a sidesman of his church, and he had no wish to endanger his position. Gradually this had dawned on Duds, gradually she had realized that he did not love her. Still more gradually, she had realized that she did not love him. There had been months of unhappiness and of disillusion, then she had met Tommy and had realized that what she had mistaken for love was indeed an ersatz' article, a utility sort of love, as she told herself now, with a smile for the girl she had been.

Henry Dumbleton's wife had died some years ago and not very long after he had taken another one, a widow with some money. Duds had met them and had casually suggested that they should come down and pay them a visit some time. She had made this suggestion as one does make such suggestions, partly for something to say, partly to show a friendly feeling and partly, perhaps, to show Henry that he had no longer any power over her.

She opened the letter.

Dear Duds,

You very kindly suggested that Irene and I should pay you a visit some time. I wonder if you would feel like having us for Christmas?

As you know, we have been living in a hotel for the last few years and Irene says, and I agree with her, that she hates the idea of a hotel at Christmas. Of course it may not be a convenient time for you, you may be going away or already have your house full. But I thought I would just write on the off chance, in case you and your husband did feel inclined to have us. Don't hesitate to say if it is the least bit inconvenient.

Yours as ever,
Henry P. Dumbleton.

Duds read the letter through twice. Did she want the Dumbletons? Eight was rather a good number for a houseparty, one could always make up two tables for bridge if necessary. And then, if she did not have them now she would have to have them later on, and it would be easier to have them when there were other people in the house than alone. There would be plenty going on all the time, and the other guests could entertain them if she and Tommy were too busy. Henry did not seem at all embarrassed at the thought of staying in the same house, so there was no reason why she should be either. The past was dead as far as they were concerned.

She went out to look for Tommy and handed him the letter. Of course he did not know about her relations with Henry, not that he would have worried if he had.

"The man like a codfish?" he inquired. "He married rather an attractive widow, didn't he? Oh well, if we've got to have them, we may as well have them with the rest of the party and have done with it. Christmas at Dingley Dell! The squire and his wife keep open house, etcetera!"

Duds laughed and went in to write to Mrs. Dumbleton. She was really very excited. A real Christmas once again! What fun it would be to see the twins and Sandy, and Henry being here would just lend a spice of . . . well, a spice of what? she wondered. Just the recollection of night-scented stock, just the recollection that once she had been young and foolish—

"Oh, Tommy," she said, when she met him at teatime, "it is going to be such fun."

CHAPTER 3

TOMMY had become quite infected with Duds' enthusiasm. They were a simple couple and enjoyed simple pleasures. The long years of war and the disappointments of the peace had left them both with a yearning for the old days of careless gaiety. Tommy had collected a fine assortment of wood and there was a really splendid fire in the hall. They had decorated everywhere with ivy and holly and the scene was truly Dickensian, with the firelight flickering on the holly berries and the tea table spread with scones and cake and homemade jam.

"This is going to be a really lovely Christmas," thought Duds excitedly. "We will all pretend to be young again." And she ran to the front door as she heard the sound of a car. She hadn't seen anything of her cousins Florence and Josephine during the last seven years except for a brief glimpse at Florence's wedding. One of them, she thought Flo, was in the W.R.N.S. and the other in the W.A.A.F.S., but she thought of them as they had been before the war, as children with whom she had played and as quite young girls whom she had taken to parties. She was glad she had thought of the stockings. They would bring back happy recollections of the old days and would create a real Christmasy atmosphere. It had been great fun collecting the things for them. She and Tommy had saved their month's sweet ration so that there were packets of chocolate in each stocking.

There was a handkerchief or two, a little vase with 'A present from Eastbourne' on it in one, and in another a funny little pincushion between two shells. There were pencils and sticks of sealing wax, packets of envelopes, lavender sachets, pocket diaries and other oddments from the village shop. These stockings were to be put in front of each of the guests at breakfast in lieu of regular presents.

"So much more fun!" Duds had pointed out. "It is so difficult to get anything decent nowadays."

"And so expensive," replied Tommy.

Florence and Josephine were now twenty-five and were both very attractive young women, but they gave Duds a shock. She had forgotten how grown up they were. She had been picturing them as they were at her own wedding, as child bridesmaids looking exactly alike in their frocks of palest pink and wreaths of tiny rosebuds. She remembered them at the Hunt Ball, the last to which she had been and their first. They had been dressed alike then, in a lovely shade of apple green. Everyone had admired them very much, but no one had been able to tell one from the other. Now they were not in the least alike—you would not even have taken them for sisters—but they were both very smart and very sophisticated, and Duds felt suddenly conscious of the fact that her own tweeds were at least ten years old.

Gordon Pinhorn, Flo's husband, was an extremely good-looking man of about thirty with very smooth dark hair and a pleasant expression. His clothes, though perfectly quiet and in good taste, made Tommy's look as though they had been slept in.

"Duds, dear," said Florence, "how marvelous to see you again, and how lovely and Christmasy it all looks!"

"Don't speak of Christmas," begged Josephine, "it makes me tired to think of it. I made up my mind to send no cards and no presents, and of course at the last moment I found that everyone I knew had weighed in with the most expensive presents, and everyone I didn't know had sent cards. It was too devastating. Do let's forget Christmas for a bit."

This was slightly damping, but luckily at this moment a diversion was caused by the arrival of the Dumbletons. They had met Jo in London and seemed pleased to meet her again. Mrs. Dumbleton was a good-looking woman of about forty, slightly plump, well dressed, and very ready to be friendly with everyone.

"What a terrible day," she remarked as she shook hands. "I never remember it being so cold as this. In fact, they say it is fifty years since we had so cold a winter, and I should not be surprised if they were right, though I remember the year twenty-three or was it twenty-four, no, it must have been twenty-three because my brother John died in the summer of twenty-three and I remember how he enjoyed the skating, which he could not have done had it been twenty-four. But I doubt if it were really as cold as this. Of course it was different in those days because one could be as warm as one liked indoors, and it was quite pleasant coming in out of the cold, not that it isn't lovely and warm here, a really beautiful fire, isn't it, Henry?"

"A log fire is always so attractive," said Gordon, kindly.

"Logs," said Henry, "are all very well, provided there is plenty of coal underneath. But there is not much warmth in wood and if you must have a log fire you should make quite sure that the logs are all oak. I should not think these are, are they?" he inquired.

"I don't know I'm sure," replied Duds. "They are just whatever we have managed to collect."

"I thought so. A friend of ours cut down his fig tree and used the wood. The result was terrible, nothing but smoke."

"Well, there is no smoke here," pointed out Gordon. "It is a beautiful fire."

"It won't last long. I could give you the address of a man who supplies oak logs," Henry went on to Tommy, "and is absolutely reliable. If you say you are a friend of mine you can be sure of getting all oak logs. He is rather expensive, of course, but it is better to pay more and know what you've got, isn't it?"

"Thanks, but we have a lot of wood about the place," said Tommy. "I don't want to spend money on buying logs."

"It might be cheaper in the long run," persisted Henry. "You have to be very careful with these old chimneys."

Duds wondered how she could ever have been in love with Henry. She glanced at Tommy. It was quite obvious that there was no chance of one of those beautiful friendships one reads about springing up between the two men. She turned to her women guests. "Would you like to see your rooms or shall we have tea first?" she asked.

"Oh, no tea for me," said Jo. "I never touch it."

"I must do something about my face," said Flo. "The cold weather is so very unbecoming."

"Absolutely antagonizing," agreed Jo.

Duds took them all up to their rooms and, telling them that tea would be ready at once, went down to the kitchen where her faithful Edith awaited her. "They have all arrived except Mr. Ferguson," she said. "We won't wait for him."

"Suppose he doesn't come till you have finished," objected Edith. "I don't see how we can make another pot for him. How I am going to make the tea ration go round as it is, I don't know."

"You forget we will have six extra books," said Duds.

"Have you got them?" asked Edith.

"Not yet. One can hardly say 'How do you do, have you brought your ration book?' all in one breath."

"And if they have brought them, as likely as not they will have torn out their tea rations before they came."

"What an awful thought! And it isn't as if any of us were over seventy."

"My auntie might be able to let you have a little," said Edith, unbending slightly.

Duds took the tray and hurried back to the hall. Everything looked very nice and probably Jo would change her mind and have some tea when the moment came. Young people often talked in that way without meaning anything. Duds did hope that they would hurry up and come down as it was nearly five o'clock and they would have to have dinner sharp at seven-thirty, as Mrs. Elphick, 'the obliger,' would not stay after nine o'clock.

Duds looked at the homemade cake and at the scones—were they such a wonderful show as she had thought? They were nothing very much, really. She thought of the old days when there would have been all sorts of cakes, crumpets, delicious sandwiches, butter galore! Oh well, it was no use thinking of those things. They had gone beyond recall and in any case no one really ate anything at teatime now.

Bother, what were they all doing? Florence and Josephine had looked quite exquisite on arrival. What could they want to do to their faces? Duds felt sure that she was unbecomingly flushed and that her nose was shining. She was very thirsty and she was rather hungry too. They had had a very light luncheon as they were saving everything for dinner. What was Mrs. Dumbleton doing? She had one of those lovely creamy skins that are never affected by either wind or sun. Had they all brought their tea rations with them? Had they brought any rations? If they hadn't, whatever should she do? Well, it was no good worrying. If she started doing that the party would never be a success.

She did hope that Sandy would turn up soon. He would be such a tremendous help. He was always so cheerful and would put everyone into a good temper. She did think Tommy might hurry up the men a bit. He knew as well as she did how important it was to have tea in good time. She had just decided to pour out a cup for herself when Mrs. Dumbleton came down the stairs.

"Well, I shall be very glad of a cup of tea," she said, sitting down at the table. "We stopped early for lunch. I was so afraid that if we left it too late we might find everywhere crowded."

"There are a lot of people everywhere nowadays, aren't there?" agreed Duds. "I can never think why, because so many people were killed in the war and they say that the birthrate is going down, then there are all the people who are still abroad, and yet there are far more people in England than there were before the war."

"I don't like crowds," said Mrs. Dumbleton. "I should always rather have a meal a little early than have to wait for it and then be uncomfortable. As I said to Henry, 'this seems a nice clean place and we do not know how long it will be before we find anywhere else as nice.' Sometimes one passes several quite decent looking places, only to find there is nowhere else on the road for miles and by then one is too hungry to enjoy one's food, and probably there is nothing left to eat, and one has to sit at a table with other people and the place is very likely dirty, stained tablecloths and so on, and perhaps nothing to drink, not that I mind that for myself, as I very seldom do take anything to drink, I find I am better without it. Don't think I am narrow-minded, but I do think it is a pity the way quite young girls have taken to spirits. It is no wonder they have to make up their faces as they do. In the old days a young girl had a naturally good complexion, but then it was unheard of for them to drink gin as they do now. Of course there were cocktails, but one did not really know what was in them, and in any case I always used to drink tomato juice. I hate the taste of spirits."

Duds was rather glad of this and hoped that Florence and Josephine would share this distaste, as spirits were hard to come by and there would barely be enough for the men.

Tommy led Henry and Gordon into the hall. He was looking rather depressed.

"I was just telling Dorothy about the place we stopped at for lunch,"

Mrs. Dumbleton informed her husband. "It was very nice and clean, wasn't it? And the fish was quite fresh."

"It was not bad as such places go," admitted her husband. "We might have gone further and fared worse. For utter inefficiency and incompetence recommend me to an English hotel."

"I don't agree with you at all," burst out Duds, forgetting that a hostess should try to agree with her guests. "I think English hotels are very good. I would much rather take my chance of a good meal at an English hotel than at a foreign one, and as for cleanliness there is no comparison." As a matter of fact she had not had much experience of foreign travel, as until the death of Tommy's uncle they had been very badly off and usually spent their holidays staying with friends. A honeymoon in Brittany, a few days in Paris and a day trip to Ostend made up her sum of continental travel, but she had a deep-rooted dislike of hearing the institutions of her own country run down, and she disliked Henry's superior manner, the more so perhaps because once she had been impressed by it.

He looked at her with amusement. "I was thinking chiefly of America," he said. "They are far ahead of anything in this hemisphere over there. But if one knows one's way about the continent, one can always find somewhere tolerable, places not known to the ordinary tourist. Tell me next time you think of going abroad and I will give you the addresses of some hotels which I think you will agree compare favorably with any hotels in our country."

Gordon seated himself beside Duds and took the cup of tea she proffered. "Well, I am sure you will never get such a nice cup of tea anywhere else," he said pleasantly. "May I have one of those delicious looking scones?"

"Foreign cooking is very nice for a change," said Mrs. Dumbleton, "but I should not like it for any length of time—it is too rich. Good English cooking is very difficult to get, of course. I remember just before the war I had an excellent cook, but she could not get on with any of the other servants. I really did not know what to do. I did not want to lose her and yet no one would stay in the house with her. It was a case of losing her or losing the rest of the staff."

"I should have kept the cook," said Duds. "After all one can do the rest of the work oneself at a pinch, but a good cook is born, not made."

"Luckily the war came and they all went," continued Mrs. Dumbleton. "I should not say luckily, because of course the war was very sad, but it solved my difficulties, and I don't think she would have been much good during the food shortage. She was rather extravagant and I do not think she would have understood cooking without anything to cook with, so we went to a hotel where we have really been most comfortable."

"There is really no food shortage," declared Henry. "It is all a case of distribution. I happen to know personally that there is plenty of everything if you only know where to go for it."

Florence and Josephine came down the stairs and Duds was thankful for the diversion as Henry was describing the dinner he had eaten the other night and Tommy was looking rather sick.

"Come along," cried Duds, looking at her cousins and wondering if, indeed, they were the Jo and Flo she had once known so well. They were looking very lovely and they seemed to have entirely changed their clothes since they had arrived and redone their hair. She had only had a glimpse of them on arrival, but now she gazed at them in wonder. It was impossible to believe that they had ever resembled each other so closely. Florence's face was rounder than that of her sister. In fact it was a perfect oval. She wore her smooth, shining hair parted in the middle and waved back from her forehead, falling rather long onto her shoulders.

Josephine was taller than her sister and wore her hair in a coronet of curls. Duds did not care for this fashion as a rule but it certainly suited Jo. Neither of the girls had a hair out of place and their makeup was exquisite.

"We have nearly finished tea," said Duds.

"I'm terrified of tea," said Jo. "I am sure it is more fattening than anything."

Duds handed her a cup, which she took doubtfully. She also accepted, even more doubtfully, a scone, of which she took two bites, then left on her plate, surrounded by jam.

Duds was not fat but she began to feel conscious of middle-aged spread as she looked at her two elegant young cousins. There seemed to be nothing of them at all. Flo was toying with a piece of homemade cake. Henry was holding forth about the food shortage—or rather lack of food shortage—and was explaining to a bored audience why the government had thought fit to import pineapples into the country at a time when she was short of bread, meat, fats and fuel.

"You are giving us a lovely tea," said Gordon to Duds.

He really is rather a dear, she thought. He wore his hair a trifle on the long side and she had never cared for suede shoes, but she was aware that she had got a little behind the times. And anyway, she told herself, he may suffer with his feet and be more shoed against than shoeing.

"Suppose," went on Henry—not that any of his audience wished to suppose anything—"that one wants concessions from . . . er . . . say Government A, one may have more chance of obtaining them if one takes something from her first, something she wants to get rid of."

"I do think that politics are too alienating," remarked Josephine, lighting a cigarette.

"I think the country behaved very badly to Mr. Churchill," declared Mrs. Dumbleton. "After all, he saved us during the war. It was only ordinary common or garden gratitude to vote for him, or for the Conservative candidate, and Henry and I both did so, though it was a very wet day."

"Don't for a moment think that I am on the side of the present government," went on Henry—not that anyone had thought anything about it. "The Conservatives ought to have got in and they would have got in if it had not been for a certain fact."

"The fact that they did not get so many votes as the Socialists," remarked Tommy.

"The trouble was," said Mrs. Dumbleton, "that a lot of people did not know that by voting Socialist they were voting against Churchill. I tried to explain to my cook but of course she thought she knew best and it was no good arguing with her or she might have given notice."

"I thought she left at the beginning of the war," objected Duds.

"This was another one. We took a house at Maidenhead for the summer and I managed to get hold of a cook and a house-parlormaid, but it was all very wearing. They were always wanting me to get things for them at the shops and of course I couldn't. We were very glad to get back to our hotel, but it is lovely being in a private house for Christmas—one does get tired of hotels."

Though no one had seemed very anxious for tea, they all sat on over it for ages, and just as Duds was hoping to shepherd them into the drawing room while she cleared away the things, Sandy arrived. She jumped up gladly, delighted to see him. A feeling of depression had been creeping over her during tea. Sandy would make everything different.

Like the twins, he looked very much older than she had expected. Still, that was not very surprising after all he had gone through in the war. What was surprising was the expression on his face when he saw Florence and Josephine. He looked at the two girls with an expression of intense resentment. At least that is how it seemed to Duds, though she told herself that she must be imagining things. She went out and returned with another pot of tea, whereon everybody else thought that they would have another cup. Gordon absentmindedly cut another slice of cake and Mrs. Dumbleton took a scone. Duds made an effort and in a joking way asked if she could have their ration books. "You know what it is," she said.

"Of course," said Florence, handing over hers and Gordon's books. "I think that there are a few points left and I have not had my tea ration this month."

"I am afraid the hotel has taken out our tea ration," explained Mrs. Dumbleton, "but I have brought a quarter of a pound with me, as Henry and I both like an early morning cup of tea and we don't want to use up all yours. They said something about there not being any B.U's left. I don't know what they are, but I hope they don't matter."

"Ration book!" exclaimed Jo. "I had quite forgotten all about it. I can't remember when I saw it last. As a matter of fact I get most of my meals out, so I never bother. I must inquire about it when I go home. I expect I slipped it inside my library book. I often lose things that way. I believe you have to hand them in when you die. Awkward if I die and can't hand it in, like going back to school without one's health certificate."

"Oh, Jo!" said Florence.

Gordon laughed pleasantly. "Don't be so gruesome," he said.

Sandy searched in his pockets and at last produced a rather grubby ration book. "I expect my landlady has taken everything she can out of it," he announced, and he expected quite right. At last Duds managed to shepherd everyone into the drawing room while she escaped to the kitchen with the tea tray and Tommy escaped to the garden with the dogs to round up the hens and rabbits. Henry accompanied him, and when Tommy came in at dressing time, he said he would murder Henry before the week was out, Christmas or no Christmas. Duds found the twins, Gordon and Mrs. Dumbleton in the middle of a rubber of bridge. She asked them if they would mind finishing it after dinner as they had to dine at half-past seven punctually.

"Everyone is dining so much earlier nowadays," said Mrs. Dumbleton, dealing the cards slowly and deliberately. "I met some people the other day who said that they always dined at seven as they only had daily help and their woman liked to get home by nine. I should not like to dine at seven. It would make such a long evening."

"Well, it is the same with me," explained Duds. "My Mrs. Elphick said that she would stay till nine to wash up, so I said that we would dine very punctually at half-past seven."

"Don't talk of dinner," begged Jo. "I feel as if I had only just finished my tea."

"We had better stop after this rubber," said Florence, and Duds felt very grateful and wondered how she could ever have thought the twins were at all alike. Florence was so much the nicer. She tried to remember which she had liked better as a child . She had always lumped them together as the twins, but now, on looking back, she had an idea that it was Flo who had been the nicer even then.

"Yes, of course," agreed Gordon. "We can finish after dinner." Duds wondered if he were really as nice as he seemed, then chided herself for the ungrateful thought. He was certainly trying to make things go smoothly, though why should anyone have to try to make things go smoothly in a family party? Surely they all understood each other and could get on together without a newcomer trying to pour oil on troubled waters.

Sandy, who had been sitting reading the newspaper, got up and walked out of the room, slamming the door behind him. Duds hoped that it was an accident.

At half-past seven she was standing in the hall with drinks spread hospitably on the table. Gordon stood by her, sipping sherry and talking to her in his pleasant voice, while Tommy lurked in the background with his crossword. At twenty to eight Sandy came down, drank two glasses of neat gin in quick succession and would probably have taken a third if he had been offered it. At a quarter to eight they were joined by Henry, who, after giving a critical look at the sherry, took some gin and lime. At ten minutes to eight Florence arrived and Sandy unbent so far as to offer her a drink.

"Not much gin," begged Florence. "Aren't you drinking anything, Sandy?"

"I'll have a drop to keep you company," he replied. Duds looked at him indignantly as he filled his glass. How far did they think her gin would go if Sandy drank three glasses every evening? Mrs. Dumbleton came down, took a glass of sherry and said she did not care for spirits. The clock struck eight.

"Except brandy of course," went on Mrs. Dumbleton. "But then I look on brandy as medicine, not that I like the taste but there is no doubt that it does one good. I remember hearing that a friend of ours had been killed in an air raid. A very nice woman, her husband had been a judge in India, and a piece of the roof fell on her. Luckily she was killed outright but I was quite upset because they lived near us, near where we used to live, I should say, because of course we moved from there at the outbreak of war. We thought it might not be very safe as it was near the coast and we were proved right. Henry insisted on me having a sip of brandy when I heard the news and I must say I felt much more comfortable after it. Well, thank you, perhaps just half a glass more, it is so very good," and she allowed Tommy to refill her glass. "You would not care for it, Henry. It would not be dry enough for you. I do not like a very dry sherry myself but on the other hand I don't like anything very sweet. I have never taken sugar in my tea, though curiously enough I always take it in my coffee."

"If you want a really good sherry, Lethbridge," said Henry, "I might be able to get you some through my man. He is very sound and has some real prewar stuff. He only sells it to people he knows personally, quite reasonably too—there is no black market about it."

"I don't want any more sherry at present, thank you," replied Tommy, shortly.

"I hope I am not late," said Josephine, coming down the stairs and looking just like a fashion plate.

"I expect you would like to finish your rubber," said Duds to Mrs. Dumbleton when dinner was over at last. The meal had not been a great success, as the soup had been lukewarm and the rabbit stew dried up from being kept hot for so long. The Dumbletons had never stopped talking, Henry instructively and Irene boringly. Sandy had not spoken at all and the twins had left most of their food on their plates.

"We could have two tables," suggested Henry. "There are eight of us."

"I always think that eight is an ideal number for a houseparty," said Mrs. Dumbleton. "Then you can always have two tables for bridge.

Six is too few and ten too many, and one does not know what to do with the two people left over."

"What about it, Duds?" asked Henry.

"I don't play bridge," announced Sandy.

"You should learn," said Henry. "Everyone should play bridge. It is a necessary social accomplishment. I tell you what, we will give you a lesson this evening. You will soon pick it up."

"I don't want to pick it up, thank you," replied Sandy.

In the midst of her anxiety about the washing up, Duds wondered again what had happened to Sandy, good-tempered, freckled-faced Sandy, always ready to join in anything. Of course Henry was enough to irritate anyone. What a fool she had been to let him come. He was enough to wreck any party with his air of knowing more about everything than anyone else. And Irene was the most crashing bore. But Sandy had been cross before he had even set eyes on the Dumbletons. What had they done to him in the prison camp? she asked herself and shivered. "I am afraid I must just go and lend a hand with the washing up," she said. "I am so sorry," and she hurried from the room.

How eight people could have used so many plates, knives, forks and glasses she could not imagine. Anyone would think they had been having a banquet instead of soup, rabbit stew, and semolina pudding. Mrs. Elphick was putting on her hat. "I am very sorry, ma'am," she said, "but I am afraid I must go now. It is half an hour past my time and Mr. Elphick will be wondering where I've got to. I thought dinner was to be at half-past seven but it had gone a quarter-past eight before you sat down. And I am afraid the stew got dried up."

"I simply could not get them to come along," sighed Duds. "I told them half-past seven but they just didn't seem to take it in. Never mind, you run along, Mrs. Elphick, and I'll help Edith."

"I nipped up to turn down the beds," said Edith, "while you were in at dinner. But I haven't done the hot water, nor the bottles."

Delightful as Old Place was, it was very old-fashioned and it had not got hot and cold water laid on in the bedrooms. Duds had not stayed in a large house since the war and she had forgotten all the details, such as turning down beds and putting round cans of hot water. In the old days a house of this size would have had at least five or six indoor servants.

"Hullo, can I help?" and Florence, looking indescribably elegant and out of place in the untidy kitchen, came in.

"I thought you were playing bridge."

"I turned over my hand to Mr. Dumbleton. He was playing everyone's hand as it was and I thought if he had one of his own it might keep him quiet. Tommy has taken Sandy to tuck up the rabbits or say good night to the chickens or something."

"Flo, what is the matter with Sandy?"

Florence had picked up a damp tea cloth with her white red-tipped fingers and did not seem to hear. "Haven't you any drier cloths than this?" she said.

"I tell you what, Edith," said Duds. "You go up and put round the hot water and bottles while Mrs. Pinhorn and I cope with the washing up." She plunged her hands into the hot, greasy water. "But you know what I mean, Flo," she said. "You must admit he is like something out of a Russian play, not a bit the life and soul of an old-world Christmas in an English country house."

"I suppose we have all changed as far as that goes," said Florence, drying swiftly and competently, rather to Dud's surprise. "The old world has gone and, it is no use trying to pretend to bring it back again."

"I thought it would be rather fun to have one week just like old times," explained Duds, wistfully.

"It would be, if one could," replied Florence. Then she kissed her cousin impulsively. "You are rather a lamb, Duds," she said. "I don't believe that you ever grow a day older."

"I am thirty-five," replied Duds, "and have several white hairs, not to mention the beginning of middle-aged spread."

"They don't show," Florence assured her. "Neither the hairs nor the spread! But it is your mind that I was thinking of. You are just the same as you were when we were children. Now we have grown up—in fact we are older than you are. Life is still a fairy tale to you."

"You make me sound mentally deficient."

"Absolutely! But you are rather nice all the same. Anything more to dry?"

CHAPTER 4

WHEN Duds at last got to bed it was well after midnight. Even when the bridge players reached the end of their last rubber they had to go over every card again and explain why they had played it, while Henry told them how much better it would have been if they had played something else. Then they took hours settling up their finances, which were not ruinous, as Duds heard Mrs. Dumbleton say, "That will be three and six. No, I am sorry, but I have no change." No one seemed to have any change and it looked as if Mrs. Dumbleton would have to go forever without her three and sixpence. Then all the men took whisky and Henry told Tommy that he knew somewhere where one could get some passable stuff. Mrs. Dumbleton asked for hot water and Duds had to go back into the kitchen for it. She found a kettle but no matches, nor could she get the lighter to work. She came back into the drawing room for a match and found that everyone had settled down for a nice chat, with the exception of Sandy, who was well through his second whisky and was looking a cross between an enemy agent and the first part of an advertisement for a patent digestive mixture.

She lay awake for some time, too tired to sleep. She wondered why Sandy had turned so queer, why she had ever thought Flo and Jo at all alike. Flo was by far the nicer of the two. She wondered if Gordon were as nice as he seemed and she wondered how she could ever have admired Henry and how on earth she was going to bear him or his wife for a whole week. The houseparty was to break up on New Year's day, and today was only Christmas Eve, no, it was Christmas Day. Next week at this time she would be on the verge of saying goodbye to them all, and very glad she would be! Except for Florence, and perhaps Gordon, she did not mind if she never saw any of them again.

Duds turned over in bed. What an idiotic idea it had been of hers to try and recapture the old prewar Christmas spirit. She had thought that Sandy and the twins would have fallen into their old places, as happy, eager children. But Josephine had turned into a spoiled, sophisticated young woman who wanted smacking, Florence into a kind but rather weary grown-up person, and Sandy . . . Sandy was the worst of the lot. Sandy, whom she had pictured as the life and soul of the party! What had they done to him? She shivered, though her head felt burning hot. When planning the party ahead, it had seemed the most natural thing in the world that they should have a game of hide-and-seek all over the house. She tried now to picture their faces if she suggested such a thing. And those Christmas stockings! She did wish that she and Tommy had not prepared them. Everyone would expect a proper present and would think she was quite mad offering round children's stockings, or they might even think they had done it to economize on presents! Kind as Florence was, Duds felt that she already found her a bit childish, and she would try to humor her over the stockings. But what would Josephine think? Gordon would be very charming, but somehow one could not imagine him enjoying a stocking with a twopenny packet of chocolate in it—and a present from Eastbourne!

Oh dear, how tired she was. If only she could sleep. There would be such a lot to do tomorrow. Mrs. Elphick could not come on Christmas Day as she was expecting all her children and grandchildren, and Edith could not be expected to spend the afternoon and evening in. Duds fell into a troubled dream. They were playing hide-and-seek all over the house, Florence and Josephine were children again, and she was running along the corridor. Someone was chasing her; she was frightened and thought she heard a voice calling for help. Was it Sandy? Or was it one of the twins? The person, whoever it was, who had been chasing her, caught her. It was Henry, no, it wasn't—it was Gordon. She woke up with her heart racing. Tommy was sitting on her bed and she clung to him.

"What on earth is the matter?" he asked.

"Only a bad dream," she replied, and she clung all the tighter.

"You were calling out. You gave me such a fright," he said.

"What is the time?"

"Seven o'clock."

"I had better get up, there is such a lot to do."

"I hope this party isn't going to be too much for you," said Tommy.

"Oh no, it will be great fun really," said Duds, her natural optimism ousting her forebodings of the night before. "But I am afraid the Dumbletons were a bit of a mistake."

"She isn't so bad, but I am afraid he will find himself bumped off before the week is out, if he isn't careful."

"I suppose she goes on as she does out of self-defense," suggested Duds, "so as not to hear him, but it is very wearing. Still it is something to feel there is someone who can be relied on to keep the conversation going. There will be no awkward pauses while she is here." She washed and dressed and went down to the kitchen to stoke up the boiler and put on the kettle for the early morning tea. Then she went to call Jo and Sandy while Edith called the married couples. She tidied the downstairs rooms and opened the windows to let in some fresh air. Tommy brought in some wood and some eggs for breakfast. Duds laid the table and put round the stockings. She had serious misgivings, but what else could she do? She had nothing to put in their place. She added a small packet of cigarettes to each stocking from her reserve cupboard, then, remembering that Mrs. Dumbleton did not smoke, she took out her packet again, then absentmindedly put her stocking in Sandy's place.

She did hope the hot water would hold out. The Dumbletons had one bathroom, the Pinhorns another, while Josephine and Sandy had to share the third. She and Tommy, not without a good deal of grumbling on Tommy's part, had forgone their own baths until later in the day. Unfortunately, when at last Josephine got up and strolled along the corridor to the bathroom, she found that Sandy had forestalled her and she was not pleased about it.

Henry was the first to appear at the breakfast table. He looked rather surprised at the sight of the stocking on his place, and Duds felt a distinct fool as she caught his amused glance. Then, remembering Tommy's words, she hoped that he had not placed a time bomb in it, for Tommy's sake, not Henry's. Personally she felt that a time bomb was just what Henry needed.

Sandy came in next and he opened his stocking gloomily, displaying neither surprise nor amusement. The little bottle of smelling salts that Duds had put in for Mrs. Dumbleton in place of the cigarettes did not serve to raise his spirits. Duds was just about to explain what had happened and to suggest changing the stockings when Mrs. Dumbleton appeared and seized her stocking with a pleased expression. She handed presents wrapped in colored paper to her host and hostess, then started opening her stocking. The first thing she found was Sandy's packet of cigarettes, which she at once handed over to her husband, who in return offered her his packet of chocolate, saying that he never ate anything sweet.

"Well, this is a nice idea," said Irene Dumbleton. "It quite takes me back to my childhood. I remember when I was a tiny little mite I always hung up my stocking and I believed in Father Christmas. I used to lie awake hoping to see him come down the chimney. I must have been a quaint little thing, but it is so nice to keep up the old customs. I remember when Henry and I stayed with Alida Bray for Christmas in 1937—no, it must have been my first husband, he did not die till 1939 but I think perhaps it was 1938 because there was snow on the ground and there wasn't any snow in 1937, unless I am mistaken. I always think there is something seasonable about snow at Christmas-time, don't you? Not that anything is much pleasure now with all these restrictions. Well, as I was saying, the Brays had a Christmas tree all lit up with candles and a star on the top, and I had a box with six pairs of silk stockings in it. One could not get anything like that now, could one? The stockings you get these days ladder the first time one wears them, especially in church. And Henry—I should say Robert—got a silver cigarette case."

Henry was still poking about in his stocking and Duds wondered whether he was hoping to find a silver cigarette case in it. She caught Tommy's eye and he choked into his napkin. She turned to her own parcel, and on opening it, found a cut glass bottle of expensive bath salts. She felt rather embarrassed, as Mrs. Dumbleton had just come across the pincushion between two shells and was murmuring something about it being just what she wanted.

Josephine arrived, shivering ostentatiously, but she remembered to wish everyone a Happy Christmas and to present Duds and Tommy each with a book token worth a guinea. She looked at her stocking in surprise, then glanced round the room as if in search of some children.

"I am sorry I was in the bath," muttered Sandy. "I didn't realize we were using the same or I should have waited."

"It is of no consequence," replied Jo coldly, "but you might have left me a little hot water. It is the only thing that warms me up in the morning."

"I didn't use any hot water at all," protested Sandy, indignantly. "I never have a hot bath in the morning."

Florence appeared, kissed Duds, and presented her with a large parcel, which turned out to be a really beautiful handbag of pigskin with a zip fastener, and offered a smaller parcel to Tommy before turning with delighted cries to her own stocking.

"Oh, it is all nobbly in some places and squishy in others, just as it used to be," she said. "Don't you remember, Jo? We always used to open our stockings together, taking out one thing at a time. Let us do that now. You can start—mind you play fair."

Josephine took out her packet of cigarettes, lit one and lost interest in the rest of her stocking. It was lucky she liked cigarettes, thought Duds, though it wasn't much of a present, and she looked at her own bath salts, handbag, and guinea book token, then at Tommy's large box of Turkish cigarettes (not that he ever smoked them), at his silver cigarette lighter (not that he would use it) and at his guinea book token (which he might change if he remembered, but would more probably leave in his pocket until it was out of date). She felt that their own offerings were rather mingy. However, Florence was exclaiming gaily over the pencils, India-rubber, and diary. She really seemed to be enjoying herself in spite of Josephine's marked lack of interest. Unfortunately both girls had quite forgotten their breakfast and as it was real eggs and bacon, it seemed rather a pity. Duds wondered if she were to eat up one of their helpings whether anyone would notice. She would never get the washing up done in time to go to church, and she did so want to go this morning.

Sandy had just unbent to the extent of handing round book tokens to the assembled company, rather in the manner of a Bow Street officer serving summonses, when Gordon arrived, and Sandy bent his head over his toast and marmalade once more.

"I am so sorry I am late," he said in his charming voice, "but Florence took all the hot water and I had to wait till it got a little bit warm again. A Happy Christmas everyone! You don't mean to say Father Christmas has brought me a stocking! How too lovely. Cigarettes, hurray! And a diary. That is just what I wanted."

Oh dear, thought Duds. I shall have to wash up the breakfast things in cold water.

"I don't expect your hot water system is run by electricity, is it?" asked Henry.

"I don't expect so," replied Tommy. "I must go and see to the animals," and he left the room.

At last the breakfast things were cleared away and Duds plunged into the business of washing up. When she came back into the dining room she found Mrs. Dumbleton putting away the clean silver while she discoursed on the servant problem to anyone who happened to pass by. Duds found that Flo had made her bed and Gordon's and done their room. He had probably helped her; he seemed very good-natured. She was glad that Florence had got such a nice husband and wished that poor Jo had got one too.

Rather to Duds' surprise, the whole party came to church and she felt much happier about everything. The church was not beautiful; it had been built in the latter days of Queen Victoria and therefore was not one of those lovely old village churches that one so often finds in the countryside. The pews were of pitch pine and the stained glass was crude in color and design. All the same, there was a real atmosphere of devotion, and Duds wondered why she did not attend more regularly. The hymns were sung with fervor if not with musical ability, and there was the genuine churchy smell, mingled with that of evergreens. Perhaps her houseparty was going to be a success after all.

"I do think that there is something very alienating about church," remarked Josephine, stopping in the middle of the village street to rectify her face.

"I must say there is nothing very uplifting about a village service," agreed Henry. "That organ would be enough to shatter anyone's faith, even without the false notes sung by the choir."

Duds felt as if someone had poured a jug of cold water over her and she could not speak.

"I liked it," said Flo. "It was all so simple and Christmaslike and reminded me of being a child."

"Some of us don't wish to be reminded of those days," said Sandy.

Florence went scarlet. The others looked at her in surprise, for the modern girl does not often blush.

"I thought it was a very nice service," said Gordon. "So genuine."

As it was Christmas Day, there were drinks in the hall when they got back. Tommy and Duds had agreed only to have them in the evening, but they felt they must make an exception on Christmas Day. Besides, Tommy would have to do something to keep the guests quiet while Duds helped Edith dish up the luncheon, or rather dinner, for they were having a real old-fashioned Christmas dinner in the middle of the day, just as they had done when Duds had been a girl staying with her aunt and the twins were tiny girls, allowed to come downstairs as a great treat.

She cheered up a little when she saw all her party gathered round the table and a real, fine-looking turkey roasted to a turn in front of Tommy. She had brought out all her best china and glass for the occasion and she liked her central arrangement of holly berries and fluffy old man's beard. The Christmas pudding was a masterpiece, considering that it had been made with dried eggs, and beer instead of brandy. But she had sacrificed a little of her precious brandy to pour over it at the last moment so that it was able to make its appearance in flames in the traditional manner.

Of course Josephine refused pudding outright and said that she never touched it. Florence consented to have a tiny piece, "Just for luck," she explained. Gordon said that he could not resist it, it looked just like a prewar pudding, and Henry, while eating a large helping, told them of some friends with whom they had spent last Christmas who had produced some real brandy sauce made with real butter. "They got it from Ireland, I believe."

"Eire," grunted Sandy.

Mrs. Dumbleton ate her helping placidly and discussed the number of points needed for dried fruits and the difficulty of getting suet. "What a relief it is to live in a hotel these days," she added.

Tommy got the thimble and remarked that he believed that was why Jo had refused the pudding. Poor Tommy, thought Duds. He is trying to be facetious and make the party go, but it doesn't really come naturally to him, and I don't think it has gone very well.

"She might have got the ring," pointed out Henry. Sandy got the ring. He just pushed it to one side without a word and gave a meaningful look at Flo, whose eyes filled with tears.

Mrs. Dumbleton remarked how funny it was the way things happened—one year she had had the ring, and two years later she had got married, and, one year she had had the threepenny piece and not long after that, it might have been that spring or the one after, she had won ten shillings on the Grand National. Not that her horse had won. But she had backed him for a place so she had got her money back.

"Who has got the threepenny piece today?" asked Tommy.

"Flo got it last year," remarked Jo meaningfully. There was a stunned silence. Flo blew her nose and Gordon said how pretty the old man's beard looked on the table.

Tommy asked Mrs. Dumbleton to have more pudding. Duds went out for the dessert, which consisted of dates, oranges, apples and cob nuts, and there was a decanter of port. She had tried to get Christmas crackers and failed, but now she was glad as she felt that they would have fallen rather flat. She could not imagine either Henry or Josephine pulling one, nor Sandy putting on a paper hat. No, even her optimistic nature could hardly describe this Christmas dinner as a riot, although the food had been exceptionally good. Jo was bored, Flo unhappy, Henry superior and Sandy sulky—so much for her merry party of old friends, living once again in the good old days!

Tommy and Gordon carried the things out into the scullery, and Florence helped Duds with the washing up while Edith went to her home in the village for the rest of Christmas Day. Mrs. Dumbleton went to her room for a rest and Tommy went out with his dogs. What the rest of the party were doing Duds did not know nor did she much care. She and Flo had the scullery to themselves and worked for some time in silence.

Suddenly Florence broke the silence. "I really did enjoy this morning—church, I mean. It took me back for a little while, but as I said last night one can't go back. If only one could!" She stopped and polished a spoon with a piece of chamois leather.

After an interval Duds said, "I am awfully sorry, Flo. I hoped that you were happy."

"I expect that I am as happy as most people, but no one is really happy once they are grown up, are they?"

"Well, I think I am. Of course I was terrified in the war, when Tommy was away, but now he is back and I have got this place and everything, I really am most awfully happy. Naturally I should like to have had children, but one can't have everything."

"No, one can't, and I am quite happy really. I am just being silly. It is all this feeling of Christmas and everything and thinking of the old days when Jo and Sandy and I were children. Seeing you brings it all back. You remember how Jo and I always told each other everything and how nothing was any fun unless we could do it together. I thought it would always be like that, but now Jo is changed. She does not want to share things with me any more."

"Has she had any trouble? I mean she may have been fond of someone and he may have been killed in the war, or he might have gone off with someone else. Or . . . I don't know, but such a lot of queer things do happen nowadays."

"I rather think that she is in love with someone, or has been, but she has not said anything to me about it. As I say, she doesn't tell me things now." She paused a moment. "And I don't tell her things, as she wouldn't be interested. I wish Grandfather had not left me that money. I believe that is at the root of it and yet I never thought of it making any difference to us."

"You wanted to share it with Jo?"

"Well, naturally! As a matter of fact I never thought of anything else. He said the eldest grandchild, and I thought, well, there are two eldest grandchildren! There weren't any others as it turned out, and I thought how funny it was that he should not have known that we were both the same age. I don't think I'd ever realized that I was the older of the two. I always thought we were the same age, but it was then she turned so queer. She said she wouldn't touch a penny of it, and she could earn plenty of money for herself. Grandfather had not intended her to have the money and she did not need to live on charity. Charity—when it was me!" Tears filled her eyes as she rubbed ferociously at a silver fork.

"She had been hurt," replied Duds. "When people are hurt themselves they want to hurt the people they like best, like a dog in a trap. I remember how terrified I was when Tommy was out at sea on D-Day. I didn't hear anything for a month and I imagined everything under the sun. I worked myself into such a state that when he did come home I quarreled with him before he had been in the house for twenty-four hours."

"Yes," agreed Florence. "I think I understand. Jo is hurt about something. Some man has let her down, I feel sure. If it were a case of his being dead she would be terribly unhappy, but I think she would turn to me. It would not be a bitter sort of unhappiness, if you know what I mean. But this, whatever it is, is bitter and she can't bear to talk about it, so she pretends it is the money she minds about and she is horrid to me. Thank you, Duds, for making me see it."

"She will get over it," said Duds hopefully. "We are all worn out with six years of war and two years of peace, and lack of fats, and everything seems much worse than it would have been at ordinary times, and I do think it is especially bad luck on people like you and Jo. It's not so bad for us older ones, because after all we did have a lot of pleasure, but you haven't had any of the good old life, have you? There was just that one Hunt Ball you came to with us. Do you remember it?"

"Rather! Jo and I were in green, rather lambs, those frocks! There was an awfully nice man called Harry. He was rather smitten, but of course as fast as he found himself making headway with one of us, he found it was the other. We used to have frightful fun in those days muddling people up. I remember a woman in the village asking Jo to tea, and explaining that she had got a man coming who was a world-famous pianist. At the last moment Jo asked me to take her place, and she forgot to tell me about the man, and I asked him if he liked music! We would never be taken for each other now," she added wistfully.

Duds went up to her room to lie down. She was very tired, and she did wish that she had not embarked on this houseparty. Only twenty-four hours gone, and there were six whole days to come! What would she do with them all? She had not realized what an awful lot of work people made. There never seemed to be a moment that she wasn't making beds or washing up or laying the table. If only the guests had shown some sign of enjoying themselves she would not have grudged the trouble. She had imagined them all taking part, perhaps breaking a few things and letting the milk boil over, but laughing all the time. She did not think that anyone had laughed since the party arrived. Florence was very sweet but very sad, and Gordon was nice and helpful, but rather as he might be at a funeral, helping people in and out of the mourning coaches and talking in a soothing manner. She fell asleep thinking of him.

She woke up panic-stricken. She had no idea how long she had slept and her watch had stopped. It must be teatime, and she had not done a thing about it. She poured some cold water into the basin and washed her face and hands, then hurriedly applied some powder. There had been a time when she had taken her complexion as seriously as did Flo and Jo, but that was a long time ago. She put a comb through her hair and hurried down to the kitchen to put on the kettle. She filled it and lit the gas, then while it was boiling she felt she must have a breath of fresh air as she was still feeling so heavy and sleepy. She went out of the back door and took in several deep breaths of cool fresh air. That was better. She turned to go back, then wondered if Tommy were in yet. She went to the window of the study and peeped in. There were two figures in the room. One was that of her cousin Jo, seated in Tommy's armchair, and the other was in the shadow. Duds could just see that it was a man's form, but she could not see the face. Suddenly Jo jumped up and threw her cigarette into the fireplace. Just as Duds was about to tap on the window Jo was seized by the dim form, who caught her tightly in his arms, and they both melted into the shadows.

CHAPTER 5

THERE was a meet nearby on Boxing Day. Tommy was able to mount Flo and Gordon and a friend of his found a horse for Sandy. They hacked over while the Dumbletons took Duds and Jo in the car. Jo sat in the front with Henry, and Duds wondered if it had

been he who had been embracing her the day before. It didn't seem
very likely that it would be Sandy, but it might have been. Perhaps his
sulky behavior was the result of being in love. It did take some
people that way. On the other hand, he had been just as sulky
throughout the evening and would not the embrace have cheered
him up? It had appeared to be a pretty thorough one. Of the three
remaining men she certainly hoped it was Henry, though it seemed
queer of Jo. She could not be really in love with Henry; he was old
enough to be her father. Probably she had had a love affair that had
gone wrong and now just flirted with anyone who came along, for
something to do.

Duds felt rather sad thinking of the young untouched Jo in her
apple-green frock. Still, one could not remain young and untouched
forever. Jo was twenty-five, and seven years of war did not help to
keep one young and untouched. All the same, Duds would have expected her cousin to be rather more choosy. Not that she could say
much herself where Henry was concerned, but her affair had been a
long time ago and she was ten years nearer him in age.

Duds was able to let her thoughts wander unchecked while Mrs.
Dumbleton kept up a slow steady monologue. She had never really
cared for riding, not that she disapproved of hunting, and she thought
the men in their pink coats looked charming, but she was rather ner-
vous. She had had a fall when she was a young girl and had never really
got over it. "I must say I was very much surprised at the result of the
general election," she went on. "Most ungrateful! I am glad we had
decided to live in a hotel, though of course one misses having one's own
sitting room. They are hard to get nowadays, as naturally the management likes to turn all the rooms into bedrooms."

Duds wondered if Jo had refused to hunt because she wanted to
stay behind and flirt with Henry or because she wanted to draw attention to the fact that she was the poor sister and Flo the rich one. She
really had turned into rather a poisonous little brute and in any case she
was not a pauper, even without her grandfather's money. She had at
least five hundred a year of her own, apart from what she earned in a
publisher's office. But of course she must spend a good deal on her
clothes and her hair, etc. You would need a big income to look like that.
Duds sighed. She was afraid she had let herself go a bit, but what with
the housework and the garden and the animals, there was not much
time nor money to spend on oneself and one's appearance. And the last

time she went to London and had her hair done at the most up-to-date place Tommy had said, "I say, darling, hadn't you better do your hair? There are some people coming to dinner."

"I don't call ten guineas a head a week at all expensive," Mrs. Dumbleton went on. "After all you get everything thrown in, no wages, no weekly books, no rates. We have not got a private bath at present, but have been promised one as soon as there is one vacant. It is all right at the moment as all the people on our landing take their baths at night, but it would be very awkward if any of them wanted it in the morning and one found it occupied just when one wanted it oneself."

Jo was laughing and talking to Henry. Perhaps she was not a really poisonous little brute, but had been badly hurt and could not help being horrid. If only one could get her to tell one all about it! Duds remembered taking her on her knee as a child and comforting her in some childish trouble.

It was a very pleasant day and the meet presented a delightful spectacle. It was quite like old times. Duds moved about, greeting friends and forgetting all about her unsuccessful houseparty. Flo was looking very pretty, mounted on Mona, Tommy's mare. Even Sandy had stopped glowering for the moment. Duds and her party stayed to see the field move off, then drove round the country lanes, getting glimpses now and then of the pink coats and of the baying hounds. How nice life could be if only everyone would be happy, thought Duds.

After luncheon, Irene Dumbleton retired to her room and, rather to Dud's surprise, Jo asked her to go for a walk with her.

"I feel I want some exercise," she said. "You do give us such a lot to eat."

Duds looked at Henry. She could not help it, but his face was quite impassive. Politeness forced her to ask him to accompany them, but to her relief he replied that he had letters to write and he retired into Tommy's study.

Duds and Jo started off together down the wintry lane. The hedges were bare, but then it was Boxing Day. The shortest day was over and spring was on its way. "Once Christmas is over one feels spring may be here any moment, doesn't one?" remarked Duds.

"I don't feel that it will ever be here," replied her cousin. "It will always be winter with me now."

"I am so sorry, Jo," said Duds, simply.

"You have always been awfully decent. You are more like an older sister than a cousin. I wish you were my older sister."

"Well, as long as you feel that I am—" began Duds.

"No, I don't mean that. But if you had been our older sister, you would have come in for the money and it wouldn't have come between Flo and me."

"But I can't see why it has come between you. Surely you and Flo have always shared everything."

"That is just it. We always shared everything because we were on equal terms. We aren't on equal terms any longer. She is Sir John Radstow's heir and everybody knows it. She is ready to be kind to me, and I couldn't bear that. I should hate for anyone to be kind to me, but Flo more than anyone. Can't you imagine how everyone would talk about how she shared her fortune with her poor sister and what a wonderful person she was?"

"It would be you who would be wonderful, if you took it. Couldn't you be a bit wonderful? There is a greater generosity, I think, in taking than in giving, sometimes."

"Yes, and I am not generous enough for that. I wonder if Flo would be? It is easy enough to give half your goods and have everyone admiring you, but to be the poor relation receiving charity is not so good, and I don't think Flo would like it either. We are neither of us saints. I think we both have enough decency to offer a share to the other, but I don't think either of us would have enough generosity to take it."

"I wonder."

"Oh, of course you think Flo would. You have always liked her best. Everyone does. She is much nicer, I admit that. But then everything has always gone right for her. Life has been easy for her from the word go. Love, money, everything! She has got it all. Now she is the kind elder sister trying to help the ungrateful younger one. Money has altered her. She is patronizing. She can't help it. She doesn't mean it, but I can't stand it. I have given up hunting altogether because she was always wanting to hire a horse for me and pay my subscription, and whenever I went out people would think, 'There is that poor Harnet girl—her sister must be treating her.' As a matter of fact, I could pay my own way, I'm not stony, but no one would believe I wasn't sponging on Flo."

"I don't expect anyone would have thought about you one way or the other," replied Duds. "You are a fool, Jo, thinking that everyone is bothering about you and how much money your grandfather left and whom he left it to. People don't take all that much interest in other people. In any case, when you are out hunting you are not thinking at all. You just seem to cut off your nose to spite your face. Why on earth can't you hire a horse and go out hunting when you want to? Tommy could easily have got you one today. It would be much better than staying here and brooding about the place like someone out of a Greek tragedy."

Jo laughed bitterly. "You shouldn't have asked me to this party, Duds. I am spoiling it for everyone. I don't mean to, but I can't help it. It isn't just the money, I don't really care two hoots about that, except that it has made Flo different. But you happily married people are so smug. Everyone thinks you are marvelous and such an example to others and if there were only more couples like you the country would prosper. It never seems to strike anyone that most people would like to be happy, if only they had the opportunity. One isn't unhappy out of depravity of character. There is nothing so frightfully heroic about being happily married, if you are lucky enough to marry the man you care for. Anyone would think that you had done something frightfully noble and self-sacrificing."

"I am frightfully sorry," replied Duds, "and I didn't mean to be smug. I guessed that you had got some trouble and I knew it couldn't really be about the money. If there is anything I can do, Jo, you have only to tell me. Sometimes it is a relief to talk things over and get them off one's chest. Use me as a safety valve or exhaust pipe whenever you like. But I wish you could confide in Flo. That would be a really generous act on your part, much more so than her sharing her money with you."

"I wish I could. I should like to be generous. I should like things to be as they used to be. But we have grown apart. She is happily married, she is prosperous, she is popular with everyone and a success all round. She does not know what it is like to wish oneself dead."

"Don't talk like that, Jo. As I said just now, the longest night is over, spring is on its way, and you will have another spring, too. You have been badly hurt and it will take some time for you to get mended, but you know one does get mended. The trees will put on fresh leaves and so will you, if you know what I mean. I thought I was in love once before I met Tommy. He was married and I was awfully unhappy for a bit."

"For a bit, yes, but it wasn't the real thing. You don't understand,

Duds. I have lost everything that makes life worth living and I may have to live for another fifty years. I don't want to see another fifty springs. I don't want to see one. I am only twenty-five, though I look and feel forty. Isn't it funny to think that Flo and I are the same age? She looks about eighteen and feels fourteen, I should say."

Duds sighed. She could not think of anything else to say. Suppose something were to go wrong between her and Tommy. Would she want to see another spring? But then what could go wrong between her and Tommy? She looked up and there were Tommy, Flo and Gordon trotting slowly down the lane towards them. Jo was right about Flo; she didn't look a day over eighteen. Her sad worried look had gone and she was flushed with health and pleasure.

That evening there was a pantomime broadcast on the wireless. Duds had been looking forward to it. She would like to be going to a pantomime on Boxing Day, as had been the custom of her childhood, but as she couldn't do that she would enjoy listening to it at home. But it was not a success. To begin with, it did not come through well. Henry stepped forward with a knowledgeable air, and Tommy, who was naturally the most good-tempered person in the world, said he never allowed anyone to touch his wireless set. Duds wished that she had not let him in for this ghastly party. It was getting even him down, and no wonder. But how was she to know that the twins had quarreled, that Sandy had some dark and secret sorrow, or else unbearable indigestion, and that Irene Dumbleton would turn out to be the world's worst bore. She ought to have known about Henry. How awful to think that she had once been so blinded by love for him that she had not realized that he was a menace.

The program had at last started to come through, but it would have been better if it hadn't. A pantomime wants to be seen to be enjoyed. The jokes seemed pointless and the songs lacking tune or rhythm. One by one the houseparty left the room, except Mrs. Dumbleton, who sat on talking through the wireless. Duds longed to turn it off, but after Tommy had taken so much trouble to tune in for, her she was afraid of hurting his feelings, already ruffled by Henry. At last, Irene said that she would go to bed and Duds escorted here there, then went down to the kitchen to fill her own hot water bottle. There was a light on in the study; probably somebody had left it on by mistake. She was just about to turn the door handle when she heard Jo's voice, "I'll be able to get hold of it, all right."

CHAPTER 6

THE HUNT BALL took place on the Friday of Christmas week. The Lethbridges had arranged to take their guests to dine at a hotel in Fordham, their nearest town. It will be a relief not to have to bother about dinner, thought Duds. She rather wished she could stay at home and go to bed. She had been looking forward to this ball for weeks—it was the first since the war—but the last few days had tired her so much that she had no interest in it left. If only her houseparty had been a success, she did not believe she would have noticed being tired. If only there had been laughter about the house, she would have enjoyed every moment, but there was no laughter, no silly chatter, unless you counted Mrs. Dumbleton's which was the wrong sort, dull and not funny. Henry talked a good deal, but he would have been better if he had kept quiet, as his conversation annoyed everyone, except presumably his wife and perhaps Josephine, who was inclined to encourage him. Gordon was very pleasant and very soothing, but a houseparty should not need soothing. Flo had seemed to enjoy her day's hunting on Boxing Day, but otherwise she had been quiet and sad, though anxious to be helpful. Jo was bitter, and Duds would have said that she was spiteful if she had not known that the poor girl was desperately unhappy. Sandy— well, Sandy did not bear thinking about. Duds only hoped that he was not on the verge of some really bad illness. She would not be surprised to hear that he had a tumor or even worse.

In the morning Henry and Jo went off to play golf. Duds was afraid that they were having an affair, but she did not see what she could do about it. Irene was such a frightful bore that one could hardly blame her husband for seeking amusement elsewhere. All the same, she did not like to feel that this kind of thing was going on in her house. Perhaps she was old-fashioned, but she had not pictured this being that sort of party when she had made her plans. On the other hand, if it took Jo's mind off her troubles, that was all to the good, and it was not likely to go very far, from what Duds remembered of Henry.

Flo and Gordon went for a ride and Sandy disappeared, no one knew where, but his absence was a relief. Tommy was busy about the place so Duds was left with Irene Dumbleton. She very kindly offered to help with the housework and to Dud's surprise she was quite effi-cient at it. She talked the whole time whether Duds was in the room or not, but she was no trouble at all. In fact she was distinctly helpful, and it was nice to get the place cleaned up a bit. Four days and eight people had made a lot of dirt. Everyone except Sandy returned to lun-cheon and Duds was too tired to worry about him. She went to her own room with a book and was soon fast asleep. If Sandy committed suicide or Jo and Henry eloped, it would be just too bad, she thought as she dropped off.

After tea she went round the henhouses, then went up to dress. She had seen that the boiler was stoked up so that everyone could have a hot bath, and she went straight to hers, determined for once that she would have one herself, whether her guests went short or not. She felt less tired and depressed after it, and she looked at her dress with satisfaction. It was really quite a good dress, and though it was prewar she had only worn it twice. She did not think that she looked too repulsive in it. The village dressmaker had let it out a tiny bit but no one would know that, she decided.

Tommy came in, looking very nice in his pink coat, and she tied his tie for him. "There is hardly anything left to drink in the house," he remarked rather gloomily. "We won't offer anyone a drink before we start. We can have them at the White Swan."

"Good idea! I am afraid Sandy drinks rather a lot. I wonder what is the matter with him?"

"I don't know," replied her husband. "But Henry is enough to make anyone commit murder and Mrs. D. isn't very bright company."

"I'm frightfully sorry, darling. I am afraid this party is an awful washout."

"Such bad luck on you," grumbled Tommy. "You put yourself to all this trouble and they mooch about the place as if they were in quod. I should like to strangle the lot. You look a perfect wreck."

This was not very bright news when one had just dressed oneself up in one's best to go to a ball. She put on some rouge and thought of the old days and of how excited she had been at the idea of a Hunt Ball and of how nice she used to look and how she hadn't had to bother about rouge or whether her dress was well cut, as her figure had been good enough to look right in any dress. Perhaps she was imagining things. Middle-aged people often thought that when they were young they had been radiantly lovely and a frightful success. She had never been anything very striking. It was her friend Lupin who had been so pretty. On the other hand she did not think she had been too revolting herself and anyway she had always enjoyed herself enormously.

Everything had been such fun when she and Lupin had been together. If only she could have come to this ghastly houseparty it would have all been quite different. Why on earth had she had to go and marry a clergyman and bury herself in the country or the seaside or wherever it was, preparing people for confirmation and encouraging young mothers to be good wives or the other way round? It was seven years since she had seen Lupin—would she have altered? She was two or three years younger than Duds but she was no longer a girl. She had two children but it was difficult to imagine her with a spreading figure or a tired skin. But everyone had changed, so she had probably done so too, and had settled down to being a frumpy clergyman's wife, and if they did meet she would talk about the food problem or her children's insides or the difficulty she had in getting the young people to church.

Everyone was rather late in assembling, but eventually they got off and arrived at the White Swan, where Tommy ordered drinks. Gordon was looking very handsome in his pink coat and Flo was quite lovely in a dress of pale gold. Jo might have been considered the more handsome of the two in a dress of very dark red, which just did not clash with the pink coats. Irene Dumbleton looked very nice in black velvet. While she sipped her sherry she talked without ceasing. Sandy looked sulky as usual and the drinks that he took in rapid succession did not make him any less so.

Duds enjoyed her dinner. It was a treat to eat one that she had not first had to scrounge and then to cook, or at any rate to serve up, and whatever the more sophisticated members of the party might think, the three courses tasted to her like manna. There was the usual trouble afterwards of moving the party on from the hotel to the ball. She wondered if Lupin's Sunday school treats and mothers' outings were as difficult to cope with as her houseparty. They lingered over coffee and cigarettes, then Flo and Jo were ages in the cloakroom, and then, though it had been arranged beforehand, no one seemed able to decide in which car they were going and stood arguing on the steps.

However, at last they really did arrive at the country house which had been lent for the ball, and Duds found herself dancing once again. Her first partner was Gordon. He was very nice and refused to believe that she had not danced for seven years. He was a very good dancer himself and Duds thoroughly enjoyed herself. It was delightful to be in a well-lit room full of well-dressed people with nothing to do but to enjoy oneself. Her party was really extremely nice-looking, whatever their other shortcomings might be, she thought to herself complacently. Jo was the most striking girl in the room and Flo the prettiest, and though Henry certainly did resemble a codfish, it was a distinguished-looking codfish.

"I do think Flo is looking simply lovely," she said aloud, as her cousin passed with Sandy.

"So do I," agreed Gordon, and he sounded pleased. "She is enjoying this week with you so much."

"Is she really? I am afraid things aren't so nice as I should have liked. I mean it is difficult scrounging food and drink, and one can't have people waited on as they used to be, but Flo has been a perfect angel about helping."

"She is loving every minute of it," said Gordon. "She is very devoted to you, you know, and she was delighted at the thought of spending Christmas with you."

"I can't get used to her and Jo being so grown up. You see, I didn't see them during the war except at your wedding, and one does lose touch with people. I keep remembering them both as they were before the war. Tommy and I went to stay with my aunt—their mother, you know—and it was their first Hunt Ball and they looked such darlings, dressed alike in frocks of apple green. No one could tell them apart. It does sound funny because they are not a bit alike now."

"No, I can't imagine them ever having been alike. Of course I can see that Josephine is very good-looking, but she is quite a different type from Flo."

"Yes, isn't she? It is funny how people grow up."

"I do wish that she had let Flo share that money with her," went on Gordon, in a confidential voice. "You know she wanted to, of course."

"Naturally, and I think it is dreadfully bad luck on Flo. I think Jo would do it if she could, but she just feels she can't. I don't understand it myself, but then I've never been proud."

"I wish Jo wouldn't be proud, because it hurts Flo."

"I think she has had something to make her very unhappy," explained Duds, "and it makes her difficult about everything, poor little thing."

"I should not be surprised if you are right," agreed Gordon. "In fact, I have had that impression myself, not that I know her at all well. She doesn't often come to stay with us, and when she does I never seem to get to know her any better. It may be that she is very sad and finds it hard to be natural, but I do wish she would confide in us. Isn't it funny how you get to know some people at once, while others you never get to know any better even if you see them every day? If you don't mind me saying so, I feel as if I'd known you for ages, though we met for the first time last Monday."

Duds felt rather touched. Gordon was really very nice and he was obviously devoted to Florence. "I was at your wedding," she reminded him.

"I didn't see anyone there except Flo," he replied.

Duds met several old friends, people whom she had known when she and Tommy used to stay with his uncle. She danced with them and introduced Sandy to two very pretty girls. She wondered if he had had an unhappy love affair. What a pity that he and Jo could not take to each other. They were both very unhappy and might be ready for the rebound, as people called it. But of course they knew each other too well and would not be likely to fall in love, she was afraid. Josephine was dancing with a little bald man with a clever face. Duds was just wondering who he was when Jo brought him up and introduced him.

"This is Mr. Veazey," she said. "My boss."

"Might I have a dance?" he inquired, and Duds rather reluctantly agreed, for she had hoped it was nearly time for her to dance with Tommy without being a bad hostess. She looked round for him, and saw that he was dancing with a tall commanding-looking female with a beaky nose.

"That is my wife dancing with your husband," said Mr. Veazey proudly. "I daresay you may have heard of her, she is Olivia Ordemar."

Duds vaguely remembered having seen the name in advertisements of novels, but could not remember ever having read any of them. "Oh, is she really?" she exclaimed. "How thrilling! I haven't had her last book yet. Let me think, what is it called?"

"*Love Knows No Law*," he replied.

"Oh yes, of course. I shall get it with one of my book tokens," and she sighed, for being of a truthful nature she would now feel obliged at least to ask for it in the bookshop. With any luck it will be out of print, she told herself, and I'll be able to get something I want.

"Did I hear Miss Harnet say that she was your cousin?" asked Mr. Veazey.

"Yes, she is staying with us for Christmas,"

"How very nice for you both. You live near here I expect."

"About ten miles away. Our village is called Pickering."

"We are staying with some relatives of my wife's in the neighborhood, Sir John and Lady Holroyd. I expect you know them."

"We have met them quite often. We used to stay down here a lot when my husband's uncle was alive. He died during the war and we came in for the place. Not that it is really a place, just a farmhouse, you know, and a bit of land. But it is a very favorite neighborhood of ours."

"I hope I may bring my wife to call on you while we are here. We are staying till the middle of next week."

"Oh, that will be awfully nice, and you must all come to the little party we are having on New Year's Eve. It will be awfully mad, I expect. We rather thought of having fancy dress—optional, of course."

"That will be delightful, thank you. I have heard so much about you from Miss Harnet. She is a very clever girl, as I expect you know. I have never had a secretary who was such a help to me."

Duds knew as soon as she started dancing with Sandy that he had had quite enough to drink. He was not drunk, but 'he had drink taken,' as the Irish expression goes. Oh dear, she sighed to herself. She had hoped that the evening was going to be a success after all. Supper had gone quite well. The Veazeys and Holroyds had joined their party and she had enjoyed her conversation with Sir John. Olivia Ordemar had rather taken away Tommy's appetite, but Sandy had been almost in good spirits for him (Duds was afraid it was the champagne) and had thrown himself nobly into the breach and had diverted most of her conversation to himself, allowing Tommy to talk to Lady Holroyd about cows and pigs, so Duds was feeling grateful to Sandy and ready to forgive him for having made so free with the champagne.

"What a woman!" he exclaimed. "What a priceless woman! She told me that a Hunt Ball was a barbaric survival, but to her as a writer it was an interesting spectacle. She said that you young men (I don't think there are a dozen in the room under fifty) have come home from the chase bringing your spoils with you. I said that one did not bring the fox home as a rule. I think she had got it mixed up, and meant 'sheaves with you.' You know 'the valley stands so thick with corn that it doth laugh and sing.' " He started to sing himself in a high falsetto voice. It was not so bad as it might have been, as the band was playing loudly and some of the dancers were making hunting noises as they revolved round the room. Many were taking the floor who had not taken it since before the war and were too occupied in what their feet were doing to notice the vagaries of other people. All the same, Duds felt it was very tiresome of Sandy.

"I feel as if I could do with a breath of fresh air," she said. "Let's go outside for a bit."

"All right, let's. But you had better have a wrap."

"Yes, but wait here a minute. Don't move."

Sandy laughed. "What do you think I am likely to do? Elope with Olivia? I tell you what I think . . ."

Duds dived into the ladies' cloakroom and found her old fur coat. Sandy was waiting for her where she had left him, and they went out into the garden. The midnight air was cold but very refreshing.

"I know why you suggested coming out," remarked Sandy. "You thought that I was drunk and that the night air would sober me down."

"I don't think you are drunk but I think you have had quite enough," replied Duds. "Why do you behave like an undergraduate, Sandy? You must be—let me see—twenty-six or -seven by now."

"Twenty-seven last November, if you want to know."

"Well, there you are, and yet you behave as if you were going through the adolescent stage, either sitting about in the sulks or else drinking—well, drinking enough to make you talk in a very loud voice."

"Have I aspersed a woman's fair name?" demanded Sandy. "I assure you I have no designs on Olivia's virtue. I wish I could say the same for her husband and my cousin Josephine."

"Josephine? What are you talking about now?"

"Didn't you notice them at supper? I don't think Henry liked it very much. After all he has been making the running so far, this Christmastide."

"You are like a gossiping old woman, Sandy. You make me sick."

"First I am an adolescent undergraduate and now I am an old woman. I wonder what I will be next—an expectant mother, perhaps?"

"I hope you will turn back into the nice reasonable person you used to be. What is the matter, Sandy? Has something beastly happened to you? I really am most frightfully sorry if you are in trouble."

"What makes you think I am in trouble?"

"Well, I hardly think you would have been as rude as you have been to Tommy and me during the last few days unless you were in trouble," retorted his cousin.

"Well, you tried me pretty high. You never said a word to me about Flo and Jo coming to you for Christmas."

"Didn't I? No, I don't believe I did. I wrote off to all of you at the same time. So I didn't know if they were coming or not. If I had said they were coming, and then they had refused, you might have thought I was luring you down here on false pretenses."

"Do you think I *wanted* to see them?"

"Didn't you? Surely you used to be tremendous friends in the old days."

"Friends! I never liked Jo. Even in the nursery she was a self-opinionated grabbing little beast."

"Sandy, I am sure she wasn't. I thought they were both perfect dears."

"Forgive me for mentioning a painful subject, but you have just told me I am an old woman. We all seem the same age now we are grown up, but in those days you were our big cousin. You did not see the twins in the nursery when they were being natural. You didn't see Jo being beastly to Flo. You didn't see her when she took Flo's kitten and threatened to drown it unless Flo gave her half-a-crown. She is being beastly now. She is trying to pay her out for inheriting her grandfather's money. I don't quite know what she is aiming at. I never knew what people meant when they said they were alike to look at. I never saw the slightest resemblance, even when they were children, and now you wouldn't even guess that they were related. But their natures are even more different than their looks. Flo was always a perfect angel and Jo was always a perfect fiend."

"Sandy!"

"Well?"

"Oh, nothing."

"Were you going to ask me if I were in love with Flo?"

"It is no business of mine."

"No, it isn't, but I don't mind you knowing. I am not ashamed of it. I have been in love with Flo ever since I can remember. Of course I did not know it was that when I was a boy. I just knew that I liked being with her better than with anyone else. I can only have been about seventeen when I first did realize it. It was my last year at Eton and she came down for the Fourth. She had a frock with poppies on it. Jo didn't come, thank goodness. I was so glad and then it suddenly came over me that I was in love with her. She could not have been more than about fifteen. Then I think it was the next Christmas I got the ring out of the pudding and I gave it to her."

Duds remembered dinner on Christmas Day and the way Sandy had pushed the ring to one side and the look of distress on Florence's face, which had puzzled her at the time.

"I always took for granted we should marry when we grew up. Well, as you know, I went abroad for a year when I left school instead of going straight to Cambridge. Then when I came back war broke out, so I never was an undergraduate, in spite of your kind remarks. Well, I didn't see Flo for over two years, and by then she was in the W.R.N.S., but she was still wearing my ring, and we took for granted that we should get properly engaged some time. I had nothing to offer her as I had no job except the army and I did not know what I should be doing after the war. I hadn't even been to Cambridge. But we had a wonderful time during three leaves, going about everywhere together, and I am certain then that she was as sure of us being together always as I was.

"Then I was taken prisoner and I was in Germany till the end of the war. It wasn't nice but it wasn't too bad. I was much luckier than many people. It wasn't at all like Belsen. Of course letters were very irregular, but Flo kept on writing and I just lived for the peace. I got friendly with a chap who was in business and he promised to find me a place in the firm. He said my languages would be useful.

"Well, I'm in it now, though I've a good mind to chuck it up and go to Canada or something. But anyhow, then I was frightfully braced, because I thought I would really be in a position to marry Flo and live happily ever after. I sent her a wire the minute I landed and she wired back, 'So glad, longing to see you, letter following. Flo.' I thought she would be there to meet me, but I supposed she couldn't wangle leave, especially as we weren't officially engaged. Then— well—then I got the letter and learned that she was engaged to Gordon."

Duds squeezed his arm, "Oh, my dear," she said.

"Yes, it was a pretty bad blow. All the time that I had been a prisoner I had been thinking of her and planning for her. But she had forgotten all about me and got engaged to someone on the staff, someone who had never been out of England."

"You know, Sandy, those boy and girl affairs don't often come to anything. Don't you think that perhaps at ordinary times, when you had been meeting people in the ordinary way, you might have got to like someone else? You see, you poor old thing, you were in your horrid prison all the time and you had nothing to do but keep on thinking about Flo."

"No. I should have gone on thinking about her whatever I had been doing and however many girls I had been meeting. She is the only woman in the world for me, always has been and always will be. I can't really believe that she cares for that sleek, two-faced, safety-firster."

Duds rather liked Gordon. He was always pleasant, always polite and deferential, a relief after Henry's maddeningly superior manner and Sandy's sulkiness, but she knew better than to say so. If someone is running down someone else, unless loyalty compels you to stand up for them, it is much better not to, as it only adds fuel to their anger. It is much wiser to agree with them, as that may help to cool them down, and Duds had no qualms in agreeing that she wondered what it was about Gordon that had attracted Flo. As a matter of fact, tiresome as Sandy was, she could not help feeling that she would have preferred him to Gordon if she had been in Flo's place. Surely there would be more glamor about a man who had spent four years in a prison camp than about one who had never been out of England, even though that may not have been his fault. Aloud she said, "I can't think why she took to him—he is very pleasant but he never seems to count much one way or the other. I suppose it was propinquity. . . Goodness! that is 'John Peel!' We must have been here ages, the dance is nearly over. Come on, I insist on having this with Tommy."

They hurried back to the ballroom. Florence was standing by her husband. Sandy went straight up to her and took her by the arm. "Come on, Flo," he said.

She looked up at him and laughed, and they went off together. Gordon approached Duds, but before he could reach her Mr. Veazey had invited her to dance, and Duds nearly giggled to find herself galloping round the room in the arms of the serious bald-headed publisher, though she was very disappointed not to be dancing this last dance with Tommy. Gordon, not a whit embarrassed at being deprived of two partners, took Olivia Ordemar and joined the noisy capering throng, al-

though Olivia wore a remote expression, as if she were really somewhere quite different. Henry had secured Jo and Tommy was burdened
with Irene.

Suddenly people started to form lines. Tommy caught Duds' hand.
There they were in one line, Mr. Veazey, Duds, Tommy and Irene, all
dancing madly down the room, singing at the top of their voices, "Yes, I
ken John Peel and Ruby too." Mr. Veazey was puffing loudly. Duds
caught sight of Flo and Sandy with Jo and Henry; the two girls were in
the middle hand-in-hand.

Everything was all right, no, not all right for poor Sandy, but surely
it would come all right, he would get over it. In this gay, noisy throng it
was difficult to believe in tragedy. Then she saw his expression as he
looked at Flo and she knew he would never get over it. She could not
see Flo's face. Then she felt Tommy's hand gripping hers and she tried
to get a glimpse of the famous novelist being propelled along between
Tommy and Gordon, who had now joined their line. Tommy's voice was
upraised, "From the drag to the chase, from the chase to the view, from
the view to the death in the morning." Gordon was singing quietly in
his charming baritone, Mr. Veazey managed a "View halloo."

The war was over, everybody was safely home and they were at a
real old-fashioned Hunt Ball once more! The last seven years dropped
away. Suddenly the band broke into "God Save the King," and everyone pulled themselves together and tried to stand to attention, very red
in the face, very short of breath, but still full of loyalty and trying to sing
the National Anthem with as much fervor as possible.

CHAPTER 7

SATURDAY was not a very bright day. For one thing, everyone was
feeling rather tired after the dissipation of the night before. For another,
both the whisky and the gin had run out.

"I am frightfully sorry," announced Duds, "but I am afraid the drink
has run a little low. There is still a drop or two of sherry and there is
some beer."

"Oh, hell!" exclaimed Jo, and Duds felt that it would really be better to have a houseparty which did not include any relations.

Irene said she did not want anything to drink, she thought that she was better without it, and Sandy gave one look, as though to say "It only needed this," and left the room and the house. Duds hoped that he had not gone to commit suicide, but remembering his confidences of the night before felt that it was more than likely. Flo and Gordon were out hunting and Tommy was busy about the place.

Jo turned to Henry. "What about a pub crawl?" she suggested.

"Good idea," agreed Henry. "What about you, dear?" he asked his wife. "I know Duds will be busy with her household duties."

"Not for me, thanks," replied Irene. "After the champagne last night I would rather stick to water today. Not that I had too much, nor that I feel any bad effects, but I had not tasted champagne since nineteen-thirty-nine—no, I am wrong, there was the Carruthers' wedding in nineteen-forty—or was it forty-one?—and the Dudleys' and one or two others. But anyhow, except just for one sip at weddings, I had not touched it since the outbreak of war. I never take much at a wedding. I do not consider it a suitable drink for the middle of the afternoon. I should much rather have a cup of tea or coffee, but I suppose it would not seem like a wedding without champagne. What are you doing this morning, Dorothy? May I help you with the housework again? I enjoyed it so much yesterday. Have you a Hoover?"

Duds quite enjoyed the next hour. Irene really was a good worker and they Hoovered the carpets and the armchairs and felt a feeling of satisfaction when they saw how much dust they had collected in the bag. Duds had got used to Irene's flow of conversation and found it rather soothing than otherwise.

"I always have enjoyed housework but I have never had much opportunity because maids don't like one interfering, and of course now that people can do their own work I live in a hotel. But I do remember once when I was married to my first husband we had a tiny house at the seaside and I did nearly all the work myself except for a daily woman. I enjoyed it very much. I cooked all sorts of things, and Henry— I should say Robert—said they were very good. Of course we were young then and it was like a picnic. I don't think Henry would have cared for it and of course I could not have dusted the rooms if he had been there. The least speck of dust starts off his asthma. Once in the hotel I did not think that the mantelpiece had been properly dusted and I took an old handkerchief without thinking and started to work on it and poor Henry who was sitting in the room began to choke at once."

Duds remembered Henry's asthma from earlier days and how frightened she had been once when she had been alone with him and he had had a bad attack. "How *is* his asthma?" she asked.

"It really is marvelously better. I hardly dare talk about it but he has been a different man since he has had these heroin injections."

"Heroin? Oh yes, I have heard of that. It is frightfully strong, isn't it? I mean you can't get it without a doctor's prescription?

"No, I think it is a form of morphia, at least its other name is di-amorphine. It has to be measured very carefully. Luckily I have had a good deal of experience of nursing and I am able to give him an injection when I see an attack coming on and it always settles him down. But I am so frightened of leaving the bottle about, as there is enough in it to kill anyone and it would be awkward if he got it mixed up with his cough mixture or his cascara or his tonic."

Duds tried to picture Henry's washstand with its array of bottles. There would be a hair tonic too, she was sure, and perhaps a soothing solution for applying after shaving, a mouthwash or gargle and Sterodent for his false teeth. She was recalled from this fascinating picture by the entrance of Tommy clamoring for his lunch. He asked where the rest of the guests were and seemed rather relieved by their absence.

"I hope that Henry will give Josephine lunch out," said Irene. "It is a great help when people have meals out, isn't it?"

Duds also hoped that they were lunching out. If they did, she thought, there might be enough meat over for rissoles tonight. It would be a frightful nuisance if they came in late and wanted everything warmed up again. They might have let her know one way or the other, bother them! Then there would be all the washing up to do. Mrs. Elphick went home at three and came back in the evening to help Edith with the dinner, so if the others came in late and wanted lunch it would mean Edith doing it all or else leaving the washing up till Mrs. Elphick came back, and she would not be too pleased at the sight of a mass of dirty things piled up. Edith was an angel, but she was getting a bit sick of this houseparty and no wonder. Nothing like as sick as I am, Duds told herself. I suppose I shall have to do the washing up myself. After all, I asked them here, fool that I was—it isn't Edith's fault.

Duds was very tired after her unaccustomed late night and her hard work this morning, but after Tommy had gone back into the garden and Irene had retired to her room, she went out to the scullery and helped Edith wash up and put away the things. Even then she decided against going to her own room for a rest. She felt that if once she lay down she would never get up again.

She went into the drawing room and put some finishing touches to her work of the morning. Then she went into the hall. The decorations were getting rather disheveled. She removed some of them and rearranged the others. She emptied several ashtrays that seemed to pile themselves up miraculously. She and Irene had emptied them all that morning. She made up the fire and wondered if the supply of wood would hold out, not that it gave out much heat by itself, and there was very little coal. Still it looked bright and cheerful, and she applied the bellows. Oh dear, how tired she was. She sat down for a moment on the big chair behind the hearth and before she had time to think about it she was fast asleep. She awoke to the sound of voices.

"You are such a tantalizing little devil. Why can't you say yes or no?"

"Do you want me to say no?"

There was a moment's silence. Duds did not know whether to make her presence known or not. What a ghastly situation in which to find oneself. She felt pretty sure that they were embracing now. Then she heard Jo laugh.

"You witch, you little witch," said Henry, hoarsely.

Duds would have given all she possessed to be elsewhere.

"Did you say witch?" asked Jo. "I hope you said witch!" and Duds could hear her light steps running up the stairs. She heard Henry walk to the foot of them. His heavier tread was quite audible, so was his labored breathing. What on earth was she to do? Should she confront him? After all, Jo was old enough to look after herself. She had been younger than Jo when she had had her brief affair with Henry. He was married then, so she really had no right too feel shocked. She was growing old, she supposed, but she did feel rather annoyed. It was not the way she liked people to behave in her house. She had meant this to be a happy, homey Christmas party, not a society comedy. After all, she had been in love with Henry, or thought she had, while she was quite sure that Jo had no illusions on that score.

But what about Henry? Was he taking it seriously? She thought how decent Irene had been the last two mornings, helping her with the housework. After all when it came to being a bore, Henry was in the first class, while Irene was only among the honorably mentioned. In fact, when one got used to her voice it ceased to irritate and became rather soothing. The stairs were creaking. Duds peeped out cautiously. Yes, there he went slowly, like an old man. Could it be that he was really in love with Jo?

As soon as he was out of sight, Duds got up and went to see about tea. Flo and Gordon came back and of course she had to give them eggs, though she had been counting on them for breakfast tomorrow. Sandy came in and asked for whisky and had to be told that there wasn't any and was given beer instead. The evening seemed interminable and the supper was not at all nice. The rissoles were hard and the sprouts soft.

"I am too sleepy to play bridge," announced Flo. "I should only revoke."

"Well, we were all up rather late last night," replied Duds, hopefully. "An early night won't do any of us any harm."

"I think it is very tiring going to bed early," remarked Jo. "One can never get to sleep and one tosses and turns and tires oneself much more than if one sat up and played something."

"Well, I am not going to play bridge," said Sandy.

"The perfect guest," murmured Josephine, sweetly.

"What about a game of rummy?" suggested Irene. "I always think that is such a nice quiet game. It does not tax the brain at all. I am feeling rather sleepy myself, I must admit. Henry and I are not used to late nights, are we, dear? I remember in my young days I used to think nothing of being up late six nights a week, but I am not as young as I used to be."

"Same here," agreed Tommy. "Duds and I are not much of a hand nowadays at missing our eight hours. I think a quiet game of rummy would just fill the bill. And we will all go to bed at ten."

"Oh, Tommy," grumbled Jo. "You are growing into a hermit. I can remember when I was a young girl I thought you were quite a thrilling young man. And I envied you and Duds, because you were always running off to night clubs and things and now I come here and find you both absolutely middle-aged."

"The perfect guest!" retorted Sandy. "Such sweet manners!"

"After all, you will be middle-aged yourself one day," added Tommy.

"I hope I'll die first," exclaimed Jo.

"You would be pretty ghastly as a middle-aged woman," agreed Sandy. "You would be one of those kittenish ones who are always trying to seem younger than they really are."

"Sandy!" protested Flo, reproachfully. "And in any case," she went on, "no one could possibly call either Tommy or Duds middle-aged. And as for wanting to go to bed early, I know I shall be as glad as anyone to go at ten."

They sat round the table and argued about how to play rummy. "Properly played," declared Henry, "rummy can be a real gamble."

"Don't let's play it properly," begged Tommy. "We don't want to start gambling."

"I can see Tommy with a beard reading prayers and making all his children be in bed by ten o'clock each evening," remarked Jo. "Ugh!" It was obvious to all that Flo had kicked her sister on the shin. Duds was grateful to her for her consideration, but she had hoped that her disappointment at having no children had not been so widely known.

"I am sorry," said Jo, making things worse. "I wasn't thinking of what I was saying." Duds felt that Irene was throwing her a commiserating glance.

Spiteful little cat, thought Duds. I believe she said that on purpose.

"Is the two of spades the joker?" asked Irene.

"Yes," replied Tommy.

"No," said Duds. "There are two real jokers in these packs. At least I think there are."

"There is one anyway," said Flo.

"The first hand we all have to put down one three, next two threes, then one four, two fours, one five and last of all two fives," explained Duds.

"This is quite a new game to me," said Irene.

"Yes, that is not rummy," announced Henry.

"It is the way we play it," said Duds. After all, it was her house she told herself, so she supposed she could choose how to play rummy.

"I have played it in Japan," said Henry.

"I wish you were playing it in Japan now," muttered Sandy.

"Aren't you thinking of mah-jong, dear?" asked his wife. "That comes from Japan, I believe. Such a quaint game. A pung was it of winds? Very pretty. It is strange how unpleasant the Japanese have turned. I had always thought of them as such cultured people, cherry blossom and Madame Chrysanthemum, so charming. But I sometimes think war brings out the worst in people, especially among one's enemies."

"Three knaves, remarked Tommy. "And the peace brings out the worst among one's friends," he added.

"Three queens," said Irene. "Oh, I never took a card. Thank you, that is right. Now I discard one. Take, put down, discard. Now I remember quite well."

"Three kings," said Jo.

CHAPTER 8

SUNDAY dawned cold and dreary. Mrs. Elphick did not come that day and Duds was very busy all the morning helping Edith with the rooms. Florence was very good and helpful, but she seemed depressed. Was it because Jo was so horrid to her, or was it anything to do with Sandy? Gordon was very delightful—attentive, handsome and courteous—but Duds felt that he would pall on one after a bit. Disagreeable as Sandy was these days, Duds felt that she would rather be married to him. Charm is all very well at a party, she thought, but it would be an unsubstantial thing to have to live with, rather like a continual diet of meringues and trifle.

Irene Dumbleton tidied her own bedroom, but by twenty minutes to eleven she was dressed and ready for church with her prayer book in her hand, and Duds felt that as a good hostess she ought to escort her there. On the other hand, she did not see how Edith was going to cook and serve the luncheon single-handed. Henry put his foot down. "My dear Irene, I do think that one should have a complete holiday when one is about it. After all, I always take you to church in London and hand round the plate. I think I deserve an occasional Sunday off."

"Not the plate, dear. I don't think any churches have plates now, and of course it does say that one should not let your left hand see what your right is doing, but I think they got larger collections in those days. After all it is very easy to slip a threepenny bit into a bag, but one would hardly like to put it into a plate for all to see. And then there is that text about letting your light shine before men. It is very confusing how some of the texts seem to contradict each other. I remember when they first started to use colored alms bags at our parish church, my father refused to attend there any longer. He said it was the thin end of the wedge and we should be having incense before we knew where we were, but we never did, and personally I can't see any harm in incense—it has such a nice smell, though I believe it makes some people feel a little faint, and it is a disinfectant, I believe, so necessary in some of the churches abroad! But our vicar says we must be careful not to give offense to our weaker brethren. He is the most broad-minded man."

"Florence and I shall be delighted to come to church with you, Mrs. Dumbleton," said Gordon. "Won't we, Flo?"

Duds was very relieved and felt how ungrateful it was of her to think she would rather be married to Sandy, who was sitting glowering out of the window—not that there was any likelihood of her marrying either of them.

"I should love to," agreed Flo. "I do like the church here. It reminds me of the one at my old home. I am different from Mr. Dumbleton. I like a few wrong notes occasionally. There is something too much like a concert about some of the London churches, don't you think so, Sandy?"

"I have never thought about it," replied Sandy shortly. Then as he caught sight of Florence's face, he relented. "But I see what you mean," he added.

"What about you, Duds?" said Flo. "Won't you come?"

"I am afraid I have rather a lot to do this morning, but it will be awfully nice if you and Gordon will go with Irene."

Josephine and Henry started out together soon after the churchgoers had left, and Duds guessed that they were going for another pub crawl. "You will be back in time for lunch, Jo, won't you?" she called after her. "Because Edith wants to go out this afternoon."

"Oh Lord, Duds," exclaimed Josephine, "you are turning into the most frightful old maiden aunt, always thinking about the servants. What is the good of having servants if you are going to spend all your time waiting on them and worrying about them?"

"Need you be so offensive, Jo?" inquired Sandy.

"I could be much more offensive than that if I liked," replied Jo.

"I have no doubt of it."

"Oh, don't quarrel, you two," begged Duds. "Everything is bad enough without that." She had forgotten for the moment that a hostess does not lament publicly that her house is full of uncongenial guests. "Of course I don't mind in the least what Jo says to me. I know she doesn't mean it."

"Doesn't she?"

"If one only said what one meant," remarked Jo, "one would not say much."

"That would hardly be a disadvantage," retorted Sandy, and Jo slammed out of the room.

"You are a beast, Sandy," said Duds. "I know that Jo is very trying, but she is in trouble and that is why she is so horrid to everyone. You ought to feel for her. After all you are in the same boat."

"Heaven forbid," exclaimed Sandy. "The truth is, Duds, that I loathe the girl. I always have. I told you the other night how poisonous she always was to Flo, trying to get everything for herself. I told you about the kitten. I'll never forget. I nearly drowned her then and I wish I had."

"Don't you think she may have been joking about that? A beastly joke, of course, but I don't believe she would really have done it. After all, Flo has forgotten all about it."

"I wonder."

"Besides, if she has such a grabbing nature as you make out, why won't she take her share of her grandfather's money, as Flo wants her to?"

"I don't know. But I am sure she has some good reason, by which I mean some rotten reason. She will take it in the end, but she likes tormenting Flo by refusing at first. Or perhaps she thinks by holding out to start with she will get more in the long run. I don't know, but she did not like the idea of it being left to Flo. She does not like the idea of Flo being the heiress. She wants everything—money, kudos, perhaps she wants Gordon, just the sort of thing she would want. And I believe he was her friend first. I wish to goodness he had married her. Oh well. I'm sorry, Duds, Jo and I both want kicking. Something seems to tell me that you are not enjoying your houseparty much. It is too bad. I have been so busy thinking of myself and my own grievances that I have forgotten your side of the picture. I'll go and help your husband round up the chickens and rabbits and whatnots like a perfect guest. And if you take my advice, you will forget all about your chores and will put up your feet and read the *News of the World*. You may find some people in that even worse off than yourself. At least no one as been murdered in your house yet."

Mr. and Mrs. Veazey turned up that afternoon, just as they had all finished tea. Duds went out to make a fresh pot, inwardly swearing.

"This is a delightful place you have here," the publisher said to her on her return.

"There is atmosphere," announced Olivia, in her deep, thrilling tones. "I can always detect atmosphere at once."

Does she mean that the house smells, wondered Duds. It was difficult to keep a house as clean as one would like when there were six people staying in it. Six such people! she thought to herself savagely. Her usual good temper had almost exhausted itself.

"Something has happened here," went on Olivia, fixing Tommy with her great amber eyes.

"We don't talk about it," replied Tommy gravely.

"Ah, so I was right. Something has happened, I always know. I could work here. If you will let me, I will come and stay with you while I write my next novel. I need a place like this in which to work, a place that will stimulate me. I shall be no trouble to anybody if I can just have a room in which to work and peace and quiet in which to concentrate. A chop or a piece of steak is all I want to eat. I do not care for food—and above all, atmosphere!"

"Well," said Tommy, reflectively, "perhaps if you are really coming to form one of our little home circle, I ought to tell you the true history of our house. It is a very long time ago when my great-uncle first married. After three months of wedded bliss, his wife was found dead in her bed. It was brought in as an accident. After a time, a decent time of course, he married again and the same thing happened. No one was very surprised, as my great-uncle was an eccentric old man, and no one could stand him in long doses, but when he brought home his third wife and she followed the example of her predecessors and made the great change within three months, people began to wonder a little. A detective was brought down by the brother of the last wife and introduced into the house as a butler. He slept in the room in which the deceased ladies had lost their lives and he was awakened in the night by a rat running across his face.

"He awoke with heart thumping and the perspiration running down his forehead. He told several people afterwards that it had been one of the most gruesome experiences in his long and varied life of detecting. I have never been awakened so far by a rat running across my face, but ask anyone who has, and they will tell you it is not so good. Well, the long and short of it was that my great-uncle was fond of money, so he chose wives with a nice little bit of their own who also had weak hearts, and put them to sleep in a certain room and left the rats to do the work for him. You couldn't exactly call it murder."

"I don't like rats," said Olivia.

"No?" replied Tommy, politely.

"Why did all the women with the money and weak hearts marry your eccentric old great-uncle?" asked Sandy.

"Like all the Lethbridges, he was extremely fascinating," replied Tommy.

"I suppose by now you have got rid of the rats," said Olivia.

"Alas, no," said Tommy, "in fact they are now more numerous than before as they have all had large families."

"You want to put down some rat poison," suggested Mr. Veazey.

"That is no good," announced Henry, in his most authoritative manner. "The only thing to do is to ring up your town hall and ask for the official ratcatcher or rodent destroyer, as I believe they call him, to come and attend to the matter for you."

"I don't believe a word of the story," laughed Florence.

"I can never get rid of the rats," explained Tommy. "A fortune-teller once told me that the luck of the Lethbridges would depart from the house if the rats were to leave it. So I keep them with us."

"I could not stay in a house infested with rats," said Olivia Ordemar, decisively.

"Too bad," replied Tommy.

Irene Dumbleton turned from Sandy, to whom she was relating a full description of the food, terms, and other guests at the hotel in which she was at present residing, and turning to the famous novelist, she said, "Don't you like cats? It is an extraordinary thing about cats, either people are very much attached to them or else they dislike them. An aunt of mine had six cats to which she was inordinately attached. She had two children and she did not care for them nearly so much. Unnatural, I call it, don't you? I mean, however fond one was of animals, I think one ought to put one's own children first. After all, they are human. Though I remember being very fond of a kitten once when I was a child. I used to take it up to bed with me."

Duds happened to look up and catch sight of Flo's face. She had gone very white. She remembered Sandy's story about Jo and Flo's kitten. So Flo had not forgotten!

"We were talking about rats," explained Tommy.

"Rats. Are you fond of rats? I have never heard of anyone being fond of rats before, though one of my brothers used to keep white mice when he was a little boy."

Duds did not hear what the publisher was saying to her. She was listening with half an ear to the conversation of the others, wondering what she would do if the Veazeys stayed to supper, wondering whether she would have to ask them to have a glass of sherry before they left, provided they did leave, deciding that she would never have another houseparty as long as she lived,, and wishing that she had not got to wash up the tea things. She pulled herself together, "I am so sorry," she said, "I did not quite hear what you were saying."

"Will you think me very discourteous if I ask to have just one word with Miss Harnet? I do not like talking shop on Sunday, especially at such a delightful teaparty. But I had a letter from one of my novelists yesterday and I should particularly like Miss Harnet's views on it. I will not keep her ten minutes."

"Yes, of course. Jo, will you take Mr. Veazey into the study? He wants a word with you."

Henry glowered at the departing figures of Jo and the publisher. Was she carrying on a flirtation with her employer? wondered Duds. Well, each to her choice. But how anyone could choose either Henry or Mr. Veazey was a puzzle to her. Poor old Jo. She must have been badly hit by the love affair, or whatever it was, and was just getting her own back by flirting with one and all. One could not blame her, but she was not an easy guest. If only Flo and Gordon had come by themselves it would have been quite a pleasant Christmas. But Josephine, Sandy and the Dumbletons were all in their different ways distinct trials. As a matter of fact Duds quite liked Irene, but there was no getting away from the fact that she was a terrible bore.

What a frightful suggestion of that Olivia woman's that she should come here to write a book. It would be over my dead body, thought Duds grimly, and that would be worse than rats. She wondered if the novelist had really swallowed Tommy's ridiculous story. It was pretty bright of him to think it up on the spur of the moment like that, because imagination was not usually his strong suit. Desperation lent him supernatural powers, she supposed. Well, if any more suggestions were made they would have to pretend they had gone away and shut up the house. They would only be able to go out after dark and Tommy would have to grow a beard and she would have to buy a red wig and a pair of dark glasses.

Oh dear, she was going potty herself now. It must be the influence of Olivia. It seemed to inspire both her and Tommy, a humdrum couple if ever there was one, to invent fairy stories at a moment's notice. She stretched herself wearily and started stacking cups and saucers.

Henry kindly took the tray from her, explaining as he did so that she should put the heavy things in the center of the tray and arrange the lighter ones round them. He said that there was really nothing in housework if one went the right way about it. He was surprised that she had not an electric machine for washing up. It would have made all the difference, he said. They understood that sort of thing so much better in America. The wives there did their housework scientifically and were able to reduce it to a minimum. Of course they had all the latest gadgets. He had known one woman with a husband and four children and no servant who ran her own home perfectly and yet found time to be president of one of the leading women's clubs, and to give lectures twice a week. She was also an expert bridge player and gave a great deal of time to the studying of economic problems.

As by this time Henry was drying up her china, Duds did not retort that she wished he had stayed in America, as he seemed to like it so much better there. He went on to say that it was a pity she had not got a different sort of cloth for drying, and that he knew a place in London where you could get a special kind of tea cloth, coupon free, for fifteen shillings each. He also pointed out that the water in which she was washing up was lukewarm, which she knew already, and he wondered at their not having a more up-to-date boiler, although there was no real reason why the present one should not heat the water adequately if only they understood it. He offered to overhaul it for her. She thought of Tommy's face if she were to accept the offer and refused politely. After all he meant to be kind.

At last the washing up was done. The putting away of the china took ages, as Henry had so many suggestions as to how she should rearrange the dresser. He was surprised that she had so many good things and even more surprised that she should eke them out with cups and plates from Woolworth's.

"But these are really good, Duds, you should never use anything else."

"As there are only six cups left, I don't see how I can give .en people tea out of them, unless of course I gave two people one cup between them."

"No, of course you can't do that, and naturally you would find them very hard to replace nowadays, but sometimes at sales one can pick up good china. So many people are having to sell things. You ought to attend sales, it is well worth while. Even if you could not get anything to match, you might find something that would blend. Look at this plate, really lovely. Royal Worcester. Would you like me to keep my eyes open and see if I can find some things for you?"

"It is frightfully good of you, Henry, but I am afraid I cannot afford to buy good china. I use what I've got, but when it goes I just replace it from Woolworths."

Henry shuddered. "You shouldn't. Look here, what could you go to? Sometimes one can pick up a real bargain."

"Oh, I don't know, I'm sure. We are awfully short of ready money just now. We are hoping to make this place pay in time, but at the moment we are having to economize for all we are worth."

"Yes, I quite appreciate that. I expect the death duties were very heavy, as Tommy was only a nephew. I wonder your uncle did not settle some money on you before he died. It is the only sensible thing to do."

"I suppose Uncle thought he would like to keep his own money until he died, and I don't blame him. After all, he needn't have left it to Tommy at all, he had no claim on him, and we are both very grateful to him. I must go and see what everyone is doing. Thank you most frightfully for helping me."

"I am only too glad to be of use. You know, Duds, I hate to see you like this."

"Like what?"

"Well, spending your whole life in the kitchen. You were such a pretty girl and you would be attractive now if only you would take thought for your complexion, instead of spending all your time among the pots and pans. You should have a face massage once a month at least, and your hair seen to, and your nails. . ."

"Thanks."

"Now don't be touchy. It is because I am so fond of you that I take an interest." He bent towards her. "We used to be great friends, Duds," he murmured. "I hate to see you letting yourself go. You could still have a very good time, you know."

"I do have a good time. I am very happy."

"Are you, I wonder. Poor little Duds!" His arms were round her.

Somewhere, quite close, a door banged and she wrenched herself free.
He would have kissed her in a minute, she believed, even though she
had let herself go. It was only because Jo was closeted in the study
with the publisher. Everyone was flirting with somebody else because
they could not have the one they wanted. What a mixup! Well, she
wasn't going to have anyone flirting with her and she hurried out of the
kitchen.

Gordon was tactfully coping with Olivia and evincing great interest in her methods of writing. Irene was sitting by placidly working at a piece of petit point. The others were nowhere to be seen.
Duds thought she would slip out and see if she could find Tommy.
He was probably doing something about the animals. She saw Flo
and Sandy sitting together in the drawing room. They had forgotten to
draw the curtains and the light fell on their faces. Duds turned away.
There was something profane about looking at them, not that they
were sitting very near each other, but there was no mistaking the
expressions on their tragic young faces. Duds moved away and as she
passed the study window, she heard Jo's voice.

"I'll let you know for certain tomorrow night."

"Very well, but five hundred is my last word."

"Is it? We shall see."

CHAPTER 9

TOMORROW at this time they will all be far away, thought Duds,
happily and hospitably, as she went up to dress for her New Year's Eve
party. Tommy would be himself again when they were alone. He had
been very grumpy all day today, poor old thing. But he had really borne
up wonderfully until about teatime (or was it suppertime?) yesterday.
Olivia Ordemar must have been the last straw when she suggested that
she should come and stay with them and write her next book in their
house. However, he had been master of himself at the time and the silly
story of the rats had been just like him. Something must have happened
after that to upset him, because at supper he was a second Sandy at his
worst, and so he had been ever since. Of course Sunday night supper is
always trying to the most cheerful disposition and this was one of the

worst. The bits of cold beef were mostly gristle and the cold shape was enough to cast a gloom over the gayest houseparty. When one adds that there were a few shriveled-looking prunes in a dish, one has said enough. It was not as if there had been cocktails to precede it or wine to accompany it. Half a glass of sherry and a little flat beer was all that was left. No, it had not been a cheerful meal and Tommy had led the field in gloominess.

Well, it could not have been Henry who upset him this time, she thought to herself, because I was holding him in play most of the time between tea and supper and I don't see how he could have got loose to annoy Tommy. And I think Gordon had taken on Olivia by the time I left the room. No, it must have been the accumulated effect of this most ghastly fiasco of a houseparty. But it is nearly over now. If only we can get through this evening with some semblance of gaiety all will be well. She did hope that Tommy would pull himself together and play the genial host.

She went into his dressing room, where he was in the act of transforming himself into Charles the Second. "Can I help you?" she inquired.

"No, thank you," he replied shortly.

And that's that, she told herself, returning to her own room and looking rather sadly at her Nell Gwynne dress. If she resembled pretty Nell as much as Tommy did the Merry Monarch, they ought to be a riot! She remembered the first time they had worn these dresses soon after their marriage—she would not like to say how many years ago. Tommy had held her in his arms and told her that the real Nell could not have been nearly as beautiful as she was. Her eyes filled with tears. Not that she would expect him to talk quite like that to her now—after all she was thirty-five—but he needn't look at her as if she were something the cat had brought in.

She looked out of the window. The moon was just out and she could distinguish two figures coming up the garden path, arm in arm. Jo and Flo. They must have made it up. Perhaps Jo had decided to take the money after all. If her houseparty had caused the twins to become friends once more, it had not been in vain, in spite of the hours of hard work, the gloomy looks, the boring conversations and Tommy's final collapse.

Luckily Tommy had been able to get hold of something to drink this evening, and not before it was needed, thought Duds. In his dress and

wig as Charles the Second, Tommy sat drinking a whisky and soda in
gloomy silence. Sandy, incongruously dressed as a jester, sat opposite
to him with a double gin. Henry had not made any drastic change to his
dress and Duds applauded his wisdom, as his was not the sort of face
with which to play about. An old-fashioned stock instead of a white tie
was his only concession to the occasion. Irene looked charming with
powdered hair and a rose-colored dress cut to display her beautiful
neck and shoulders.

Henry at once noticed several flaws in Duds' dress. She encouraged him to tell her of them, as she was afraid that he might start to
criticize Tommy's, and she felt that one crack from him would snap
the last vestige of her husband's self-control and murder would take the
place of dancing.

Just as Henry had exhausted his criticism of his hostess's dress
and was beginning to turn his eyes towards the others, Flo made her
appearance. She represented a Greuze picture and was looking very
lovely with her smooth hair parted in the center and wearing a dainty
muslin frock. Gordon followed her, very handsome in eighteenth century
dress, blue coat, white knee breeches and snowy cravat. They were a
very attractive couple and even Henry seemed unable to find anything to criticize. In any case his eyes were wandering up the stairs,
obviously waiting for Jo to appear.

He had some time to wait and Duds was beginning to get anxious
about dinner. At this rate the guests for the dance would be arriving
while the houseparty guests were still eating. She had just decided to go
on without Jo when she appeared. She paused halfway down the stairs
with one hand on the fine old bannister. She was just under the light and
was indeed an arresting vision. Her hair was piled high on her head and
had a red rose stuck in it. Her dress was black and she wore a
Spanish shawl of scarlet, embroidered in gold. She carried a fan and
as she stood gazing down at the assembled company she wore a trium-
phant smile, as if she were aware of the admiration she was causing.

"Carmen!" murmured Henry, staring at her as if he would never
be able to move his eyes.

She gave a little laugh and hummed a bar or two of "Toreador."

"Charming," said Mrs. Dumbleton, in her pleasant voice, and Duds
wondered what made her choose that adjective. She would have said
handsome, striking, glamorous, perhaps cruel, but not charming. "I remember so well going to see *Carmen,*" went on Irene. "A wonderful

opera, so full of color. I enjoyed it very much. The woman next to me was taken ill and wanted to go out in the middle, so disturbing, not of course that she could help it. I remember feeling ill once. . .”

Duds looked at the men to see what effect Jo had had on them. There was no doubt about Henry—he was staring as if his eyes might pop out of his head at any moment. Gordon had looked at Jo for a moment but had turned his eyes away almost at once and was gazing complacently at his wife, evidently finding nothing in Josephine's re-markable display to compare with Florence's exquisite prettiness, and Duds agreed with him.

Her eyes passed to Tommy. He was shaken for the moment out of his gloomy apathy and was looking with obvious admiration at his wife's cousin. Duds smiled to herself. I am glad he has cheered up, she thought. Jo certainly does look marvelous enough to raise the tempo of any party! Sandy was still drinking gin. She hoped he would not be any the worse for it. He did not seem to have noticed his cousin's entry but was gazing into the fire as if that alone had any interest for him.

The other guests arrived soon after nine o'clock. It was a very small party, thirty-two all told, and with the exception of the Veazeys all were typical country people. There was a dance band on the wireless and they had cleared the hall and drawing room for dancing. Quite early in the evening the party spirit seemed to reign supreme. It may have been the fact that most of the people gathered together were in fancy dress and felt that they could behave more lightheartedly than in their ordinary clothes, or it may have been that there were drinks to be had in the study, though Duds wondered what she and Tommy would drink for the rest of the winter.

“Capital fun this,” said Sir John, who was keeping up the old tradi-tions in a pink coat and satin knee-breeches. “Very sporting of you and your husband. I am afraid I am not much of a hand at these modern dances. Give me the old-fashioned waltz, I say. I suppose I shall have to dance with my wife's cousin next. Very clever woman, you know, writes novels and all that—to tell you the truth I am frightened to death of her.”

Duds looked at Olivia Ordemar in medieval Italian dress droop-ing in the arms of the plump little vicar, and she could well believe Sir John. The vicar did not look too happy. When the dance program came to an end they put some records on the radiogram, until at half-past ten a welcome voice announced *Those Were the Days*. Sir John got his old-fashioned waltz after all and he danced it with his own wife, a little roundabout woman as different as possible from her famous cousin. Then came the Lancers, for which there were just enough for four sets, two in the hall and two in the drawing room. The older people coyly said they did not know them, but the younger ones who had listened to them every week on the wireless were quite ready to give instructions, as they had no reason for wishing to appear ignorant of them.

As a matter of fact the announcer told them all what to do as they went along, so it was quite easy, and very soon everyone was enjoying himself or herself. The older people had quite forgotten about giving away their ages and were remembering every step quite openly, while the younger people had forgotten to feel superior and bowed and curtsied and set to partners as if they had been brought up to it.

"First lady, second gent to the center," said the announcer. "Retire to places, turn corners.

"Second figure, the line movement, first couple only waltz round. Prepare for side lines, advance, retire, number two lead. Basket movement, ladies to center, retire, gents advance," and so on until the last figure of all, the grand chain. Everyone was dancing now for all he was worth. Sir John, with his wife's cousin leaning heavily on his arm, grinned at Duds. His honest face was red, and there was perspiration on his brow. Tommy had actually cheered up and was laughing down at Jo as he met her in the grand chain. Even Sandy and Flo were smiling.

When at last the Lancers were over and a soprano on the wireless was obliging with an old ballad while the dancers rested, Duds escaped upstairs to powder her face and tidy her hair. It really is going well, she told herself, as she looked at her disheveled appearance and wondered how the twins managed to keep tidy whatever activity they took up. Everyone was enjoying the party. They would remember this evening and forget the rest of the week, all being well.

She opened her door on to the corridor which led to the big landing. There was the door of Tommy's dressing room, their bathroom and beyond that a room that they used as a box room. Two figures were approaching the door of the latter. Duds smiled to herself. It would make a very good sitting out place. Good luck to them whoever they were. The door was opened and the light switched on and in the streak of it Duds recognized her cousin Jo in her Spanish dress and with her, an arm round her shoulders as he drew her into the unused room, was Tommy. Tommy dressed as Charles the Second, beyond doubt Tommy himself!

Duds thought she was going to be sick, and she hurried back into her own room and closed the door. The floor seemed to go up and down beneath her. She had not felt like this since last time she had crossed the Channel. She remembered the first time she had seen Jo in a man's arms on Christmas Day. She had taken it for granted that it was Henry, but she had nothing really to go on. She remembered Tommy's look of admiration as Jo came down the stairs that evening. She remembered the way he had looked at her in the Lancers, then she remembered his voice and his expression when they had worn these same fancy dresses last time. She remembered the words he had said to her.

Her world was tottering but she must go down and dance. Of course Tommy had been in good spirits all through the week. She had thought that he was putting a brave face on it, but he had been enjoying this ghastly houseparty. Yesterday he had suddenly realized that it was nearly over and that was what had made him so depressed. She staggered to the dressing table. There was a flask of brandy in her handkerchief drawer that she had been saving against emergencies. There was never likely to be an emergency as bad as this one, so she found it and took a good pull. A long pull and a strong pull and a pull all together, she told herself wryly.

Duds took a look at herself in the mirror and wondered how anyone had ever cared for her. She was a terrible sight. The wonder was not at Tommy looking elsewhere but at his ever having looked at her at all, ever having cared for her, as he undoubtedly had. She was really revolting. She put on some rouge but the effect of it on her green face made her look like a raddled old woman. What did it matter what she looked like? Anyhow she must go down and make the party a success. She could still do that and perhaps after all she was making a fuss about nothing. Most people's husbands had flirtations with pretty girls. Why had she expected hers to be different? The fact remained that she had expected it.

Arrived back in the hall, she found that *Those Were the Days* had turned into a talk from somewhere by someone about something she had no idea what. She switched off the wireless and went to the case where they kept their dance records. Putting out her hand at random, she found that she had picked *Sir Roger de Coverley*. She had not even known it was there. But she put it on to the radiogram and catching Henry by the hand she swept him into the dance. Sandy and Flo followed them, then Gordon and, Irene.

"Come on, come on," shouted Duds, as, seized with the spirit of madness, she led the crazy rout. Everybody joined in and suddenly she saw Tommy with Olivia Ordemar and Mr. Veazey with Jo. Everybody followed Duds as if she were the Pied Piper of Hamelin. She found herself in the center having to give her hands to Tommy. Their eyes slid away from each other and she returned to Henry, laughing up at him in a provocative manner and behaving as if she were having the time of her life.

Afterwards they all went in to the supper room, Duds still flirting shamelessly with Henry. She danced round the room with a plate of sandwiches and a jug of cup which had been made of genuine champagne, the last of their store. She saw Jo sitting between Mr. Veazey and Sir John Holroyd, both obviously enamored of her.

Tommy was being a good host. He seemed to be enjoying himself, his glumness had quite departed. He enjoyed his time in the box room, thought Duds bitterly. He was laughing with all his guests in turn. Now that she no longer cared whether the party were a success or not, it was going better than her wildest hopes had anticipated. This was what she had been longing for, for six long years—gaiety, lights, music, people and champagne. Now she had got them she wished herself back in those dark days, those days when everything was crumbling around her. For at least one thing had then been firm. Let the buildings go if only she had got Tommy. Even if he had been drowned she would still have had him but now she had lost him.

She seized Henry's glass and drained it and then half-consciously looked at Tommy to see if he had noticed. She thought that he had just turned his head away but she could not be sure. He was flirting in an outrageous way at the moment with Olivia Ordemar, who seemed to like it, but once or twice Duds saw him look across the room at Jo and smile at her.

Henry was playing up to Duds. He might be rather embarrassed at being singled out for so much notice by his hostess, he might be longing for Jo, but still it must be apparent to all, including the latter, that he was still a very attractive man to women. Poor little Duds, he thought complacently. It really is pathetic how fond she still is of me. Irene was having a very pleasant time with one of the older guests who thought her a very fine woman, which indeed she was.

Tommy strolled into the hall and turned on the wireless, Big Ben struck twelve and at once there was a dead silence, almost a solemn silence. Then everyone was lifting his or her glass to each other and draining what was left in it. The strains of *Auld Lang Syne* came to them and they all trooped into the hall and formed a big circle, holding their hands crossed. Duds found herself between Henry and Sir John; she gazed sentimentally at Henry as they sang the words:

> "Should auld acquaintance be forgot,
> And never brought to mind
> Should auld acquaintance be forgot,
> And days of auld lang syne?"

CHAPTER 10

LUPIN caught the 6:20 train at Paddington by the skin of her teeth and owing to the help of a very nice man who gave her a lift in his taxi. He had been in the army and had only lately returned home, to find his four children quite big and rather a handful. In fact, one of his boys was being decidedly difficult. His headmaster had actually written a very serious letter. If it had been a case of getting out of the dormitory after lights out, his father would not have minded, as that was just the sort of thing that he had done when he was young, and he described at some length—and with a good deal of pride—a rag which had nearly ended in his being expelled. "No, boys will be boys," he said, "but when it comes to blasphemous poetry it is another thing."

"So it is," agreed Lupin. She received the impression that it was the poetry he minded, really more than the blasphemy, though that just added the last straw.

"Then take my elder girl," he said, as the taxi drove up at Paddington Station and he waved away Lupin's attempt to pay her share. "Of course I don't know much about girls."

Lupin was in rather a dilemma. If she did not rush she would miss her train. On the other hand the man had paid for her taxi, so she felt that common honesty compelled her to listen to the story of his children's shortcomings in return. Her heart fell as she realized that there were four of them. "Of course, young people do pass through difficult stages," she said. "Oh, there's a porter. I want to catch the 6:20 to Fordham."

"That is what I say. Of course, one expects young people to be a bit awkward. I don't want my children to be perfect. They would be little prigs if they were. I remember when I was a lad, I must have been a fair young demon. I remember. . ."

"Platform Five," said the porter.

"I must fly," said Lupin. "I do hope we shall meet again. I have been so interested in what you have been telling me and I should love to see your children." She dashed after her porter and just succeeded in finding a seat in a crowded carriage as the train started. There is safety in numbers, she thought. If I were alone with any one of these people they would start confiding in me. That woman in the corner would probably tell me about her insides and all the operations she has had. The old man would inveigh against the government and the way England is heading for communism, or of course he might be an Anglo-Israelite or have had an ulcer. The pretty young girl might tell me her love affairs, or more likely how difficult it was to get clothing coupons, or how her mum sufferers with her legs. Ailments are the things people are most interested in—their own or those of their relations. That dark girl has very likely lost her faith or may never have had one. Oh, she has got a wedding ring. I expect she is unhappily married or does not get on with her mother-in-law or wants to lead her own life. That young man would tell me about his business and what a success he was, and the other one would tell me about all the people who have got more than their share of this world's goods while others are starving. He would probably have a fling at the church and marriage and Mr. Churchill. Well, I am glad I am not alone with any of them. Why do people start telling me all their troubles the minute they see me? I can't really take any interest in anybody's troubles at the moment except poor old Duds'.

Lupin alighted at Fordham Station. Thank goodness there isn't a blackout, she told herself, as she saw one or two yellow lamps casting a sickly light over the platform. Then, under one of the lamps, she saw Tommy. His face looked pale and yellow but he was free—that was the main thing. He had not been arrested yet. "Oh, Tommy!" she said rushing up to him and seizing both hands, "I am so glad to see you."

Tommy was rather surprised at the warmth of her greeting. She hadn't been so gushing in the old days. "It is frightfully good of you to come," he said. "It will make all the difference to Duds. I thought you'd be very tired and hungry, so I arranged for us to have a meal at the White Swan here before going on."

"I shall be very glad of something to eat and drink," Lupin admitted.

They were soon seated in the lounge of the White Swan with drinks before them. Lupin felt better after a sip or two and more able to face life. "You know, Tommy," she said, "there is only one thing to do and that is to stick absolutely to the truth."

Tommy was startled. Lupin was just as pretty as ever. She was starting on her second gin and lime, but she had certainly become rather sanctimonious after being married to a parson for ten years. It was going to be a bit thick if she were going to preach sermons to them all the time. She usen't to be a bit like that. "Oh, of course," he said in an embarrassed voice. "Have another drink?"

"No thanks," and Tommy led her to the coffee room. As they crossed the lounge, Lupin gave a start and clutched Tommy by the arm.

"Is anything the matter?" he asked. Had the two drinks been too much for her? They had been quite mild, but of course she probably was not used to anything stronger than barley water, living in a vicarage. He wished he had not offered her the drinks, but he had needed them himself. He began to wish that Duds had not asked her to come. She was going to be a perfect nuisance exhorting them to speak the truth at one moment and then getting drunk the next.

Lupin was pale and shaking as she sat down at the table. "I am frightfully sorry," she said. "I suppose it is because I am hungry. Perhaps I oughtn't to have had those two drinks on an empty stomach. But I really thought I saw something as we were coming into this room."

"What sort of a thing?"

"Er . . . well, a person, at least of course it wasn't really."

"Well, I saw a person. I saw Henry Dumbleton. He was just coming out of the cloakroom.

"Tommy, did you really? Do you mean you saw him too?"

"Well, of course I saw him," Tommy replied irritably. He did wish Duds hadn't asked Lupin to stay. She seemed to have gone quite mad, as if things weren't bad enough as it was. "I am not blind," he went on. "What is the matter with you, Lupin? Do eat your soup."

"But—but I thought he was dead!"

"Dead! I wish he were. No, I don't mean that, but I never could stand the man. They are staying on here until after the inquest. I must say it was decent of them to suggest it. I had visions of them parking with us indefinitely."

"But whose inquest?" asked Lupin. "Why is there an inquest if he is still alive?"

Tommy stared at her. "Jo's inquest, of course. Didn't Duds tell you? She is terribly upset about it. She is her cousin, you know, and she has poisoned herself."

"Jo! She was one of those pretty twins. I remember them quite well. Has she really poisoned herself?"

"Yes. What made you think it was Henry?"

Lupin laughed rather shakily. "It was Duds' letter," she explained. "She said that Henry was being very tiresome and that you had said you would murder him before the week was out, Christmas or no Christmas."

Tommy laughed. "And so you thought I had."

"Well, naturally I didn't think anything of it at the time, but when I got her telegram saying that she was in great trouble, it all came back to me and I thought, just suppose he started necking with Duds and Tommy came in, he might have knocked him down and if he had hit his head in falling or something it would have been a bit awkward."

"It would." A sudden thought struck him. "So that is what you meant about telling the truth."

"Yes, of course. It would have been much safer. If you had dashed off and faked an alibi it would have all looked much worse, if you know what I mean."

"I see. Still, it didn't happen, though it might have done," he remarked thoughtfully. "I mean I might have knocked him down, but one doesn't often in real life. I am glad you weren't just preaching me a sermon on truth in the abstract."

"Did you think I was?"

"Well, it sounded like it."

"I leave the preaching to my husband, but anyway, thank goodness you didn't! I am terribly sorry about Duds' cousin, though, poor little thing. But I am glad you are not in danger of being arrested for murder. I don't know when I have been so glad to see anyone as I was to see you at the station."

"Oh, that is why you were so pleased. I thought you seemed rather effusive."

"Well, naturally. I am sorry if I made you feel shy, but I had been in an awful state ever since I got Duds' telegram and it was such a relief to feel at any rate you hadn't been arrested so far."

Tommy laughed. "You are a fool, Lupin, but it is really more good luck than good management that I have managed to keep my hands off the man. It really has been a pretty sticky Christmas, you know."

"It must have been nearly as bad as the one you spent with us when the curate got murdered."

"That was a bit grim, wasn't it? Still, we were younger then and things didn't get one down in the same way. Besides, it wasn't as if we knew the chap."

They drove up in front of Old Place and Tommy led Lupin into the hall. As he opened the front door Duds came running down the stairs. "Oh Loops!" she exclaimed. "I am thankful to see you. It is good of you to come."

CHAPTER 11

LUPIN sat up in bed sipping a hot drink while Duds, curled up at the other end, smoked a cigarette.

"It was too absolutely ghastly," Duds was saying. "I was lying in bed. I couldn't sleep, I don't know why, when suddenly Irene Dumbleton came into the room and said 'I am afraid I have bad news for you, Dorothy—your cousin Josephine is dead.' "

"What sort of time was it?"

"I don't really know. I was too upset to notice, but I should think it was round about four. I just got up and dashed along and there she was lying on her bed. She was still in her fancy dress. She had been dressed as Carmen and looked so lovely—she still did. I tried to feel her pulse but it was no good. Irene Dumbleton had done a lot of nursing and she was sure she was dead. Then Tommy turned up. He must have heard us going along."

Wasn't he in the room when Mrs. Dumbleton broke the news? wondered Lupin, but she said nothing aloud.

"And Sandy, he was next door, and it was then we saw the letter and the bottle."

"What letter and bottle?"

"I am sorry, I am telling this awfully badly, but I feel all to pieces. It was the shock of seeing her like that, with the rouge and everything still on her face and the rose in her hair—it made it all seem so much worse. But she had left a letter for me. It really was frightfully sweet of her and I felt such a beast because I hadn't really liked her very much."

"Hadn't you?" Lupin was surprised. "I thought you were awfully fond of them both. You always used to be."

"I was awfully fond of Flo. I still am, and I used to be fond of Jo, but this week she has been very difficult. Of course I realize now that it was because she was so unhappy. If only I had been more sympathetic, perhaps she would have confided in me and this would never have happened. I could have said something or done something. She did talk to me a little bit one day but somehow I never gave her another chance. Everything was such a rush with the house full and everything, but still there is no excuse and I know I often felt annoyed with her. I was a beast."

"It is silly to feel like that. I don't expect you could have done anything. What did she say in the letter?"

"The police have got that. The doctor said though it seemed a perfectly clear case he could not give a certificate and there would have to be a post mortem and an inquest. It is all so ghastly. An inspector and a sergeant, I think it was, came round. They were very nice but I got the wind up rather—that is why I sent for you."

"Very sensible! But about the letter, do you remember it at all?"

"Every word. She said: 'Dear Duds, I am so sorry that I have spoiled your houseparty. I spoil everything for everybody and will be better out of the way. If I tried to go on living I should go mad. I think my brain is going. A black cloud seems to come over it every now and then. I have made up things with Flo and we have parted friends. Please give her my best love and don't let her be unhappy. It really is better this way. Love from Jo.' It was nice of her to write. I feel a beast for having misjudged her, but . . . Oh well, I don't expect she has known what she has been doing these last few days."

"What did you say about a bottle?"

"There was an empty bottle by the letter. It belonged to Henry Dumbleton and had had some heroin stuff in it. Diamorphine, the doctor called it. He took it for his asthma. Irene gave him injections of it and she told us how frightfully strong it was and that an overdose might kill anybody. Well, she had brought down a new bottle of it and had not used any, so Jo must have taken the whole lot. I must say Irene has been awfully nice. She said they had better stay somewhere near in case they were wanted at the inquest. After all, she had been the one to find poor Jo and it was Henry's stuff."

"How was it that she found her?"

Duds stared at her for a moment. "You mean, why did she go into her room? I have not the vaguest notion. I never thought of it till this moment. I was too upset. She must have had some reason. I mean you don't usually wander into people's rooms in the middle of the night. I say, I suppose it couldn't have been Henry?"

"Why should it be?"

"Well, he was most frightfully keen. As you know," she said rather shamefacedly, "he was always having an affair with someone and it didn't usually mean much, but I think he found himself caught this time. She had the most extraordinary influence over men. They all fell for her, the most unlikely people," she added bitterly. "Anyway, poor Henry was absolutely knocked out by her death. I thought he would be telling us what to do and ordering the police about and generally running the show but not a bit of it. I am afraid he really was in love with the girl. Still, if he did go to her room, Irene knows all about it and says that it was she. She really is a good sort and, as I was saying, they have gone to the White Swan at Fordham because she knew I wouldn't want a lot of people here. After all, it is no business of ours which of them went to Jo's room. The girl was dead and there it is."

"Absolutely. But do you think she cared for Henry at all?"

"No, she played him up a bit to start with. Then there was the man she worked for—I think he was keen on her but I don't think there was anything on her side. I think what happened was that she had been very much in love with someone who let her down and she just fooled about with anyone who turned up."

"Is her sister terribly upset?"

"Yes, poor little thing. It is frightful. You see, she was absolutely devoted to her. I think there is something about being twins that makes them specially bound up in each other. You see, in spite of everything, Jo's last thought was for Flo. She made up things with her and she left that message for her in the letter to me."

"What do you mean about making it up? Had they had a quarrel?"

"Well, I don't know exactly that it had been a quarrel. But Jo had been very funny to Flo. You see, Flo had come in for some money. Her grandfather had left rather a funny will, saying that all his money was to go to the oldest grandchild. There were only two grandchildren, Flo and

Jo, so Flo took for granted that they would share it. Of course legally it was Flo's because she was actually the older of the two. I had never even known which was the older and I don't believe they had either. Anyway it went to Flo and she was going to make a deed of gift, or whatever it is you have to do, to Jo of half of it. It seemed the obvious thing to do, but Jo turned very queer and said nothing would induce her to accept it, that she wouldn't take charity from anyone. Well, it wasn't a very nice thing to say about her own sister and naturally Flo was very hurt."

"It was queer of her," said Lupin, thoughtfully.

"I didn't know anything about it till they arrived here. I had taken for granted that they had shared the money and that they were still devoted to each other. But of course I soon found out that things were strained between them. In fact they both told me their own sides of the story. I ought to have done more about it."

"My dear, when you are trying to run a houseparty in peacetime, I am sure you can't be expected to patch up quarrels between families, even if one ever could, which one can't. They only end by hating you."

"There is something in that. Besides they did make it up, as it happened. I am so thankful because it will be a comfort to Flo to remember that."

"Yes, it will. She is still here, I suppose."

"Of course, but she won't see anyone except her husband. He has been very nice and helpful, but she is completely knocked out. It isn't surprising. I can quite understand her not feeling like seeing anyone though I wish she would see me, I am so fond of her. Tommy got hold of Gordon—her husband, you .know—and he broke it to her. It must have been frightful for him. They had just made it up and she must have thought everything was going to be happy ever after. I can't think what made Jo commit suicide just then, but something must have happened that we don't know about. It is no good going over it again and again. You will wonder why I sent for you, but I felt so wretched and there was something else, but I don't want to talk about it now."

"No, of course not. By the way how did Flo's husband get on with Jo?"

"I don't think he liked her very much. Sandy has some story about his being friends with Jo first. He may have been, I don't know. Jo always had heaps of friends. I don't think there can ever have been anything between them. He is absolutely wrapped up in Flo. Of course

Sandy doesn't like him because he was in love with Flo, still is, poor lamb. I didn't know that when I invited him for Christmas. It didn't make things any easier."

"They are frightfully alike to look at, aren't they?"

"No, not now. They used to be. You remember them, don't you? It was quite difficult to tell which was which. But the war has made a lot of difference. Jo looked older and she was much more sophisticated. They are both lovely to look at in their different ways. Jo was very striking and people noticed her more at first sight, but I think Flo is the prettiest. You would have thought a tragedy like this would have drawn us all together but it hasn't. We are all at sixes and sevens as if we suspected each other of having had something to do with it.

"But after all, we know what did happen. Henry looked so sea-green I should have suspected him of having something to do with it if it hadn't been for the letter. It was his diamorphine but then he had been awake all night with asthma and a heart attack. I felt rather awful letting him go. But Irene was awfully nice and said she would be happier in Fordham as they would be nearer a doctor. I must say it would have been the last straw if Henry had died on us on the top of everything else," and Duds laughed rather wildly.

Lupin remembered the glimpse she had had of Henry when she had seen him at the White Swan. He had looked pretty awful—no wonder she had taken him for a ghost. "Have they had the post mortem yet?" she asked.

"Yes, and they say it was diamorphine poisoning. It is pretty nasty for Irene and Henry, it being their stuff, though naturally they weren't to know someone would be taking it. Sandy, too, is looking like a murderer. He did not like Jo, but he wouldn't have murdered her because of Flo."

"But we know it was suicide," objected Lupin, who was getting sleepy and muddled. If the girl had taken poison, why must Duds keep looking round for people with motives for doing away with her? Such silly motives too.

"Yes, of course. I don't know why I am talking like this, but downstairs no one says anything. There is a sort of queer atmosphere. When Jo was alive she cast a spell over everyone and she is doing the same now she is dead."

"Oh well, you have got Tommy, anyhow." Duds gave Lupin rather a queer look, but she pretended not to notice and went on. "I was so afraid when I got your wire that he had killed Henry."

"Why ever should he kill Henry?"

"You said in your last letter that he said he would, Christmas or no Christmas."

"Oh, that was only a joke. What ages ago, it seems. Henry was rather trying, I must admit. He was always talking as if he knew more about everything than anybody else. I can't blame Tommy for getting a bit irritated. I did myself."

"I was afraid that you might have been indulging in a mild flirtation with him."

Duds laughed mirthlessly. "Me! My flirting days were over some time ago and I don't think I should choose Henry if they weren't. In any case, it wouldn't worry Tommy. Well, my dear, you must be tired out. I shouldn't have kept you talking so late, but it is lovely seeing you. You make me feel better somehow. Good night."

Lupin was very tired, but she could not go to sleep. She felt worried. Of course there was something particularly sad about a young and lovely girl taking her own life. No wonder everyone was on edge. One might have expected Duds to cry on Tommy's shoulder and Tommy to have been very loving and sympathetic, but Lupin had had enough experience of life to know that it was much more natural for them to get on each other's nerves and to bicker over trifles. Tommy was thoroughly upset in his own way, there was no doubt about that. Lupin remembered the first glimpse she had had of him on the platform. It is true that the lamps had cast a yellow glare, but surely the porter had not looked so haggard as Tommy and he had been illuminated by the same light. Then he had rather repelled her glad greeting, though of course she had been a bit gushing, having expected to find him languishing in jail. Still, the old Tommy, with whom she had been such friends, would have laughed at her and said 'Why so glad to see me?' or something like that. He would not have been embarrassed. There was no getting away from the fact that he had been on edge the whole evening and so had Duds.

And what was it that Duds had said about there being something else, but not wanting to tell her just then? Well, it was no business of hers. Duds would tell her if and when she wanted. Very likely it was only something like the laundry not having come back. Bother, she had not done anything about the laundry at home, she had come away in such a hurry. She hoped the children were all right. How awful it would be if when they grew up one of them committed suicide! Had she put the fish in the refrigerator? Tomorrow was her day for the flowers in church. Would Staines think of it? She turned over in bed again.

She was sitting in the Chair at the meeting of the Good Wives' Fellowship. Mrs. Vokes, the portly wife of the verger, was dressed as Carmen, with a rose stuck in her severe bun of hair. 'Someone has been writing blasphemous poetry,' she announced. 'Oh dear,' said Lupin. She dropped her handbag; there was a hypodermic syringe in it and the fishmonger picked it up and gave an injection to a codfish. 'No cod today, thank you,' she said to him but he had gone. Oh dear, she would never catch her train, someone was standing in her way and his face was yellow.

She awoke with a start and her heart was racing. "Andrew!" she called, but Andrew was not there. She was staying with Duds. She had sent for her because her cousin had committed suicide. Lying in the darkness she went once again over the story of the tragedy. Suddenly an idea struck her: had Jo cast her fatal spell over Tommy?

CHAPTER 12

LUPIN slept soundly at last and was awakened the next morning by Duds coming in with her early morning tea. They only exchanged a few words and Lupin got up almost immediately and hurriedly bathed and dressed so as to be able to lend Duds a hand. She was in time to lay the breakfast table and had just finished the task—which had taken her some time as she did not know where anything was kept—when a young man came into the room. He was very nice-looking with well-brushed hair and a pleasant expression. He wore a very well-cut pair of gray flannel trousers and a tweed coat.

"I am sure you are Lady Lupin Hastings," he said in a charming voice.

"How clever of you," replied Lupin, rather inanely, because who else could she be? Unless of course Duds had invited several old friends to come to stay, which wasn't very likely at the moment. "Have you any idea where Duds keeps the salt?" she added, as she realized that she had neglected to put any on the breakfast table.

"Salt now. I am almost sure I saw Duds put it into this cupboard. Ah yes, here we are." and he produced a nice little tray on which there were several silver salt cellars, pepper pots and mustard pots.

"Good. Now can you think of anything else there ought to be? Knives, forks—I wonder if I ought to have put out fish knives. I think we should know if it were fish, don't you?"

"Yes, I think so, and you have done it all beautifully. I was just going to take up a tray to my wife. Might I have one of your salt cellars?"

"Yes, do." Lupin realized he must be Gordon Pinhorn. "I am so terribly sorry. I remember your wife and her sister when they were little girls. They were so pretty. It is dreadful."

"It is a ghastly tragedy," he agreed, carefully arranging knives and forks on his tray. "They were such devoted sisters. My poor wife is suffering very badly from shock."

Lupin looked at the tray and wondered vaguely why Gordon was laying knives and forks and mustard pots. Surely someone suffering from shock would hardly need so many utensils. Then she remembered the time that she was staying with her brother and had fallen ill with influenza and he with great pride had brought her up a grilled chop. "I am not surprised," she said aloud.

Tommy came in carrying a basket of eggs. "Do you think that Flo could manage a new-laid egg?" he asked Gordon. "Oh, good morning, Lupin."

"I think perhaps she might," replied Gordon, rather doubtfully. "I do so want her to keep up her strength."

"I'll tell Duds," and Tommy disappeared into the kitchen.

Presently Duds emerged with the egg and a little toast and butter which she put on the tray. Gordon took it from her and the other three sat down to breakfast.

He returned shortly. "I think," he said to Duds, "that if you don't mind, I'll take up my breakfast and have it with Flo. I don't like leaving her alone. She is very shaky this morning."

"Of course," agreed Duds. "I'll tell Edith to pop on your egg and there are some sausages if you feel like them."

"Thank you so much, Duds, but don't you bother. I'll just go out and get something from Edith and take it up."

After Gordon left the room, Tommy observed, "It would make me more shaky having him sitting beside me."

Lupin looked up. She wondered why Tommy disliked Gordon. He had struck her as a particularly nice young man, so easy to talk to. Perhaps if one saw much of him he would pall on one a bit. Tommy used to be such a good-tempered, easygoing sort of person, and now he had been on the verge of knocking down Henry and didn't seem far off knocking down Gordon. Oh well, a suicide in the house is enough to upset anyone's equilibrium, she thought.

Tommy plowed his way doggedly through an egg and sausage and some toast and marmalade, not with the air of one enjoying a good breakfast but of one with a duty to perform. I suppose he doesn't want to look as if he is suffering from nerves, thought Lupin. Duds, too, was making a great effort to eat. She left half her egg, which was a pity from Lupin's point of view, as she could have easily managed two herself if she had been pressed. Then she suddenly remembered the thought that she had had in the middle of the night about Tommy and Jo. Was there anything in that? Or had it been part of her dream? He and Duds had hardly addressed a remark to each other since they came down. That in itself perhaps was not remarkable. However, Lupin did not feel that their silence was one of friendly understanding but one of constraint if not of hostility.

The door was pushed open and a furious-looking young man came into the room. This Lupin took to be Duds' cousin Sandy, the one who was in love with Flo. Lupin saw the look of misery in his eyes, which he was trying to mask with a look of anger. Was it entirely sorrow for Flo, who had lost her sister in such tragic circumstances, or was it jealousy of Gordon, who was now sitting beside her eating his eggs and sausages, or was there something else, apprehension perhaps?

"Do you remember Sandy, Lupin?" asked Duds. "I think you met him once or twice when he was a little boy."

"I believe I did," replied Lupin, pleasantly.

Sandy grunted. He obviously did not care whether he had ever seen her before and cared even less whether he ever saw her again. He refused eggs and sausages rather as if he had been insulted at being offered them and accepted a cup of black coffee and a piece of toast.

This is a jolly breakfast party, mused Lupin. Of course it is all terribly sad and no wonder poor Flo is heartbroken, but why need everyone be so angry? "I don't think it is quite so cold today," she hazarded aloud.

"The temperature is half a degree lower than yesterday," announced Tommy.

Sandy paid no attention to the remark but lit a cigarette in a contemptuous manner.

Duds said she did not know whether it were colder or not but personally she was frozen.

Lupin relapsed into silence, feeling she had done her best. After breakfast she helped Duds with the housework. They worked for the most part in silence and behaved as if nothing out of the ordinary had taken place. Duds seemed to regret her communicativeness of the night before and Lupin rather wished she had stayed in her own home, as she did not seem very popular here. At about a quarter to twelve she volunteered to go to the village and started off, armed with a shopping list.

She was the only customer in the village shop as most people did their shopping earlier. And as Mrs. White, the proprietress, sliced up the bacon, she remarked conversationally, "A bad business this for Mrs. Lethbridge."

"Yes, indeed," agreed Lupin. "It has upset her very much."

"No wonder, poor lady, her own cousin throwing herself out of the window. I know a sister of my husband's was in service with a gentleman who blew his brains out, and she said she never felt the same again."

"I am not surprised. It must have been a terrible shock. As a matter of fact, Mrs. Lethbridge's cousin did not throw herself out of the window—she took poison."

"Oh, well, it all comes to the same in the end. Took poison, did she? That's queer. I happened to be in Mr. Tyler's shop yesterday afternoon. He is our chemist and a very clever man, just by the church his shop is. As I was saying, I went in to ask him if he had anything for my backache, something cruel it is, just catches me when I am getting up or down, and often in the night I will wake up all of a sweat. Sometimes I wonder if it has anything to do with my kidneys, an aunt of mine died of kidneys. Mr. Tyler he was ever so nice, quite the gentleman he always is and never alludes to anything that could make one feel uncomfortable. He says it is the plumbago and will pass off in the summer, if we get a summer this year that is, which I very much doubt.

When I was a girl we had it hot from the first of May to the thirty-first of September. Pardon?"

For Lupin had absentmindedly murmured, "Thirty days hath September, April, June and November."

"Yes, as you say, there is no difference between June and November nowadays."

"Perhaps it will be better this summer."

"That is what I say, but I am always one to look on the bright side. My poor husband always used to say 'Ada,' that is my name, Ada, after an aunt of mine, not that she left me anything except her prayer book, which I had one of my own already, but he always said, 'Ada would see the bright side of her own funeral,' which I don't know as I would, but I certainly saw the bright side of his as he had taken to drink during the last few years, though a good husband in spite of his faults. But there it is, there is a bright side to most things if only you look out for it. One man's loss is another man's gain, as the saying is."

"That is very true and I do hope your medicine will do you good."

"It isn't what I would call medicine, it is a stuff to rub in. My niece comes in every evening and rubs it in for me. She is a good girl and she will find I have not forgotten her when the time comes. Mr. Tyler said I wasn't to drink it on any account, which reminds there was a gentleman in the shop buying weed-killer. A London gentleman I should say, he wasn't anyone from around these parts, he was having to sign the poison book, and I thought to myself I wouldn't like to do that. Suppose someone was to die sudden, one would be accused of the murder before you could say knife, and of course when I heard the young lady was poisoned, I thought of it at once. Weed-killer is just the stuff those horrid poisoners use, especially if they want to do their wives in—still the young lady wasn't married, was she? So there wouldn't be anyone wanting to do her in, unless of course she was married secretly."

"No, and in any case it wasn't weed-killer that she took. Thank you so much—bacon, sugar, tea, and a bottle of Parozone. Oh, and two pounds of coffee."

"The fresh ground. I keep it specially for Mrs. Lethbridge. Most people prefer the Camp, I do myself, it is easier to make, but after all everyone has a right to their own taste, live and let live is what I say."

"So do I," agreed Lupin, as she made her escape. Her basket was very heavy but she did not notice that much. For one thing, she was used to carrying heavy baskets and for another, she was pondering over something in her mind. Why should anyone buy weed-killer in January or December, whichever it was? It was a very funny thing to do. And if it were a stranger it was funnier still. A Londoner would not be very likely to want weed-killer. She might discount his being a Londoner—any stranger would be a Londoner to Mrs. White. Suppose he lived in some other part of the country and wanted to buy weed-killer, surely he would buy it in his own town or village, and in any case why should he want it in the middle of the winter?

Lupin was not a very good gardener but she felt fairly sure that you did not put down weed-killer at Christmas, and the more she thought about it the more peculiar it seemed. However, it was nothing to do with her. It could have no possible bearing on the death of Josephine Harnet. She had died from taking an overdose of diamorphine—in plain language heroin—and she had left a note to say she had done it herself. Everything was perfectly simple and straightforward and very sad. Her job was to try to comfort poor old Duds, who was naturally very much distressed.

She found herself just outside an inn called the Cock and Hen and thought that it would be a good idea to drop in there for a few moments. A rest would do her good and a little refreshment would make her stronger for the succoring of her poor friend. On entering the bar parlor the first person she saw sitting in a corner by himself was Duds' cousin, Sandy. He had not shown any great enthusiasm for her company at breakfast this morning and Lupin thought that it would be more tactful not to draw his attention to herself, so after fetching her glass and agreeing with the landlord that the weather was very "treacherous but what could you expect with the present government in office," she looked for a secluded spot in which to sit and restore her energy. To her great surprise, Sandy stood up and pulled a chair towards the table at which he was sitting. This was evidently meant as an invitation and she seated herself beside him.

She remarked that she had been doing some shopping for Duds.

"Good. Poor old Duds!" he said. "I am glad you have come to be with her."

Lupin was surprised. He had not seemed glad earlier in the day but perhaps breakfast was not his meal. "Oh well, we have been friends for simply ages," she explained. "She was frightfully good to me when she was first married. I used to stay with her and Tommy a lot in London and they gave me a wonderful time. In fact I was staying with them when I met my husband, so naturally I feel very grateful to them."

"Are you?" asked Sandy. "That is more than most people would be."

"How do you mean?" asked Lupin.

"Well, I don't think many people would be grateful for having been introduced to their husbands or wives."

"Oh, I see, you are being cynical. But, you know, quite a lot of people are happily married, only you don't hear so much about them as you do about the unhappy ones. They don't put it in the papers when people are happy together, only when they are not. It must be a terrible thing to be unhappily married, but after all there are Tommy and Duds and Andrew and me and . . ." She had just been going to add Gordon and Flo but remembered that Duds had told her that Sandy was in love with Flo, so it would have hardly been tactful to draw attention to the fact of her being happily married to someone else. "And I know lots of others," she said rather lamely.

Sandy laughed sardonically and offered Lupin another drink which she refused. "Don't let me stop you," she said.

"No, I don't want any more, at least I won't have any more. Duds thinks I drink too much."

"Do you?" asked Lupin.

"It depends what you mean by too much," he replied. "I don't get drunk if that it what you want to know."

"It isn't any business of mine anyway."

"No, it's no one's business but my own. But still, it is time I took hold of myself, I suppose." He took her basket and they started walking along the village street. "I'm in a hell of a mess," he said, after they had walked some way in silence.

"I am frightfully sorry."

"It is so difficult to know what to do."

"It often is." Lupin noticed that Sandy was swinging her basket savagely as he walked. She was afraid that the bottle of Parozone would be broken all over the rations. It would not improve them, she feared.

"What is the use of stirring up a lot of mud? It won't bring the girl back to life again."

"No more it will." Lupin pondered for a minute or two. "You mean you know something and wonder whether you ought to tell anyone or not?" she hazarded.

Sandy dropped the basket, "What makes you think that?" he demanded, as he bent down to pick it up.

"What you said about not knowing what to do and not wanting to stir up a lot of mud." She looked sadly at the basket. Whether he wanted to or not he had stirred up a good deal of mud, which freely bespattered the basket.

"You are quite right," he said. "You see, I am not absolutely sure that Jo did commit suicide."

"What about that letter she left for Duds?"

"Letters can be forged."

"Yes, I suppose they can, but why should anyone want to murder her?"

"I can think of lots of reasons. I have often wanted to myself but I didn't."

"No, I shouldn't think it was you."

"Thanks."

"I mean, if it were you, you would not be trying to make out it was a murder when everyone else seems satisfied that it was a perfectly good suicide."

"Yes, everyone does seem quite satisfied. Should I leave them satisfied, or am I being an accessory after the fact if I know it is a murder and keep quiet about it?"

"If you really know that it was a murder of course you ought to tell the police. But do you know?"

"No, I don't, that is just it. Oh well, having told you so much I may as well tell you the whole thing. I saw someone come out of Jo's room at a quarter to three."

"Have you any idea at what time Jo is supposed to have died? Duds didn't tell me. Naturally she was rather confused over the whole thing."

"It was four-fifteen when the doctor arrived and he said as near as he could tell she had been dead for two hours."

"Then she would have been dead by a quarter to three," Lupin pointed out.

"There is always a margin of error each way," replied Sandy. "Half an hour isn't much. Suppose this chap had just been in with the poison . . ."

"It was a man, was it?"

"Yes," replied Sandy, shortly.

Lupin thought this over. It was not difficult to guess who the man was. Though she held no brief for Henry Dumbleton, she did not really think he was a murderer. Besides, surely, if he were, he would not have been such a fool as to poison someone with stuff which was bound to be traced back to him. "I can't see it," she said out loud. "For one thing, if he had given her the stuff at a quarter to three, it would have taken some time to act, at least a quarter of an hour I should think, if not more—not that I know much about it—but the doctor could not have been as far out as all that. Then another thing, the whole point of poisoning is to give yourself an alibi. I mean you slip the poison into something the victim is going to drink and then stroll away nonchalant like and look surprised when you hear they have passed on. You don't burst into their room in the middle of the night and wake them, saying, 'Hi, drink this!' "

"Then what was he doing there?" asked Sandy.

"I would rather not say."

"Just suppose she had been expecting him—and mind you, we don't know what time he went in, only what time he came out. They may have had a drink together and then he waited to make sure she was dead before he came out. Then he fixed the letter and the empty bottle—he would have written the letter beforehand—and out he came."

"Yes, I see," said Lupin. She thought it over. Of course it was possible. Why should Henry want to kill Jo? Unrequited passion? But then it wasn't, if she had invited him to her room. He was afraid that Jo might give him away. He had always been a very cautious sort of person. She remembered him during his brief affair with Duds. Would a cautious person commit murder? If he did, surely he would manage it a bit better and not be seen coming out of the victim's room in the middle of the night, leaving his own medicine bottle by her side. He had gone to Jo's room, perhaps by invitation, perhaps not, and when he got there he had found that she was dead. Well, naturally he did not want anyone to know that. He had looked, as Duds had said, sea-green. But as for murder, no, she did not believe it.

"As you say, it is very difficult to know what to do, but I do not think he murdered her. I think he went in and found her dead," Lupin went on. After all, it all fits in, she thought, and he went straight back and told his wife what had happened and she went to Duds.

"If he had nothing to hide, why didn't he say that he had been in?" broke in Sandy.

"He had something to hide, but not murder," explained Lupin.

"Yes, of course, so he had. Well, as long as he had nothing to do with the death, I will do my best by keeping my mouth shut, I suppose. The best for Flo, I mean," he added.

"I think so," said Lupin slowly. "She wouldn't want it to come out. The letter and everything makes it pretty clear and Duds says she had been very miserable. I don't think I should say anything about it for the moment anyway, unless of course you are asked a direct question."

"It has been a relief talking things over."

"It always is, isn't it?"

They arrived back in time for lunch and the meal went better than Lupin had anticipated. Sandy did not look quite so wretched as he had done at breakfast and he even spoke once or twice. Gordon was very nice with everyone and suggested that Duds should take a peep at Florence that afternoon. "I do think it will do her good," he said. "Once she has seen you, she will want to go on seeing you. It must be bad for her to shut herself away as she has been doing, but you know what a funny thing shock is." And he appealed to the table in general.

"Oh yes," replied Duds. "I understand perfectly and I will just creep in this afternoon to break the ice, so to speak."

"Give her my love," said Tommy.

Sandy said nothing. He seemed absorbed in scraping up the last remnants of his milk pudding.

"It is very queer the different ways shock takes people," agreed Lupin. "I know one woman who when she heard that her husband was dead went straight out and bought herself six pairs of silk stockings. She was devoted to him too. But it just took her that way."

CHAPTER 13

DUDS WENT up to see Florence after lunch and came downstairs in tears. Lupin was sitting in the hall looking at a picture paper. She got up and gave her friend a hug. "It must have been awful for you," she said. "But it won't be so bad next time."

"No, and I am glad that I have seen her. She is such a darling and I keep thinking of her and Jo as children and when they first grew up just before the war."

Tommy had to go into Fordham that afternoon to see about various

formalities connected with the inquest and the funeral and he offered to take Lupin with him. "Were you thinking of coming?" he asked
his wife. "I shouldn't if I were you."

"No, I won't," she replied. "I think I will lie down. I feel as if I
could sleep for months."

"I should," said Lupin. "Not for months but for the whole afternoon."

Lupin and Tommy drove off together. "I told Gordon I'd see to
things for him," he explained. "He doesn't like to leave Flo."

"He seems a very devoted husband."

"Yes, he is. Poor chap, I am sorry for him really, but he just happens
to be the type that irritates me. He has been very decent about everything, and it must be rotten for him, I mean his sister-in-law and everything."

"Was he fond of her?"

Tommy did not answer for a moment or two. He seemed intent
on the road, though one milk van was the only bit of traffic in sight
and that was a good way off. At last he said, "As a matter of fact,
the whole thing is rather complicated and it would be a relief to tell
you all about it."

Lupin felt that she might compete with some of those well-known
patent medicines famed for giving instant relief. At the sight of her,
strong silent men and quiet reserved women were seized with a desire
to unburden themselves. "Then do," she said aloud.

"Well, I am afraid Jo was fond of Gordon. I'm betraying her confi-
dence in telling you this and, of course, I shouldn't have done so if she
had still been alive, but I know you are absolutely safe. And it isn't as if
you were anything to do with them, so to speak."

"No, that is all right."

"It was the night of the fancy dress dance, Monday. Goodness, it is
only Wednesday now. It seems years ago. Well, when I was dancing
with Jo, she suddenly said she was awfully tired and could we sit out
somewhere. I said, 'Let's sit on the stairs,' and she said, 'No, let's go
somewhere more private.' I was a bit surprised because I did not know
her at all well. I thought she looked on Duds and me rather as back
numbers. She had never put herself out to be particularly civil and I
wondered . . ."

"Whether she were going to try to add you to her list of admirers?"

"Don't get it into your head that I am the sort of fellow who goes about thinking that all the girls are after him. In fact, it is quite the other way. I know that I am not much of a hand at that sort of thing, but just for a minute I did wonder whether Jo wanted to see what she could do with me . Then when I looked at her I saw she really was on the point of breaking down, so I took her upstairs to the box room. When we got there she burst out crying and I felt pretty silly, you know what I mean—a man does feel pretty silly when a woman starts to cry—one does not know what to do for the best."

"It is very difficult."

"Of course if it's your wife or your sister, you give them a pat or a hug, and that is what I did with Jo, as a matter of fact. After all, she is a sort of cousin. I did the big brother touch more or less and it went pretty well. She calmed down a bit and started to tell me all about it. I had not really liked her much before. I thought she had been sidy and I was pretty sick because Duds had put herself out a lot for this houseparty and been frightfully excited and it had all been a frightful frost. Henry laying down the law and his wife being a first class bore the whole time and Sandy without a word to throw at a dog and so obviously fed up with the whole thing! Now I began to understand a bit. She knew she had been a pig, she said, and she was dreadfully sorry, but she had been so unhappy, she could not help herself and then it came out. She had been in love with Gordon and she had thought that he was in love with her. Then he met Flo and she had realized at once that what he had felt for her had been merely friendship."

"Had he made love to her at all?"

"No, she was quite decided about that. He had not been in any way to blame. They had gone out quite a lot together and she had been so used to men falling in love with her that she had taken it for granted that he had too. He was the only man that she had ever been in love with, the only man she ever could love, and it seemed unbelievable that he shouldn't love her. She did not blame him. It was only natural that he should fall in love with Flo and that Flo should fall in love with him. But she just could not bear to see them together. She cut herself off from them. I expect you heard about Flo coming in for a lot of money. Well, she wanted to go fifty-fifty with Jo. They had always been very devoted to each other and it was only natural as they were twins but Jo wouldn't. We couldn't imagine why but of course when she told me about Gordon I saw it. Flo had got her man, to put it crudely, and she did not want to be under an obligation to her."

"Yes, I understand that. You don't think Gordon married Flo for her money?"

"No, I don't think so. He is very devoted to her. You have seen that for yourself today. Personally I think she is much more attractive than Jo, though I don't like to say that now that Jo is dead. Of course Gordon does not strike me as the sort of person who would fall in love with someone without money, but I may misjudge him. I am a bit allergic to him. He has really been very decent and I have no right to say that, only I think he is the sort of person who might give the impression of being in love with a woman when he wasn't, if you know what I mean."

"Absolutely. He was quite tender to me when we were looking for the salt together this morning, so different from most men, who when they really are in love behave as if they were suffering from indigestion."

"Quite! Well, the poor kid had got herself into an awful state. She had evidently taken that cooing manner to be the real thing and then he goes and marries her sister and that divides them and makes her utterly wretched. I know she gives—gave, I should say—the appearance of being very hardboiled, but I think that was just eyewash and she was quite soft and unsophisticated underneath. Anyway, she told me she had got herself into a frightfully unhinged sort of state and she had taken to drinking too much. She hated herself for it, but she simply could not sleep and did not know half the time what she was doing. In fact she thought her brain was going and felt that she could not face life any longer."

"Did she actually threaten to commit suicide?"

"Well, that is the awful part of it and why I feel so ghastly about the whole thing. She did say, 'I can't go on living, Tommy. I have nothing to live for,' but naturally I did not take it seriously. I mean people often do talk like that, especially if they have been drinking a bit. But I do feel now that I ought to have done something about it. If only I had told Duds or Flo they would have sat up with her all night and it couldn't have happened."

"It is no good thinking about that now," replied Lupin. "It is easy enough to be wise after the event, but if I had sat up all night with all the people who have told me that they didn't want to go on living, I shouldn't have had much sleep during the last ten years."

"I suppose it only happens once in a hundred times, but I shall kick myself for the rest of my life. Thanks awfully for letting me tell you about it. I am afraid I have got to go to some rather grim places. Can you amuse yourself for a bit?"

"Of course."

"Then I will meet you at the White Swan at four o'clock."

Lupin set out to amuse herself. She went into a draper's shop and bought herself a packet of invisible hairpins and into a stationer's to buy a couple of picture postcards to send to her children. She stood for some time outside a cinema wondering whether to go in, but as she had seen the film once already and had not cared for it, it seemed rather a waste of money. She went to look at the church and stood for some time in the porch reading the notices. They made her feel very homesick. There would be a special service for the Mothers' Union on Monday next, and the Good Wives' Fellowship was meeting in the parish hall on Thursday. She wished that she were back taking her part among similar activities. She walked back thoughtfully along the High Street, wondering how her children were behaving at the Sunday school treat and whether the wives would get on all right with their discussion that evening and what Staines would give Andrew for supper.

Passing a chemist's shop, she suddenly remembered she had no aspirin with her and might easily want it before this visit was over. She went in and as she was paying for it she was moved by a sudden impulse. "Have you any weed-killer?" she asked.

The chemist looked at her in surprise. She was right, then. It was a funny thing to ask for in January. "That is queer," he said. "You are the second lady to ask for weed-killer this week and I have never known weeds come up this time of year."

"Was it another lady who asked for it?" She asked with interest.

"Yes, on Monday morning, it was. I thought at the time it was a funny thing to ask for. I don't stock it in the winter. May I ask what you were wanting it for?"

Lupin hesitated. The man was looking at her suspiciously and she felt that he had guessed her guilty secret, not that she had one. "Well, you never know when things will come in useful," she said. "I mean it is as well to lay in a store of anything when you can get it." He was still looking at her queerly and she added in what she hoped was a nonchalant voice, "I hope you don't think either of us are wanting to poison our husbands," and passed out into the street, feeling a fool. It had not gone well. Still, she knew two things now:

one, that it was queer to buy weed-killer in January, and two, that a woman had tried to buy some on Monday. But then it was a man who had bought the tin in the village. Were they two quite separate people or were they working together? In any case, whatever queer deeds they were up to, it was nothing to do with her. Was she still haunted by the suspicion that Jo's death had not been suicide? In any case she had not been poisoned by weed-killer—that was established beyond doubt.

There would probably be a murder in the vicinity before long and weed-killer would be found inside the victim. Lupin would be among the suspects as she had gone into the shop and deliberately asked for it and given a very silly excuse over which she had certainly blushed and stammered. Would it affect Andrew's career if she were had up for murder? And what about the children? It was so horrid for a child to have anything odd about its parents. She remembered a friend of hers whose mother had worn trousers before everyone else did, and how miserable she had been, and murder was worse than trousers. Why couldn't she mind her own business?

She turned her steps towards the hotel. Luckily the porter remembered her from the night before and allowed her to sit down at a writing table and address her two postcards and to write to Andrew.

Darling,

I do hope that Staines has explained everything to you. Duds sent a telegram and I thought I ought to come but I don't really know why she sent for me. It is all very dreadful as her cousin has committed suicide and she was such a pretty girl. She had left a letter saying that she was doing it, so all seems plain sailing, though dreadfully sad, but no one is to blame though they are all going about as if they had a guilty secret. The inquest is tomorrow and the funeral the next day so all being well I hope to be back on Saturday. Staines said she would cope with the Sunday school and the good wives and the mothers so I expect everything will be all right but I do hate being away especially when it is for an inquest which it usually is when it's me. I think the minute I arrive somewhere, people say 'Let's have an inquest.'

All my love. L.

She did not mention the weed-killer. There was no point in worrying him unnecessarily and if the murder took place far enough away and after she had gone home perhaps she would not be mixed up in it, though it will be the first murder I haven't got mixed up in, she told herself gloomily. If there has been the least possibility, that is. Then she remembered that one of the good wives who was of a literary frame of mind had suggested that there should be a poetry competition next month. The best poem was to be published in the parish magazine. Lupin had not worried much about it as she knew hers would not be the best. However, she supposed she ought to try to write something to show that she took an interest in the activities of the fellowship, even if she didn't. What was the subject of the poem? A winter evening. Oh yes, of course.

> In the evening when it's cold
> It makes one feel so very old.
> It's really better in than out
> Unless one is young enough to run about.

She read this through critically and came to the conclusion that the last line did not scan very well. She tried again.

> It's really better to stay in
> And have a soothing glass of gin.

That scans better, but perhaps it isn't quite the right tone, Lupin said to herself, sighing. Writing poetry was very difficult and she could not see there was much object in it. It would not help them to be better wives. In fact, just the contrary, as they would be thinking of poetry when they should be thinking of their husbands' dinner. However, she had better have another try.

> On the whole I think it's best
> To keep quite clear of an inquest.
> The room is always very chilly
> And all one's friends appear so silly.
> They always seem to sag and wilt
> And be so full of conscious guilt.

That is rather good, she told herself, although of course there isn't much in it about a winter evening. Suddenly she was seized by a sudden inspiration and her pen started to scratch busily over her paper

> In a drear nighted December,
> Too happy, happy tree,
> Thy branches ne'er remember
> Their green felicity;
> The north cannot undo them,
> With a sleety whistle through them;
> Nor frozen thawing glue them
> From budding at the prime.

That really is poetry, she told herself proudly. Perhaps she would get into the parish magazine after all. She had not realized that she had got it in her. Then a horrible thought assailed her. Was it original, or was it something that she had learned by heart as a child? Her governess had made her learn a lot of poetry by heart and some of it had stuck and some hadn't. How awful if she were to be had up for plagiarism as well as trying to buy weed-killer in January. Andrew and the children would have to go to Canada.

She looked up and saw Henry Dumbleton walking across the hall. She was not as upset as she had been last night, because she knew now that he was not dead. All the same he looked as if he might die at any moment. His face was an awful color and he stooped like an old man. She had never liked him but she felt sorry for him now. As he passed her chair, she said "Hullo, Henry, do you know anything about poetry?"

CHAPTER 14

HENRY gave a start. What a state his nerves are in, thought Lupin. He was obviously the person Sandy had seen coming out of Jo's room. Lucky for him that she had committed suicide and not been murdered, as he would be eligible as first murderer at one glance. Still, as Lupin knew well, everyone looked guilty after a case of sudden death, even if they had only been to the same church as the victim on the previous Sunday or stood next to him in the fish queue.

"Why, it is Lupin Lorrimer!" exclaimed Henry. "It is a long time since we met. By the way, you are married now, aren't you?"

"Absolutely, and the mother of two. I'm now Lupin Hastings. I am glad you recognized me after all these years. You are married too, aren't you—again, I mean?"

"Yes, I was married some years ago." He looked nervously round the lounge as if he were afraid that his wife might see him speaking to Lupin. Did he fancy himself such a Don Juan, she wondered, that he could not speak to a woman without being suspected of dishonorable intentions? He did not look much like a Don Juan. He looked more like something that had been in the sea several days and then picked up. He reminded Lupin of a codfish she had seen lying on the slab the other day and had been nearly mesmerized into buying by the fishmonger.

"I am staying with Tommy and Duds," she explained. "Tommy had some business to see to in the town and he told me to meet him here. There was not much to do in the town so I came here to write to the family while I waited. And then I remembered I had to write some poetry for the Good Wives' Fellowship, and I just wondered if you knew anything about it."

"No, I don't know anything at all," replied Henry hastily, and whether he was referring to the good wives or the poetry, Lupin thought he had changed very much from the old days when he had been an authority on everything from motor cars to the revised prayer book. "I want to see Tommy," he went on. "Will he be long?"

Lupin did not feel that Tommy would be anxious to see Henry. Of course she might be mistaken, but she had not gained the impression that there was anything of the David and Jonathan touch between the two men, at any rate not on Tommy's side. "He said about four," she replied.

Henry looked at his watch. "And it is only half-past three now," he muttered. He took several steps up and down the lounge, wiped his forehead and said, "I want to go to the police station, but I must tell Tommy first."

Does he think Tommy did it? wondered Lupin. And is he going to warn him before reporting him to the police?

"Why?" she asked aloud.

An attractive-looking woman joined them. "Hullo, dear," she said to Henry. "Do you think it is too early for a cup of tea?"

"This is my wife," explained Henry. "Lady Lupin Hastings."

"Oh, you are Lady Lupin Hastings, Dorothy's great friend. I am so glad you have come. This is such a very trying time for her, for us all in fact. Just ring the bell, will you, Henry?"

Henry rang the bell. "I don't want any tea," he said. "I shall go and wait in the smoking room until Tommy comes."

"Yes do, dear," replied his wife soothingly. "But don't smoke, will you? His asthma has been so bad," she explained to Lupin. "It was unfortunate that the poor girl should have chosen that moment to take his heroin, as he had a very bad attack that night and I was unable to give him an injection. The doctor very kindly gave me another prescription and I had it made up and I gave him an injection last night. He is better today but not at all well. It could not have happened at a worse time. Still, of course, the whole thing is very tragic and I feel very sorry for the poor girl and for her sister—a sweet person—and for Dorothy and everyone concerned. The whole thing has been most distressing and such a sad ending to our happy week."

"I did not think your husband was looking very well," said Lupin, sympathetically.

"No, and then he is worried too, which is of course very bad for him. In fact the whole thing has been most unfortunate."

Lupin felt that this was a mild way of putting it, but she agreed that it was a sad business.

The tea arrived and Mrs. Dumbleton poured out a cup for Lupin and one for herself. "Do you take sugar?" she asked. "I never do, so it does not worry me it being short, but men seem to need sugar, don't they?"

"Yes. Let's save this for Henry and Tommy."

"Thank you so much. These scones look quite nice. I must say this hotel is very good for a country town and the people are very civil. People say there is a lot of communism about but I can't say I have ever come across anything of the kind."

"No, nor have I—at least I met one once, but he was frightfully nice. I don't see that it matters what people's politics are, so long as they are friendly, do you?"

"No, though I have always been a Conservative myself. I used to sing at the Primrose League concerts at one time." She took a bite out of her scone. "Those days before the war seem very far away, don't they? They were so peaceful and everyone seemed so happy. I think the war has unsettled people a good deal. That young man Sandy Ferguson appeared very depressed. Of course he was a prisoner-of-war and that cannot have been at all nice. If he had been the one to take his own life I should not really have been at all surprised, as he had been very miserable. But all the young people seem rather unbalanced. Still one cannot blame them. They have not had a very good time the last few years."

"No, poor things," said Lupin. "They sort of went straight from the nursery to the war and they missed all the years that were such fun for us."

"That is what I feel," said Mrs. Dumbleton. She surveyed a dish of rock cakes thoughtfully. "The whole trouble is that my husband is so conscientious."

Lupin was rather surprised. Of course she had not seen anything of Henry for a long time and he might have changed a lot during that period, but certainly conscientiousness had never struck her as being his outstanding virtue in the days when she had known him. "Oh, is he?" she asked, and then felt that that had not been quite the right reply.

Irene did not seem to notice anything lacking. She took a bun and went on talking. "It is being a lawyer, of course, that makes him feel he ought to keep the law."

"Of course," agreed Lupin, wondering if lawyers were the only members of the community to feel themselves thus bound.

"As I was saying, the whole occurrence was most unfortunate, and what made it particularly so was that Henry found Josephine's bag and took it along to her room."

Lupin looked with respect at Mrs. Dumbleton. She had some sterling qualities. "Oh," she said. Should she explain that he had been seen?

Mrs. Dumbleton did not give her time to speak. "The party was over soon after one and I went straight up to bed and was soon asleep. Luckily I am a very good sleeper. It must be terrible for people who suffer from insomnia. Suddenly I was awakened by Henry. He is usually most considerate, but I could see at once he was upset. His breathing was very bad and I went at once to the washstand to get his injection. The bottle of heroin wasn't there. Then I realized that he was holding it in his hand, the top was broken off, and for one awful minute I thought he had poisoned himself. I got him on to the bed and piled him up with pillows and gave him a little brandy. Then he managed to tell me, but he was gasping terribly. I was quite frightened. I wanted to go at once for the doctor, but I did not like to leave him."

"No, of course not."

"It seems that he had stayed downstairs for a bit with the other men, having a final drink, though he is really better without it. Not that he ever drinks much, but he has to be very careful about his diet. As he was coming up to bed he noticed Josephine's bag lying on a sofa and not realizing, I suppose, how late it was, he thought he would take it to her room on his way up."

"Oh, and was she dead?"

"She wasn't there."

"Not there?"

"No, he found his bottle there quite empty and a letter to Dorothy and no sign of Josephine. Of course he was very much upset and came straight to me, but the agitation brought on one of his worst attacks of asthma at once. It took me some time to get the story from him and then it was some time before I could leave him. I was very worried about Josephine, naturally, but my own husband came first."

"Absolutely."

"At last when he was a little more comfortable I went to Josephine's room, hoping that perhaps the whole thing had been a practical joke, and when I got there I found her lying on her bed, quite dead. I have had a good deal of nursing experience. I was in a hospital for part of the war and both my husbands have been more or less invalids—in fact my first husband was very ill before he died. I knew at once that she was dead. Poor soul. She was still dressed up in her fancy dress. It was terrible. I went back and fetched the empty heroin bottle and put it where Henry had found it. I thought it best to leave everything as it was. Then I went to Dorothy."

"What time was this?"

Irene pondered for a minute or two. "It is difficult to say exactly. I don't know what time Henry woke me up and I don't know how long it was before I got him quieted down. But I do know it was four-fifteen when the doctor came and he came pretty quickly, so it must have been nearly four by the time I got to Dorothy's room, but what with one thing and another I had been very delayed. I don't think it would have made any difference, though, if I had been earlier, as the doctor thought she had been dead for at least two hours."

"She can't have been dead when your husband went into the room."

"No, that is what Henry said, and of course we were very upset, as if we had found her in time we might have given her something to make her sick. On the other hand, according to the doctor she was dead, and Henry says suppose someone killed her and then put her on the bed. I said that isn't very likely because why should anyone want to kill the girl? And there is no point in thinking of such things. But he says that he is concealing valuable evidence and it is his duty to tell the police."

"I suppose a man would feel like that, especially a lawyer. Women are more for letting sleeping dogs lie," said Lupin.

"You see, the whole matter is a little delicate, because people are so inclined to think things. Of course there was no harm in his taking the girl's bag to her room, anybody might have done it, but it is no good pretending that he hadn't been a bit silly. Well, you are married, so you know what men are like. Henry never could resist a pretty girl, no harm in it you know, but he had been running after Josephine all the week."

"Had he?"

"Yes, but after all, there is always something, and I think it is better than drink or gambling. My first husband took up speculating, which is a very dangerous thing. As it happened he was lucky, but he might easily not have been. In fact if he had not died when he had, we might have lost everything." Lupin suddenly remembered of whom it was that Mrs. Dumbleton reminded her: Mrs. White of the village shop. "Well, there it is, everyone knew that Henry had been keen on this girl and I must say she encouraged him to start with. I thought it better to take no notice. These things usually die down if you leave them alone, but once you start making a fuss you never know what may happen. Anyway, this girl, Josephine, was all over Henry to begin with, but the last two days she would have nothing to do with him. I hoped at first that she realized that she was behaving badly. On the other hand another man turned up, a publisher. She was his secretary and I could not help wondering if there was anything between them."

"I wonder if there was?"

"It made Henry keener than ever. You know how men always seem to like the girls who cold shoulder them better than those who run after them."

"By keeping men off you keep them on," quoted Lupin.

"Just so. So of course things being like that, and it is no good pretending that he could take his eyes off her at the dance—she certainly looked very striking—it is a little awkward his having gone to her room. It isn't as if for a moment *I* believe there was anything wrong, but it does not put Henry in a very good light. And one does not want people to think one's husband a fool."

Lupin did not see how anyone could think her husband a fool, except of course for marrying her. She had an idea that most of his friends had thought him a fool then. Aloud she said, "No, rather not."

"You are so understanding," said Irene, taking another scone. "I am sure you would feel just the same if it were your husband."

Lupin tried to imagine herself and Andrew in such circumstances and failed. "Well," she said, diffidently, "of course being a clergyman he doesn't run after girls much. I mean it's not the sort of thing that goes down frightfully well in a parish." Then, fearing she might seem to be boasting, she added, "But he does eat his food rather fast."

"There is always something," said Irene, companionably. "There it is. Henry is determined to go to the police, but he feels he ought to tell Tommy first as it all happened in his house. There is nothing really we can do about it, but I think it is a pity from everybody's point of view." And she poured herself out another cup of tea.

"Didn't the police ask him any questions?"

"No, he was still pretty bad and I saw the inspector and told him about the heroin and how the girl must have taken it from our washstand. I said I went straight to her room and was going to ask her to go to Dorothy to ask if she knew anything about it. I made the excuse that I did not like to go to her room myself because of disturbing her husband. Josephine, being a cousin, would not mind. Of course it was not exactly true and I should not have minded in the least about Tommy. I am not embarrassed about that sort of thing, and in any case Tommy was not there. He was in his dressing room, because Dorothy banged on his door and I noticed his bed was empty."

Lupin's mind was in a whirl. It was a quarter to three when Henry had been seen coming out of Jo's room. His wife may not have realized how late it was, but it was certainly too late to take people their dropped handbags. If he had taken it on his way up to bed that would be a fairly normal thing to do, though not frightfully wise if he and Jo were being talked about. But at a quarter to three, no!

Of course Irene was the person who had a motive for putting Josephine out of the way and there was something about her pleasant discursive unemotional manner that made her a not unbelievable murderess. "Such a pity I had to murder the girl, I hate murdering people, it seems so unkind," and she would take another scone. But if she had done it she wouldn't be telling Lupin this long complicated story; she would have kept quite quiet. It was an obvious suicide and no one would question it if people did not talk. But that story of Henry's about the bag almost rang true. Surely no one would have invented such a silly story. Had they murdered the girl between them? No, they would keep quiet if they had.

Had Irene murdered her without her husband's knowledge and was Henry unwittingly going to queer her pitch? Possibly. Had Henry murdered her without his wife's knowledge? No, because it was he who was insisting on going to the police.

"Henry says he should not tamper with the truth and of course I agree with him. I have always had a great horror of lies. My father brought us all up very strictly and would never allow any of us to tell an untruth. In fact if we instructed the parlormaid to say 'not at home,' we had to go into the garden. Of course he believed in hellfire."

Lupin shivered. "Any kind of fire would be rather nice," she remarked. "But I agree with you about the truth. My husband is very particular, too, and the police usually find out everything in the end and it makes you look awkward if you have told them something that is not true."

"That is the unfortunate part, because I have already told them about going to Josephine's room to look for the heroin."

"I think if your husband tells them the true story they will understand why you said that. As a matter of fact, if you don't mind me saying so, it didn't sound frightfully convincing in the first place. I mean you wouldn't really be very likely to be shy at the idea of seeing Tommy in bed."

"No, nor I should. I daresay Henry is right, though it will make him look a little silly. Oh, here they are. I wonder if we had better have some fresh tea. This has not been made very long. On the other hand stewed tea is never very nice. I think perhaps we had better have some fresh."

"I've told Tommy," said Henry.

"Have you, dear? Perhaps Tommy you would be so kind as to ring the bell as you are nearest to it. Oh, there is the waiter. Might we have another pot of tea? Thank you so much."

"It is very difficult to know what to do," said Tommy, sitting down by Irene.

"Isn't it?" agreed Lupin.

"We must speak the truth," said Henry. "There is no question about that."

"What is truth?" asked Lupin, "As Julius Caesar said. Oh dear, no, it was Pontius Pilate. I am so sorry, I did not mean to be blasphemous."

"Lady Lupin means that if you tell the truth, dear, it may give a wrong impression," explained Irene.

"People have such nasty minds," said Lupin.

"I can't help that," said Henry.

"Of course, it is a bit uncomfortable for your wife," said Tommy, taking a cup of the fresh tea and stirring it round thoughtfully, "and for Flo too, if people think things about her sister. On the other hand I think you ought to speak."

Lupin thought out aloud, "You see if Jo poisoned herself, how did she get back to bed after she was dead?"

"Well, I'll be getting along," said Henry. He put down his cup and left half a scone on his plate.

"Oh, do finish your tea, dear. You will feel so much better after it."

"I'll come with you," said Tommy.

He felt almost drawn to the man, now that he was in trouble, and he certainly had a strong sense of honor, yet Tommy remembered opening the kitchen door and seeing him and Duds. He remembered the night of the dance and Duds and Henry laughing together and drinking out of the same glass . . . yet all the time Henry had been thinking of Jo, planning to go to see her as soon as the dance was over. Or was it just a sudden impulse on seeing her bag? Anyhow, whatever it was, he was suffering now and he was an ill man. It was Tommy's business to help him through the ordeal and to hand him back intact to his wife.

The inspector was very nice. He appeared to swallow Henry's story about the handbag without having what Lupin would call a nasty mind. He accepted Mrs. Dumbleton's apology for her false statement. "My wife was very much upset," explained Henry. "I had been very ill in the night and she may well have forgotten what

exactly did happen. She was very worried at finding my diamorphine gone. She did not say anything about my having gone to the room
with the bag. She may have thought it sounded a little unconventional."

"Quite," said the inspector. Henry looked ill enough; he was not
inventing that. The woman had seemed a decent type, though inclined to talk too much. She might not like it known that her husband
had gone to the girl's room, though looking at him it was probably
quite an innocent visit. Very funny that the girl wasn't there. It was
two o'clock, Henry thought, or a little later. He had been taken ill
when he returned to his room and his wife had been too concerned to
go along to see. She had really thought the whole thing a practical
joke. It might have been an hour later before she got there; he did
not know, nor did his wife, but the doctor arrived at four-fifteen.

"Luckily your wife only made an informal statement, so we need
not take it into consideration," said the inspector, "but I must ask
you to read yours through and sign it. It looks as if the lady had
taken the drug, then gone along to her sister's room and died shortly
after her return to her own."

"If only I had gone straight to Florence's room," said Henry,
"and told her what I had found, we might have done something, or if
my wife had gone to her when I told her, but I had that stupid attack
just at the critical moment. I shall never forgive myself."

"It can't be helped now," said Tommy. "I might have done something, too. I knew she was very unhappy. It doesn't bear thinking
about. Here we are," and he helped him out of the car and into the
hotel. Lupin and Irene were sitting by the fire and the latter was
describing a trip she had made before the war to Egypt. The hotel was
really most comfortable, she said. In fact it was very up-to-date. "They
had Vi-spring mattresses, which some people like very much, but I did
not find them very restful—too resilient, if you know what I mean."

"Oh yes, bouncy. I know. And how did you like the Pyramids?"

"Very much—and the food was good too. Oh, here they are."

Tommy and Lupin said good night to the Dumbletons and started on
their homeward journey. They drove for the most part in silence, but
just as they were nearing home, Lupin said, "I never did care much for
Henry Dumbleton, but I felt sorry for him today."

Tommy grunted. Lupin went on, "I thought his wife was awfully
decent about everything."

"She is a good sort," replied Tommy. "A bit of a bore, but

she was very kind about helping Duds with the housework over Christmas."

"Yes, and some wives might have turned nasty about their husbands going to a girl's room, even with a handbag as a chaperone, but she took it all in her stride, like the Pyramids and the Vi-spring mattresses."

"What?"

Lupin told Tommy about Mrs. Dumbleton's reactions to Egypt, but like Queen Victoria, he was not amused. The old lighthearted Tommy had gone and this staid, rather disapproving stranger had taken his place. Lupin sighed and relapsed into silence until they reached Old Place.

CHAPTER 15

THE EVENING was not very cheerful. No aperitifs were forthcoming as everything had been finished on the night of the dance. The supper consisted of fish (just the sort of fish I would get landed with, thought Lupin sympathetically, but luckily I have Staines to vet things for me). The fish was followed by bottled plums. These were very sour and Lupin foresaw a bad night for them all. Tommy went to have a last look at the animals and Sandy disappeared. Now was the time, thought Lupin, for she and Duds to have a good heart-to-heart, but Duds did not seem anxious for confidences. Last night she had seemed pleased to see Lupin and anxious to tell her everything—well, not quite everything, there had been something left unsaid, but Lupin had thought it would only be a matter of time before that came out too. But now Duds seemed to regret having sent for her. She showed no wish to confide in her nor to hear any of the facts that Lupin had learned that afternoon. On Lupin saying that Henry had looked ill, she replied that she believed he suffered from asthma and on being told that Irene had been friendly, she had said she had found her very nice. At last Lupin could bear it no longer and remarked that she was very tired and would Duds mind if she went up to bed.

"No, do. I shall be coming up soon, but I won't disturb you. Are you sure that you have got everything you want?"

Lupin was not at all sure. In fact she knew she hadn't. For one thing she wanted her husband, for another she wanted her children. She also wanted something to eat and something to drink, for the evening meal had been far from satisfying. She wished that she were taking the chair at the meeting of the Good Wives' Fellowship. She suddenly remembered the poem she had been writing for the competition. She had been on the track of something really good. How strange it would be if she were to blossom out into a famous poet! She believed there were people who developed late in life. The people of Glanville would be surprised to find they had been nursing a genius in their bosom.

> In a drear-nighted December
> Oh, horrid, horrid fish
> I always will remember,
> You made a nasty dish.

No, that was not up to the lines she had written in the White Swan. Besides, it would not be very grateful. Her nurse had always taught her that you should not criticize the food in other people's houses. Had those lines she had first written been her own? That was the trouble. It would be terrible if she tried to pass off one of Shakespeare's works as hers.

She saw Sandy crossing the hall. "I say, Sandy," she said, "do you know a poem beginning 'In a drear nighted December?' "

"Yes, why?"

"Who is it by?"

"Keats."

"Oh, Keats! Of course it would be. I didn't really think it could be me. By the way, I wanted a word with you."

"Did you? Where shall we go, into your bedroom? We could take our hair down and recite poetry to each other."

"I am not really very hot at poetry. I only know bits and pieces and I can never remember who wrote them. And in any case I think it is best to keep out of bedrooms."

"Just as you say, but I wasn't going to take advantage of you."

"I didn't think you were, but what about the box room? You never know what will come out at the inquest and a box room sounds better than a bedroom."

The room was rather dark and musty, but there was one

rather inadequate electric light and they sat down on a couple of trunks.

"Well?" asked Sandy inquiringly.

"It was about what you told me this morning," explained Lupin. "I saw Hen . . . I mean the person you told me about and he has been to the police station and told them that he went to Jo's room on Monday night. He says he found her bag on a sofa and took it to her room on his way to bed. When he got there she wasn't there but the letter and the empty bottle were lying on the dressing table. He hurried along to his wife to tell her about it and had a very bad attack of asthma. Of course she was very agitated, especially as Jo had taken his stuff, so it was some time before she was able to do anything about it, but as soon as she could leave him she went to Jo's room and found her lying fully dressed on the bed, quite dead."

Sandy stared at her. In the dim light Lupin could see that he was very much surprised by what she had told him.

"Of course he has been very ill," she went on. "That is why he did not say anything before, but now he has insisted on going to the police, so I don't think he can have had anything to do with it, because if he had he would keep quiet. And in any case it sounds a bit awkward his having gone to her room."

"Who are you talking about?"

"Henry Dumbleton, of course."

"But it wasn't Henry Dumbleton that I saw coming out of Jo's room."

Lupin stared at him. "Not Henry!" she gasped, "but you said it was a man!"

"I know I did, but I never said anything about Henry Dumbleton."

The full meaning of what Sandy's words implied was dawning on her. He had seen Tommy coming out of Josephine's room. No wonder he had not wanted to say anything about it!

Had Tommy gone in after Henry came out? He had seemed so natural when he told her the story of the scene in this box room, but he had never said anything about going to her room afterwards. He said he wished he had taken her remarks about taking her own life more seriously. Perhaps he had taken them seriously and gone along to her room to make sure she was all right. Well, if so, why make a mystery of it? Surely he knew Lupin well enough to know she wouldn't think anything horrid. She felt quite indignant with him at the idea. The most natural thing would have been to confide in Duds, but there was something queer there, a sort of undercurrent. If, as she thought last night, he had fallen under Jo's spell and Duds suspected it, it might make for strained relations. And it would have been difficult for them to discuss the girl.

All the same, Henry had fallen under Jo's spell and he had not hesitated to go to his wife when he found himself in a similar fix and, fool though she might be in some ways, she had had the sense and loyalty to sympathize with him. Lupin was sure that Duds had as much sense and loyalty as Irene. Why hadn't Tommy trusted her? Then again, Tommy had been so sympathetic with Henry, even going round to the police station with him. Had he been acting all the time, knowing that he had also gone into Jo's room? She had known Tommy for fourteen years. She could not believe that he had been acting as a hypocrite. Then his story to her about his interview with Jo in the box room had rung so true, all about giving her a hug in a brotherly way. Had he been acting? Tommy acting seemed impossible, he had always been shocking in the old days when they got up amateur theatricals.

"I see," she said rather faintly to Sandy, after a pause. "Well, there is nothing we can do about it."

"I suppose not," he replied doubtfully, "but it does complicate things a bit, Dumbleton having been there too."

"It does," agreed Lupin, thinking of the old happy days with Tommy and Duds. They had radiated gaiety and affection. She had read about the war breaking up marriages, but she had not thought of it breaking up Duds' and Tommy's any more than hers and Andrew's. Had Tommy met Jo before this houseparty—lately she meant? She knew he had known her in the old days. But even if he had fallen for her he would not ask her, or allow Duds to ask her, here for Christmas and have an affair with her in his wife's house. That would be impossible for the Tommy she had known and liked, in fact loved, for years. Was there anything worse still? Her mind shied away from the thought. He could not possibly have had anything to do with Jo's death. That must have been as much a shock to him as it was to everyone else.

"Are you feeling all right, Lupin?"

"Absolutely. This light makes one look like death warmed up. You look awful, too, but I think I will go to bed all the same."

"Right you are. We had better sleep on it."

"Yes," she agreed, but she did not think that she would sleep.

"Good night, Sandy." She stood up then and looked at him. "I say, I suppose you don't think it would be a good idea to tell Tommy what you saw."

Sandy pondered a moment. "Perhaps you are right," he said.

CHAPTER. 16

DUDS CAME in again the next morning with Lupin's cup of tea. She did not look as if she had slept much, but then neither had Lupin herself. "You shouldn't bother," she said as she took the cup and wondered how much Duds knew. "I could easily come down and get it."

"Oh, that's all right," replied her friend. "I am always up anyway. There is not much object in lying in bed."

"No, there isn't really, is there?" And Lupin swung her legs over the edge of the bed. "I expect you are brooding over the inquest a bit."

"Oh, that," said Duds airily, as if an inquest were a mere nothing to her, and so it probably was, if she had lost Tommy.

If only, thought Lupin, as she got into her bath, she would talk it over. I don't expect it is as bad as she thinks. After all, Tommy may have been very silly, but so was Henry and his wife isn't worrying. As she says, if it isn't one thing it is another, and Jo does seem to have been a sort of *belle dame sans merci* type of person, whatever it was. She dried and dressed and hurried downstairs, where she laid the breakfast table as she had done the day before. Tommy and Sandy came down. I saw pale knights and warriors too, thought Lupin. They are both death-pale, as the poet puts it. Gordon, on the other hand, looked quite normal, though with the subdued air suitable to one about to attend the inquest of his sister-in-law. He took up his wife's breakfast, then came down and ate his own with the others. He and Lupin made a little desultory conversation but the other three did not help them.

"Were you thinking of going to the inquest?" Gordon asked Lupin as he was helping her to clear the breakfast table.

"I suppose so, if Duds wants me to, I mean." She was not at all sure that Duds would want her and she wondered for the hundredth time why she had sent her that urgent summons by telegram and wished very much that she had ignored it.

"I was only wondering if by any chance you weren't going you would feel like staying with my wife. The doctor has given her a certificate so that she will not have to appear, but of course I will have to go and I don't much like leaving her alone. Of course I quite understand if Duds wants you."

Lupin's heart leaped. It would be lovely to escape the inquest. She was dreading the disclosures that would come out. It would be awful sitting by Duds while Tommy admitted, if he did admit it, that he had been in Jo's room at a quarter to three. "But do you think she would see me?" she asked aloud. "She does not like seeing people, does she?"

"She said she would like to see you. It would be easier for her to see a stranger—not that you are exactly a stranger, but someone she has not seen for a long time—rather than one of the houseparty. She is devoted to Duds, but the sight of her brings it all back to her so much. I found her in tears yesterday afternoon after Duds had been in, but of course you will not mention this."

"I quite understand. Oh, here is Duds. I say, Duds, what about it? Do you want me to come with you or would it be more useful if I stayed with Flo? Mr. Pinhorn says she would not mind seeing a stranger so much as one of her own family. I know what he means, don't you? So unless you specially want me for the inquest, perhaps you would like me to stay with her. Just as you think."

"No, that would be a very good idea. There is no point in you coming to the inquest and it would be pretty grim for Flo all alone. I wish I could stay with her myself, but I daresay as Gordon says it will be easier for her to talk to a stranger."

Lupin said goodbye to Duds just before the inquest. "Goodbye, my dear," she said, "and honestly I don't think things are as bad as you think they are." She wished she could impart some of Irene Dumbleton's philosophy to her friend. But she just gave her a hug and said, "Bless you, old thing."

Duds gave her rather a queer look. "Thank you, Loops. I am sorry I have been a bit prickly the last two days but the thought of this inquest has been hanging over one and—well, other things, too." She hesitated, then, "I must fly," she said.

Flo was sitting up in a chair by the window. She was wearing a housecoat of a very pretty shade of blue, buttoning down to her slim ankles. Her smooth hair was waved back from her pale face and hung to her shoulders. Her beautiful blue eyes were shadowed as if she had been sleeping badly. She gave Lupin a welcoming smile, which was a relief, as Lupin had not been sure if she would resent her visit or not.

"I do hope you don't mind me coming in to see you, but your husband thought that you would let me come for a little while."

"It is very good of you," she replied. "As a matter of fact, I am very glad to see you. Somehow it is easier to talk to someone from outside than to one of the family, if you know what I mean."

"Yes, I can understand that. The others bring things back too much. Duds understands too and isn't the least bit hurt. She has got imagination, you know."

"I did see her for a minute or two yesterday but I could not talk to her. She is too mixed up with everything and I knew I should break down at the least thing. All the same, you are not a stranger. I remember you perfectly."

"Oh, do you? Good. I didn't think you would. Of course I remember you as an infant."

"I never thought you would marry a clergyman."

"Nor did I. It was a terrible shock to me when I realized what I had done and a worse one for him I expect. As for the parishioners, they nearly passed out. In fact the curate did." She then remembered that sudden death was hardly a tactful subject in the circumstances and went on hurriedly, "It is a funny thing that a clergyman's wife is the only one who is expected to take part in her husband's work. A soldier's wife does not go into battle, a plumber's wife does not come and hold the tools while he is mending the sink, nor does the gardener's wife weed the lawn, nor the lawyer's wife advise you about your will. But a clergyman's wife is expected to help with everything—to visit the sick and those who have lost their faith, to count the number of communicants and to lead the responses when there aren't any. Once in the war we had a very small congregation and I had just counted fifteen when I realized that there was an awkward pause, so I said 'Sixteen' in a loud clear voice instead of 'Lord incline our hearts to keep this law.' It was very awkward, but after all the doctor's wife isn't expected to come and say 'Ninety-nine' while her husband is sounding your chest."

"But you are very happy, aren't you?"

"Rather! Frightfully. I don't really mind what I do so long as I have got Andrew. I do think being married to the right person is the one thing that really matters." She felt that she was safe in saying this to Flo, because there was no doubt that she was very devoted to Gordon and he to her.

"That is what I feel," replied Flo. "I shouldn't mind what Gordon's profession was, so long as we could be together. Though I have sometimes felt rather a beast for being so happy when Jo was so miserable."

"I know," said Lupin gently.

"You see, sometimes I have an awful feeling that she was rather fond of Gordon to start with. You know he was her friend originally, but I never had the least idea of their liking each other, and then she introduced him to me and we fell in love practically at first sight and got married very soon. It was after that she turned, well, a bit queer. I thought she had not liked it because I had come into Grandfather's money, but it was all so silly. He left it to the eldest grandchild, so as there were only two of us and we were twins I took for granted we should share it. But it seemed that legally it was mine because I had been born first. I didn't see that it mattered, as naturally we should share it whatever the lawyers said. But to my astonishment she would not touch any of it. She was so funny with me, sort of offhand and quite different. It worried me dreadfully.

"Then Duds asked us both down here for Christmas. I never thought that Jo would come but she did. I was so thrilled about it. I thought everything would come all right between us. Gordon and I motored her down and I was so happy. I had always been fond of Duds and I thought it would be just like old times, us all spending Christmas together.

"And then as soon as we arrived I realized that things were wrong. In spite of everything Jo wasn't her old self. She was terribly blasé and she didn't try to fit in. It was all a pose, of course. I think she really wanted to be nice but couldn't bring herself to begin. Then she started flirting with that awful Henry Dumbleton and it was most uncomfortable. She was like a travesty of her real self. She was pretending to be hardboiled. The man she worked for, a publisher called Veazey, came down and she dropped Henry for him. Of course, it may have been that she was interested in her work and liked talking about it, I don't know, but Henry sat about glowering and all the nice Christmasy atmosphere was spoiled."

Flo paused for a minute and looked out of the window. "Then on Monday she suddenly came to me and said, 'Do come and look at the moon, Flo!' and we walked round the garden together. It was a wonderful evening, the stars were out and though it was cold, somehow I felt spring wasn't far off. I don't know if you know what I mean but I felt tomorrow is New Year's Day and it will be a much nicer year than we have had for a long time. Jo said she was afraid that she had been rather a beast lately but that she had been very unhappy and it made her want to be horrid. I said I quite understood and she said she would come to my room when the party was over and we would have a nice talk about everything and I said, 'We are twins again, aren't we?' and she said 'Yes.'

"I enjoyed that evening. It was such fun and I was so happy because Jo was herself again. She came to my room when everyone else had gone and we had a lovely long talk. It was then that I first wondered if she cared for Gordon. She did not mention his name, but she said that she had grudged me something, not the money, but that it had made her feel spiteful and that she did not want to take the money from me. I said it wasn't me, it was Grandfather, and she said 'Nothing matters now except our being friends.' I said, 'And we will share the dibs, won't we?' and she said, 'Of course.' Then Gordon came along and said we would both look sights if we did not go to sleep and Jo said she was so sleepy she couldn't move. Do you think she had had the stuff before she came to talk to me?"

"I suppose she might have done," said Lupin, wondering whether she should tell Flo about Henry going to the room and finding the empty bottle and the letter. She decided it wasn't really her business to say anything. Gordon would tell her whatever he thought fit.

"Gordon chaffed her and said she had had too much champagne and insisted on escorting her back to her room. I heard them laughing together, then he came back and I went to sleep feeling so happy and all the time she . . ." Her voice broke.

"Don't talk about it if you'd rather not," begged Lupin.

"It is a relief in a way."

I wonder how many more people will use that word about talking to me? reflected Lupin to herself.

"I have been brooding over it all and yet I couldn't bear to talk about it even to Gordon. And poor Duds would be so upset. She has always been so fond of us both. But you are a nice person to talk to, Lupin. Anyway, Jo and I parted friends. That is the one thing I shall always be thankful for, and she wrote that sweet letter to Duds and then I suppose she just went to sleep."

Lupin thought over the story. It was obvious that Henry had gone into the room while Jo was with Flo, but when did Tommy go in? Gordon had seen her back into her room, so Tommy couldn't have been waiting there for her. He must have either gone into the room while it was empty, or afterwards when, in all probability, she was dead. If he had found her dead he may have felt that no object would be served by his saying he was there. After all it would not have been very nice for Duds or for Flo. He might have been genuinely worried at her telling him she did not want to go on living and gone along to see she was all right, only to find she was dead. But surely Duds would understand. She looked at Flo. Her eyes filled with tears as she thought of the twin bridesmaids at Duds' wedding and she felt a sharp pang of sorrow. "There is nothing one can say at a time like this," she said aloud. "One feels so terribly inadequate, but if there is anything at any time, I mean if you feel like talking and want a stranger to talk to, or anything like that, I shall be awfully glad."

"You are so kind, Lupin. I remember Jo and I thought you were the loveliest person we had ever seen when we were all bridesmaids together at Duds' wedding. I remember so well that I lost the brooch that Tommy had given me as a bridesmaid's present and you insisted on giving me yours."

Lupin started. Yes, she remembered quite well. Duds had been married from her aunt's old house in the country. The smell of the lime trees came back to her. It is funny how one can remember smells when sight and sound and touch have all gone. They were standing together in a group outside the church, the two lovely little child bridesmaids in their frocks of pale rose. One of them had given a horrified cry as she looked down and found her brooch gone. They had all looked on the path and under the lime trees, but there was no sign of it and Lupin had felt so sorry for the child, who had looked so happy a few minutes before and who now looked so disappointed, that she snatched off her own brooch and hurriedly pinned it on to the child's frock just as the bride's car drove up the narrow lane.

Lupin remembered the episode vividly although she had not given it a thought for years. It had been a little awkward because she had gone to stay with Tommy and Duds when they came back from their honeymoon and they must have thought it funny that she never wore the brooch. Then, what had happened? There was something else. She tried to think back.

"I can't think what happened to it. It never turned up but you have always been a sort of heroine to me from that hour," went on Flo. "I was frightfully thrilled at the thought of seeing you again."

"It is most awfully nice of you to see me," replied Lupin, wrenching her mind back from the past, "and if there is anything I can do for you or any message I can give to anyone, please let me know. Everyone is so terribly sorry for you." She could not help rather wishing that she would send her love to poor Sandy, though perhaps as his love for her was so hopeless it would be better not to encourage him in any way. The sooner he forgot her the better. If only he could meet some nice girl and get married. He really was rather a dear. It was quite natural that he should be a bit sulky being in love with Flo and having to see her married to Gordon. It was a pity he had come to this party. In fact the whole party had been a bit of a pity. Poor old Duds.

"Thanks awfully," said Flo. "If you could explain a bit to Duds. I should so hate to hurt her feelings. but she is so associated in my mind with Jo. Yesterday when she came to see me after lunch it reminded me of how Jo and I used to be sent up to rest in the afternoon and Duds used to pop in and give us chocolates and tell us a story and make us laugh, and Nanny would come in and send her away. And there was I lying down just the same, but there was no Jo."

Lupin was spared a reply as the noise of Tommy's car coming up the drive could be plainly heard. She was glad not to have to speak, for there was a lump in her throat. She squeezed Flo's hand and left the room. She met Gordon on the stairs and it struck her that he was looking quite cheerful. He put on a serious expression as he met her and with a hushed word or two walked into his wife's room. After all there was no particular reason why he should feel sad.He had never cared for Jo and probably did not know that she had cared for him. He would soon be taking his wife away from this house of gloom. The inquest was over and there was only the funeral left, no wonder he was feeling cheerful, but he spoke gravely enough. "A bad business," he said, "but everyone was very decent—it was brought in 'Suicide while of unsound mind.' "

"Thank goodness," said Lupin, relieved. She did not quite know what she had feared, but she had been afraid that both Henry and Tommy would be involved in some awkward way, if not actually accused of murder.

Gordon looked rather surprised at her relief but he merely said, "How is Flo?"

"She is very unhappy," replied Lupin, "but I think it did her good to talk a bit. I should get her right away as soon as you can."

"I will," he said with his charming smile and went on his way.

Lupin went down to the hall where the others were gathered together. A kind neighbor had given them a bottle of sherry and Lupin accepted a glass thankfully and said that Gordon had told her the verdict.

"Yes," replied Tommy, "they could not very well say anything else and I honestly do think that she was quite unhinged when she was talking to me."

"What about Henry Dumbleton?"

"Oh, that passed off all right," said Sandy. "Irene was the star turn of the whole show. No one had a leg to stand on once she had started. They would have said anything or done anything to stop her talking."

"As a matter of fact," said Tommy, "Henry showed up very well. You remember what a dither he was in yesterday. He spoke up quite sensibly this morning and did not seem at all embarrassed. He said he had found Miss Harnet's bag and not realizing how late it was he had taken it to her room, only to find that she was not there. Some of the jury were inclined to look a bit old-fashioned but when Irene got up and started off, no one had time to think of anything they shouldn't. Besides, the way she spoke of her husband having taken the bag to the dear girl's room made it sound as if she were a sort of adopted daughter of them both. And then of course there was a lot about his asthma and how awkward it was that Josephine had taken his heroin, not that she grudged it, and how if she could have given him an injection she could have warded off his attack. Then she went on to other attacks that he had had and I think something about her first husband too, but I am not sure. The coroner tried to keep her to the point but he might as well have tried to stem a raging torrent. By the time she had finished everyone was wanting a drink and wasn't in the mood for asking awkward questions. I'll never grumble at the woman for talking too much again."

Lupin looked at Sandy, half raising one eyebrow. "Oh, that was all right," he said, answering her unspoken question. "Tommy and I tackled Gordon last night and he said that he had taken Jo back to her bedroom. He had found her with Flo and he admitted to us that he thought she had had one over the eight, but of course he realized afterwards that it must have been the drug. She was decidedly light-headed and uncertain on her feet, so he saw her back safely into her room. That was when I saw him coming out, of course."

"You saw Gordon!" exclaimed Lupin.

The others looked at her in surprise. "I thought Sandy had told you all about it," said Tommy. "He came to me last night and said he had been talking it over with you."

"Yes, but he didn't say who it was, except that it wasn't Henry."

"Who on earth did you think it was?"

Lupin blushed. She thought she had outgrown the age of blushing, but as she saw the three pairs of eyes fixed on her in a puzzled manner and realized what a fool she had made of herself she grew hot all over.

Sandy began to laugh. "I believe she thought it was you, Tommy."

"Me!" gasped Tommy. "I told you all about my scene with her in the box room. Did you think that I wanted any more? I was sorry for the girl and as it has turned out I am glad she did confide in me, as I could witness to the fact that she was pretty well off her head. But if I had gone along to her room afterwards, which I wish I had done, to make sure she was all right, why should I have made a secret of it, unless you are suggesting. . ."

"Lupin, how could you!" said Duds reproachfully.

"Well," said Lupin, indignantly, "you have both been going on in the most extraordinary manner ever since I arrived. I could not help feeling there must be something wrong and I had heard such a lot of Jo's spell over men that I thought she had cast it over Tommy and that that was why you were behaving like something out of the Frigidaire. I shouldn't have thought about his coming out of Jo's room if Sandy hadn't said he had seen a man. Naturally at first I took for granted it was Henry but he must have been earlier while she was still with Flo. I never thought of Gordon, though I suppose it was quite natural, his being her brother-in-law, and after all there is not likely to have been any harm in it, so I don't see why Sandy got so het up over it."

"I don't know," said Sandy, "but they weren't on very good terms. I couldn't think why he was coming out of her room. I suppose his story is true."

"Of course it is," said Duds. "It was absolutely natural. For goodness sake don't try to think out some new plot. The whole thing was quite obvious. It is terribly sad, but there is it."

"Yes," agreed Tommy. "I feel pretty awful about it and it's bad enough for Flo as it is, without trying to make out that Gordon had something to do with it, or that he was flirting with Jo, which I am sure he wasn't."

"Right you are," agreed Sandy, and he walked out into the garden.

Lupin turned to her host and hostess. "Now look here, you two, it is no use expecting me to behave in a reticent, well-bred way. Whatever I may have been before, I have been a clergyman's wife for ten years and interfering is my job. What is the matter with you? I can understand your being sad, anyone with a spark of decent feeling would be sad, but why be cross? You ask each other to pass the salt as if you were citing each other for a divorce."

"I didn't know we were," replied Tommy feebly.

"Rot! Two things struck me. One, that Tommy thought you, Duds, had been having an affair with Henry. Well, that seemed too dotty for words. You said in your letter that he was too perfectly frightful and whatever you may have thought when you were young, you can't possibly have been attracted to him now. Besides, everybody knew that he was having an affair with Jo. Duds is too old to have an affair with anyone."

"That is an absolute lie. I could flirt quite easily if I wanted to."

"You did on the night of the dance," said Tommy.

"Yes, I did, so there, Lupin. As a matter of fact I only did it because I saw Tommy going into the box room with Jo and I decided to show him that two could play at that game."

"Duds, you fool," said Tommy. "You didn't think there was anything between Jo and me?"

"Well, you had your arm round her, and I couldn't think why you should choose the box room to sit out in."

"If it comes to that you were sitting on the same chair as Henry and drinking out of the same glass."

"I only did that to annoy you."

"Duds!"

"Tommy!"

"I do hope you haven't caught asthma," said Lupin, unromantically. "Or fish poisoning," she added.

"Why fish poisoning?" asked Tommy, baffled.

"I know," giggled Duds, "Henry was always rather like a fish, even in his younger, more fascinating days."

Lupin heaved a sigh of relief. Anyway, these two were all right again. That was the great thing. After all, they were her friends and Duds had asked her to come. If she had succeeded in getting them to kiss and be friends, she felt her work was done and she could return to her family and parish with a clear conscience. She was very sorry about Jo and for poor Flo, but it was Duds who was her business, and anyway Flo had a very nice husband and Henry had a nice wife—bore or no bore, she was a brick. Sandy was the one she was sorriest for. It must be awful being in love with someone who was in love with someone else. But time was a great healer, so she had heard, so perhaps he would get over it and marry some nice girl. She might ask him to stay and introduce him to some girls. Satisfied with her morning's work, she turned towards the staircase. Tommy and Duds would obviously like to be alone for a few minutes to put the finishing touches to their reconciliation and she would like to read Andrew's letter once again.

Just as Lupin reached the foot of the staircase Edith came into the hall. "Oh, please, sir," she said to Tommy, who hurriedly moved two steps away from Duds, looking very sheepish, "this parcel came for you yesterday, but what with the reporting gentlemen, not to mention the policemen, I got all in a fluster and forgot about it."

"That is all right," said Duds. "Naturally we were all a bit upset. I forgot to write to my aunt for her birthday and had to send a telegram."

"Better late than never," said Tommy, cheerfully.

"A Christmas present, I should think," said Lupin, who had paused on the stairs.

"What on earth!" Tommy dropped the paper and string and, with a look of amazement on his face, held up a tin of weed-killer.

CHAPTER 17

THERE WAS a moment's stunned silence, then Lupin spoke. "There is something funny going on about weed-killer," she said. "I don't know what or why and I don't see how it can have anything to do with the death of poor Jo, unless of course there is diamorphine in weed-killer."

"I think it is chiefly arsenic," said Tommy.

"The stuff people use for killing their wives," added Duds.

"But Jo wasn't anybody's wife," objected Lupin.

"Well, of course she wasn't and we all know what she died of. The inquest is over and everything," said Tommy. "What on earth are you babbling about weed-killer for?"

"You know, Loops," put in Duds, "you do like to make mysteries where there are no mysteries."

"I was only just wondering why Tommy had had a tin of weed-killer sent to him at the beginning of January. I did not know that weeds came up then, not that I am very hot at gardening."

"I can't fathom that," admitted Tommy.

"Well, I expect there is some quite reasonable explanation," said Duds. "Perhaps it is a late Christmas present or something."

"Yes, so it may be," agreed Lupin, "but what I was going to say, when you both sat on me—and as a matter of fact you are both quite wrong about me liking mysteries because I don't—was that when I was in the village shop yesterday getting rations, your Mrs. White told me that she had been into the chemist's on Monday afternoon to get something for her back, it wakes her up in the night, and there was a man there buying weed-killer and signing the poison book for it. You must admit it is a bit of a coincidence."

"Who was he?"

"However should I know? Mrs. White said that she thought he had come from London, so I imagine he must have been wearing a bowler hat."

"Why?" asked Tommy. "I don't wear a bowler hat when I am in London."

"And even then I vaguely wondered why somebody should have been buying weed-killer in the middle of the winter, but as I said I don't know much about gardening and for all I know there may be a sudden influx of weeds at the New Year and I didn't like to expose my ignorance by asking about it. Well, anyway, when we were in Fordham in the afternoon, I went into a chemist's shop to buy some aspirin and just out of interest I asked the man if he had any weed-killer."

"What did you want weed-killer for?" demanded Duds.

"Is this your weed-killer?" asked Tommy.

"Oh, do let me explain. I wanted to see what he would say and whether I was right in thinking that it was a funny thing for somebody to buy just now. I thought I should be able to judge by his manner whether there was anything queer about it or not."

"And did he seem surprised?"

"Yes, very. But what was even more extraordinary, he said another woman had asked for some on Monday morning and it was a very strange coincidence, which of course it was. I said was he sure it was a woman, because if it had been the man who afterwards got some at Pickering it wouldn't have been so strange. I was going to confide the whole story to him when I suddenly realized that he was eyeing me a bit and that probably the thing struck him as being as queer, as it did me, but that I was part of the queerness, if you know what I mean. I made some perfectly fatuous remark and escaped from the shop, but of course if someone does now die from weed-killer, I shall be suspect number one."

"But did you get a tin of weed-killer?" persisted Tommy.

"Oh no, he doesn't keep it in the winter. I was quite right about it being a funny thing to ask for."

"But I don't see what all this has to do with my tin."

"Only that it is rather a coincidence that a woman should have asked for it at Fordham on Monday morning and that a man should have asked for it at Pickering the same afternoon and that you should have received a tin today."

"I don't see what they have to do with me," said Tommy. "But just as a matter of interest I will stroll down to Tyler's and find out who signed the book for it. Perhaps it has been sent here by mistake."

"I don't see what else it could have been sent by," remarked Duds.

"No," agreed Lupin, "but it will be rather interesting to find out who signed for it and why."

"Lunch will be ready in a few minutes," complained Duds.

"Bother lunch," replied Tommy. Then ignoring Lupin and Sandy he kissed Duds and hurried from the room.

Duds went out to the kitchen and Lupin wandered into the dining room and started to lay the table.

They were just sitting down when Tommy returned. Three pairs of eyes raked him anxiously, but he paid no attention and remarked that he had had to go down to the village to see a man about something. His manner was somewhat furtive and the dullest of listeners would have grasped that he did not want to be questioned in front of Gordon.

Gordon's tact was, as usual, equal to the occasion. He made

polite conversation until coffee time gave him an excuse to return to his wife and to allow the four conspirators to discuss their private affairs. He had hardly left the room before Tommy, who had been on the verge of bursting all through the meal, came out with, "What do you think? It was Veazey, that publishing fellow."

"I am not surprised," said Sandy. "I never liked him."

"Why ever not?" asked Duds. "I thought he was rather a lamb."

"I wonder why he should want to send you weed-killer?" reflected Lupin.

"But do we know that it was the same weed-killer?" inquired Sandy.

"Yes, that was the extraordinary part of it," replied Tommy. "He said to Mr. Tyler, 'Be sure to send it to Mr. Lethbridge at Old Place.' Tyler says his boy must have forgotten all about it as there it was the next morning on the shelf where he had put it, with all the other things to be delivered. But it was just about then that he heard about Jo and he thought to himself, 'Well, she can't have taken weed-killer,' which was a relief to him and he could not bring himself to be angry with the boy, though of course it was extremely careless of him and it might have been something really important. He thought that in the circumstances I would not want to be bothered about it, so he kept it back till this morning, but he was very glad I had called in so that he could clear the matter up and he hoped I hadn't been put to any inconvenience."

"Did you say, no, you had managed quite well with diamorphine?" asked Lupin. Then she realized this remark was in very doubtful taste and began to sing, "We plow the fields and scatter," why, neither she, nor anyone else, could have said.

"I have just remembered something," said Duds. "It was on the Sunday evening when they all came over. I had just been washing up the tea things," and remembering who had helped her, she went rather red. "I came to the study to look for Tommy and Jo was there with Mr. Veazey. He had asked to have a private word with her, business, he said it was. And just as I opened the door, I heard him say, 'Five hundred is my last word,' and she said 'We'll see.' I crept away and I don't think they either saw or heard me. I took it for granted that they were discussing terms for some novel, but could . . .I mean . . . well . . . of course it can't have been anything like that."

"Blackmail," explained Sandy. "Of course it was. I can't help it if she is dead. She was always like that. I told you about Flo's kitten, Duds. I don't know if you have told the others but—"

"Don't," said Duds. "Please, Sandy."

"Anyway," said Lupin, "I don't see how that explains anything, even if what Sandy says is true, which I don't believe for a minute— sorry, Sandy. Jo wasn't killed with weed-killer and I don't think the tin has ever been opened."

Tommy turned the tin round in his hand. "No," he said, "unless someone has sealed it up again, which I don't see how they could as it has the trademark on it, unless of course they were in the trade. Did Veazey think I wanted to kill her and that if he put a nice tin of weed-killer into my hands I'd do the job for him?"

"If he had sent it to Duds it would have been more to the point," remarked Lupin.

"Why?" asked Duds. "Oh, I see what you mean."

"I wonder who the woman was who asked for it at Fordham?" said Sandy.

"It wasn't me," protested Duds. "You all know quite well that I never left the house that morning. I was so busy getting ready for the party and Irene was helping me, so it wasn't her either."

"It is all very queer," pondered Lupin. "Mr. Veazey had a motive for wishing Jo out of the way so he bought a tin of weed-killer but he didn't use it. She died of something else in the meanwhile, luckily for him, I suppose. But did he buy it for that purpose and if so why did he send it to Tommy? Then was the woman who asked for it at Fordham anything to do with him or not? It is all very queer and I don't see how it can possibly have any bearing on the death of poor Jo. All the same, it would be rather satisfactory to clear it up. I mean, tins of weed-killer flying about the place at this time of year are just a bit sinister, even if no one has died, and in the circumstances we are all naturally rather on edge."

"But what does one do?" demanded Tommy, getting up and striding up and down the room. "Do I write to Mr. Veazey and thank him for his kind present which was just what I wanted, or what?"

"I bet you anything Jo was blackmailing him," reiterated Sandy.

"What is the good of going on saying that all the time?" grumbled Duds. "You don't know anything about it and I don't think it is very nice to talk like that now."

"I like that," said Sandy, "considering it was you who started the whole idea by bursting into the study and overhearing what they were saying. That is what you thought, though you don't like to say it."

"And in any case it hasn't really anything to do with it," said Lupin, "so there is no point in quarreling. You are a bit like a character in a Russian novel, Sandy, not that I have ever read one. But what I was going to say was: have you ever heard me speak of Mr. Borden?"

"Your sleuth friend?" replied Tommy. "Of course we have, your letters used to be full of him. I gather he is a sort of Sherlock Holmes, Hercule Poirot and Father Brown all rolled in one."

"He is not very like Father Brown," replied Lupin reflectively, "and I don't think he is very like Hercule Poirot. He is clean-shaven. And I don't think he is really much like Sherlock Holmes, but he is quite bright in his own way and he is discreet and all that."

"I don't want it to get about that I bought a tin of weed-killer the day before Jo poisoned herself," said Tommy.

"But you didn't," pointed out Duds.

"No, I know I didn't, but you never know what things will be brought out on these occasions, and we don't want to find ourselves divorced or anything by mistake."

"Honestly, Mr. Borden—I don't know why I call him Mr. Borden because I have known him for ages, but I have simply no idea what his Christian name is—what was I saying? Oh yes, I know, you are perfectly safe with him unless you have actually committed a crime. Of course I don't expect he would want to be an accessory after the fact, whatever that means, but you haven't, have you? Honestly, he would never breathe a word that might be awkward—he is most understanding. Shall I write to him?"

"If you like."

"I don't know what you are all fussing about," said Duds, irritably. "Poor Jo poisoned herself, we know all about it and the coroner was quite satisfied. What on earth are we talking about murder and detectives for? It is your fault, Lupin. You are always getting yourself mixed up in those sort of things and they are getting on your brain."

This remark struck Lupin as rather unfair. It was not her fault that she had been mixed up in certain unpleasant cases. She had disliked them extremely and it certainly was not her fault that she had got mixed up in this case. It was Duds who had sent the telegram asking her to come. She would have very much preferred to stay in her own home with her husband and children, even though it meant taking the chair at the Good Wives' Fellowship. However, she contented herself with saying, "I don't see how it can very well be getting on my brain, if what they said at school was true."

"There is something in that," agreed Tommy, "and if Lupin likes to write to this brilliant friend of hers, I don't see that it can do any harm, darling," he added to Duds.

Why on earth they are putting it all on me, I don't know, thought Lupin. I don't want to write to anybody or to do anything except go home.

"After all," went on Tommy, "of course it can have no bearing on the death of poor little Jo. All the same, I should like to know why Mr. Veazey chose to send me a tin of weed-killer as a New Year's gift."

Sandy laughed rather sardonically and left the room, and Lupin sat down to write to Mr. Borden.

Dear Mr. Borden,

    I am up to my ears again in intrigue and sudden death. I think it is a perfectly straightforward case of suicide but as you know nothing ever comes out straightforward, it seems, when I am involved, so you never can tell. I don't know if you saw a case of a Josephine Harnet taking an overdose of diamorphine. There was a bit in the paper. Anyway the inquest is just over and it all seems quite clear. 'Suicide while of unsound mind,' I think they said, though luckily for once I wasn't there. But just as we were sitting quietly afterwards imbibing a glass of sherry, a tin of weed-killer was brought in and Tommy, that is my friend's husband, hurried to the village and found that it had been sent to him by a publisher named Veazey, you'll know of him, and Josephine was his secretary. We think that she may have been blackmailing him but this is in the deepest secrecy, so don't breathe a word. I don't like saying things about people when they are dead. In any case the tin had not even been opened and she didn't die of weed-killer, so it can't have had anything to do with it, unless there is a new weed-killer made of diamorphine and even then they would have had to open the tin, at least one would think so. But Duds, my friend and Josephine's cousin, heard Mr. Veazey say, 'Five hundred is my last word,' and she said, 'We'll see' or something. But of course it might have meant anything, but if you feel like worming your way into Mr. Veazey's office as a window cleaner or an author or something of that sort, I should be most awfully grateful as we do

all feel it is the kind of thing that it would be interesting to
get to the bottom of.

I hope to go home tomorrow night but will be at my club
between five-thirty and six-thirty in case you were able to drop
in and talk things over.

With all good wishes,
Yours very sincerely,
Lupin Hastings.

P.S. My club is the Lady's Chatsworth, 103 St. James's
Street.

CHAPTER 18

LUPIN WAS just about to get into bed that night when there was a tap
on her door. She was rather glad, for she had seen so little of Duds
since she came and would enjoy a talk with her. It would probably
be her last opportunity as there would be the funeral tomorrow and
she was hoping to get away directly after it. Duds had been a perfect idiot and she would tell her so, though for the matter of that
Tommy had been just as bad. What a mercy that they had come to
their senses. She said "Come in" mechanically while these thoughts
were passing through her head and was surprised to find Sandy in
her midst.

"I say, Lupin, I must talk to you," he said.

Lupin felt that it was a queer time and place to choose, but to do
the boy justice it would have been difficult to find anywhere else so
private. She made a resolve never to stay anywhere again without
her husband—one was so vulnerable to confidences if alone. "All
right," she said aloud, in a resigned voice. "Have a cigarette?"

"You see, it is like this."

"You'd better have the armchair, and I will lie on the bed. We may
as well be comfortable."

"It is my belief that Gordon murdered Jo and that he will murder Flo
too."

"Oh dear," said Lupin. "I thought we had cleared up everything
so nicely, except of course the weed-killer."

"You think that I am mad and am imagining things."

"One can imagine things without being mad."

"It is no good being a gentleman now. Things are too serious. At the expense of seeming a cad I must tell you everything."

"All right."

"Well, I expect Duds told you that I have always been in love with Flo. I know women talk about those things and in any case I am not ashamed of it. I have loved her ever since we were children and I thought she loved me too."

"I am terribly sorry."

"But she did. That is what I meant about being a cad. I came back from Germany as I daresay you know and found she was married to Gordon, and then to my horror I met them both here. But on the night of the dance, Flo and I got together and she told me everything. I don't think she meant to but she broke down a bit and I lost my head and—well, you know how those things happen. Naturally I shouldn't have said anything about it but as things have turned out I must."

"I see."

"Well, it seems that she did have an infatuation for Gordon. I suppose he is very good-looking and attractive to women."

"He wouldn't be to me."

"No, but I suppose he might be to a girl. You see, Flo had always taken me for granted. I was a part of her life and I think at one time she had concluded, just the same as I had, that we should be married one day, but she had never been consciously in love with me. She liked being with me better than with anyone else, but she hadn't realized that that is being in love. Oh well, I can't tell you all she said, but the gist of the matter is that as she grew up, she grew out of childish, things—meaning me—and took for granted that I had done the same and never thought of herself as being engaged to me. She imagined herself in love with Gordon and got married to him, only to realize, almost at once, that she had made a terrible mistake. She had played with the idea of leaving him before she met me again. But—well, you know Flo, she is frightfully good. But then she met me again and I know you won't misunderstand me when I say she realized that we really belonged to each other. It seems impossible that she should care for me and I wouldn't have said . . . I feel awful talking about it, but I am in such a funk."

"I understand. Did you ask her to leave her husband?"

"Yes, of course, I did all I could to persuade her, but she said she could not make up her mind in a hurry about a thing like that and even if she left him she didn't think she could come to me. You see she had promised in the wedding service to forsake all other—"

"Yes, I know the wedding service."

"As I said just now, Flo is frightfully good, not priggish but straight and loyal, and she would hate to do anything wrong. Most people would have just buzzed off when they found they didn't care for their husband, but she did not want to break her vows. I wouldn't have her different. It is because of that that I care for her as I do. There is no one like her."

Lupin hoped there were a few like her in not liking to break their vows but did not feel it necessary to say so.

"Still, there it is," Sandy went on. "She did admit that she, er, liked me and that she wished she had waited for me. Her feelings for Gordon had just been a passing madness. Everyone thought the reason she was unhappy was that she had quarreled with Jo and though that did make everything else much worse, because she was so fond of Jo, I can't think why. What . . . why . . . what was I saying? Ah yes, it wasn't really her quarrel with Jo that was getting her down so much as being tied up with Gordon. That was what was really making her so miserable."

Lupin was puzzled. Only that morning Flo had said that nothing really mattered to her so long as she had Gordon, that whatever his profession had been she would gladly have helped him in any way she could. Was Sandy deceiving himself? What could Flo really have said to him? She must have said something. Or was she acting a part this morning, pretending to be a devoted wife, whereas really she was nothing of the kind?

"I do feel terribly sorry for you both," she said aloud.

"I shouldn't be telling you all this if it weren't for what happened after," explained Sandy.

"But why should Gordon kill Jo because Flo was fond of you?" asked Lupin.

"If he killed Jo, it was because he found out that she and Flo had made it up and he knew that would mean Flo dividing up her money with her. It is my belief that he engineered the quarrel from the beginning so as to prevent any such arrangement. I admit I never cared for Jo, so I can't blame Gordon if he didn't, but that is different from murdering her to prevent her getting the money."

Lupin was beginning to feel rather sleepy and Sandy did not explain things very lucidly. But a thought suddenly struck her. If Gordon really murdered Jo, it was a very clever murder and very well thought out.

"If, as I have gathered, Flo and Jo had only just made it up," she said, aloud, "I don't see how he can have possibly organized the whole thing. I mean, if it was done, it wasn't done on the spur of the moment. I don't think it was done but if it was, it took a lot of thinking out and couldn't have been done suddenly like that."

"Well, he may have seen the reconciliation coming and made his plans accordingly. He must have known that Flo didn't like the quarrel and as soon as he realized that they would be here together for Christmas he decided what he was going to do. What worries me about the whole thing is that having murdered Jo for half the money he may murder Flo to get the rest."

"But Sandy," said Lupin, sitting up, "you really are letting your imagination run away with you. What earthly reason can you have for thinking these things? You don't like Gordon and naturally you don't like his having married Flo, but that doesn't make him into a murderer. Suicide is much more natural and surely the coroner having said so, we needn't think anything more about it."

"I must think about it if Flo is involved in it."

"But he really does seem to be a very good husband. I don't say that he is a type I care for frightfully, but I should have said he was a quiet, well-meaning person, not at all likely to commit a murder. To put it quite crudely, I don't think he'd have the guts."

"You can never tell about murders," said Sandy, getting out of the chair and walking up and down the room. "Such very unlikely people do them. I admit I haven't much to go on, but suppose Gordon saw Jo back to her room, as he said he did. Then why did he go in with her and shut the door?"

"Oh, I don't know. The door may have shut itself—wind or something."

"Of course you think I am a fool, but why won't Flo see anyone but Gordon? He wouldn't be the natural person for her to turn to in trouble. No, I don't mean me. She might not like to ask for me, not till she has made up her mind anyway, but surely she would want Duds. It is my belief that Gordon is preventing her from seeing anyone. He may be drugging her for all we know. Perhaps he has guessed about me, perhaps he is afraid of her leaving him and taking her money with her. Somehow he is keeping her shut up in her room. If only her wretched grandfather had not left her that money. Oh, you do see there is something queer about it, don't you?"

Lupin hesitated.

"You think that I am inventing the whole story about her caring for me or that I was drunk at the time and misunderstood her?"

"I don't think anything of the sort," replied Lupin. She felt her way carefully. As a matter of fact it was a little odd if Sandy's story were true, and she believed it was, that Flo should have spoken of Gordon as she had done this morning. Yet was it? "Flo has had a terrible shock," she went on.

"Well, we all know that," retorted Sandy.

"Yes, but there are lots of different ways in which shock may affect people and I am wondering whether perhaps she is suffering from remorse."

"Why on earth?"

"On Monday night she was with you and she was wrapped up in her own and your affairs. Jo was in the depths of misery, but she wasn't thinking of her."

"How was she to know? She thought everything was all right with Jo. They had made up their quarrel. She was going to give her half her money. I don't quite see what you have to got to blame Flo for."

"Oh, do be your age, Sandy. I am not blaming Flo, bless her. I am just trying to put myself in her place. All I can get at present is that she was thinking chiefly of you on Monday night. Then this happens and she keeps wondering what she could have done to help Jo and she is filled with remorse that she was so full of her own troubles that evening that she had not realized her sister's feelings. Also, I should think she is the sort of person who would take the marriage service seriously, not that I know much about her, and would realize that she had made a very solemn promise and that she had been contemplating breaking that promise. No, I know she hadn't broken it and probably never would have done, but all the same she wishes she had not chosen that particular evening for—well—talking about it and so on. She sort of feels that she will atone for her sister's death by devoting the rest of her life to Gordon and to making him a good wife. Do you see what I mean?"

"I suppose so, in a way, but are you sure that it isn't Gordon who is preventing her from seeing anyone? Perhaps she knows something or suspects something?"

"Rot. I saw her this morning. We were absolutely alone. Gordon was at the inquest, so she could have said anything she liked. She wasn't under the influence of drugs, either. I should have known if she had been. She was quite normal, though of course very sad. She won't see Duds because the sight of her brings back too vividly the old days. Even seeing her yesterday afternoon, for that minute, made her think of when she and Jo used to lie down as children and Duds came in and brought them chocolates and told them stories. Surely you can understand. Naturally she won't see you. She has had to give you up, Sandy. I am dreadfully sorry for you, for both of you, but she has realized that she took Gordon for better or for worse and has decided to do her job."

"You may be right," said Sandy, very doubtfully, "but the whole thing seems sinister to me."

"There has been a ghastly tragedy," agreed Lupin, "and it is only natural that all of you who have been concerned in it should feel thoroughly shaken up. You will none of you feel quite the same again and caring for Flo as you do, you feel worse than anyone else. Is there any chance of you getting away, right away I mean, for a time? If your firm had a branch abroad or something like that, I believe you would be helping Flo if you could disappear out of her life for a bit."

"Do you really mean that?"

"Yes, I don't believe she is in any danger in your sense of the word, but I do believe that her only way of obtaining peace of mind is for her to do what she thinks is right, and so long as you are about she is torn in two."

"I think I could get sent to Canada. In fact I had got sort of half fixed up to go before I met Flo again, but now I cannot bear the idea of leaving her."

"You can if it is best for her, but please believe me, Sandy, when I say how terribly sorry I am for you both and how much I wish things were different." She longed to hug the poor boy, as Tommy had hugged Jo on the night of the dance, but it wouldn't be much comfort to him, she reflected, and might embarrass him. "Good night, Sandy," she said.

"Good night," he replied, and left the room.

Lupin got into bed feeling very unhappy. She lay in the darkness going over again and again first her interview with Flo that morning and then her interview with Sandy that evening. It was quite obvious that Flo had put Sandy out of her life and was determined to devote herself to Gordon. It would be a very good thing if Sandy could go to Canada for his firm.

She remembered the scene of Duds' wedding, the loss of the brooch, and the grief of the little bridesmaid. She remembered her own embarrassment on her first visit to the newly married couple because she had not been able to display Tommy's pretty present. Then she remembered what had evaded her this morning. She had returned from that visit to find a little registered parcel awaiting her at home and there was the brooch, with a sweet little note from Flo, explaining that hers had been found after all, and thanking her for what she had done. It was funny that she should have said this morning that it had never been found. She must have forgotten all about it.

CHAPTER 19

FLO ATTENDED her sister's funeral, but as she walked up the aisle, supported by her husband, her head bent, everyone averted their eyes, not wishing to pry on her grief.

Duds walked with Tommy and Lupin and Sandy followed behind, each in their several ways torn with sorrow and pity. It was during the singing of "Abide with me" that Lupin, for absolutely no reason whatsoever, thought of the words, "Infirm of purpose, give me the dagger." Now why on earth? she asked herself as she sang "Shine through the gloom and point me to the skies."

She sat down to listen to the lesson, but her mind wandered. Why had she thought of those particular lines? Where did they come from? Not the Bible, she was sure. Shakespeare? Yes, of course. She had learned them at school. *Macbeth*, that was it. She remembered how they had all enjoyed saying "Out damned spot!" But why should she have suddenly thought of it after all these years and in the middle of that particular hymn? She could only suppose that they had been singing it one morning at prayers just before a rehearsal of *Macbeth*.

But would they have been singing "Abide with me" at morning prayers?

It was not until they were all filing out of church that an idea came into Lupin's head, an idea so wild, so fantastic that she was afraid she must be taking leave of her senses.

Jo was laid to rest in the little country churchyard. Gordon took Flo away as soon as the ceremony was over, but the others stood for a moment as the last rays of the winter sun shone through the bare branches of the elm trees. The Dumbletons were there. Henry still looked very ill, but Irene was her usual placid self. She refused Duds' invitation to come back to the house for some tea, saying that she thought the sooner they were on their way to London the better.

"I shall be glad to get Henry's own doctor round to see him," she said, "though the one here has been very kind."

Lupin looked at the pleasant, comely figure, subdued but composed, then at the haggard face of her husband, and she wondered if her wild idea had been wrong, and whether these were the two people that had brought *Macbeth* into her head. Certainly if there were anything to be done Irene would be the one to do it. Henry would be of little or no help. From what the others had told her, Lupin gathered that he would have cut a poor figure at the inquest yesterday if his wife had not been there to get him out of all his difficulties.

"Such a very pleasant Christmas, Dorothy dear. And I am sure the change will prove to have done Henry good in the long run, though of course the sad occurrence at the end has pulled him down, as indeed it has all of us. You look far from well yourself and no wonder. It has been a very sad time. I have not spoken to poor Flo. I felt she would prefer to be quiet, but please give her our fond love and tell her that if there is anything we can do for her when she is back in London we shall be delighted. I could easily slip round any time she feels up to seeing a visitor."

Sir John Holroyd and his wife came up with grave faces and shook hands with Tommy and Duds. "A bad business," he said. "Such a sweet girl and she seemed so full of life and spirits the night of your party. *Carmen!* Ah, well, tut, tut. My wife's brother-in-law was so sorry not to get down today. He asked us to represent him—the publisher you know. I think your cousin helped him with his work."

"She was his private secretary," explained Duds. "He has sent a beautiful wreath."

"Good. Quite right. I'm glad to hear it. No, we won't come in.

Give our regards to Mrs. Pinhorn. She is quite overcome, I expect, poor girl! Shocking, shocking!"

They walked back to the house and Lupin tried to banish the ridiculous idea that had risen unbidden to her head in church. As Duds would have said, she was liable to imagine mysteries where none existed.

On their return they found that Flo had gone to her room. Gordon was bringing round his car. "I think I'll take her straight home," he said to Duds. "I know she would love to be with you, but everything here reminds her too much of Jo. You are so understanding," and he gave Duds a very charming smile.

"I think you are quite right," replied Duds. Personally, she felt that the sooner they all went away the sooner she would be able to feel comfortable. She rather regretted having asked Lupin, fond as she was of her. She really had been a little trying the day before about the weed-killer. If it had not been for her story about the stranger buying some in the local chemist's shop and the woman asking for it at Fordham, they would not have thought about it themselves. Probably Tommy would not have gone down to the village and found all about Mr. Veazey and the added complications. She forgot that these were mostly of her own suggesting. "I will just slip up and say goodbye to Flo," she said. "She must have a cup of tea before she starts."

Gordon took her hand. "My dear," he said, "you are so sweet, but do you know, I believe it will be better if I take her straight off without seeing anyone. I don't want her to break down again. She was so wonderfully brave during the service, but it was a terrible strain. Your kind little Edith has taken her a cup of tea. It seems ungrateful to slip off like this, but I do hope you and Tommy will come to see us in London when Flo is a little stronger. I don't know how to thank you for all your kindness."

"Oh, don't talk like that," begged Duds. "Just send me a line any time you think Flo could bear to see me."

"I will indeed and thank you, my dear, for everything." He stooped and kissed her affectionately, then turned to Tommy and wrung his hand in silence. Sandy had disappeared, so he could not perform the same office by him, which was perhaps just as well.

Lupin was rather afraid that he was going to kiss her too. Instead, he took her hand in a very meaningful way as he said, "Goodbye, Lady Lupin, and thank you for your kindness to my poor little wife. Her talk with you yesterday did her a lot of good." Lupin wondered if this were true, but murmured something about being glad if she had been of any use.

"I wish we could give you a lift to town," he went on, "but I shall have to drive very slowly. I don't know how Flo will stand the journey and if, as I believe, you have a connection to catch we might miss it. I know you will understand."

This seemed to be his favorite remark, but Lupin replied that she did and that Sandy was taking her to the station and that she must be off at once. Her good-byes said, she ran Sandy to earth in the drive and took her seat in his car.

"Look here," she said, as they drove through the gates. "I don't really agree with the things you were saying last night, but there is no harm in being on the safe side. I did get a sort of idea in church. It is quite mad, but would you like to follow Gordon's car, discreetly of course, and ring me up at my club if anything out of the ordinary happens. I shall stay there till I hear from you. If they arrive at their London house you will know all is well, so just ring up and say O.K. Here is the number." She thrust a card into his hand and jumped out of the car. "Don't wait, here is a porter. I must rush. Tell Duds what you are doing if you like. Goodbye for the present."

Sandy returned, parked his car in a side road and kept an eye on Tommy's gate. Gordon's blue Sunbeam was drawn up before the house. No one was about to speed the parting guests and as he watched from behind a hedge, Sandy saw Gordon help his wife into the car and drive off.

Sandy walked into the house and opened the study door, where Duds and Tommy were lurking. "I am following that car," he announced.

"Why?" asked Duds. "Honestly, Sandy, it is no use. We would all much rather that she had married you, but she hasn't and there is nothing to be done about it."

"Lupin says she has a sort of idea and wants me to follow the car," explained Sandy.

"Loops said so?"

"Loops has an idea!" said Tommy and Duds, simultaneously.

"Come on," said Tommy. "What are we waiting for?"

"Loops may be half-witted," said Duds, "but when she does get an idea it is usually worth while taking notice of it, though it may be rather tiresome."

Disregarding the tea things lying about, Duds left her house in company with the two men and the three of them packed themselves into Sandy's M.G.

It was not long before they picked up Gordon's Sunbeam ahead of them on the London Road. There was a good deal of traffic and luckily he had been held up by some lorries carrying prefabs. But once he got going again it did not look as if Flo's nerves needed slow driving, at least they were not getting it.

"What a rate they are going!" exclaimed Duds. "Still, I think sometimes when you are feeling upset fast movement helps one."

Sandy followed desperately. He saw something sinister in Gordon's rapid driving. It was not easy to keep the Sunbeam in sight. As they did not want Gordon to turn round and see them following him, they had to keep some way behind, letting other cars pass them or come between them, thus giving them a little cover. They passed along the wide street of Beaconsfield, past the Saracen's Head. Every car out this afternoon seemed to be a blue saloon. They went through Gerrard's Cross, where, judging by the number of lorries carrying building materials, bricks, cement, gravel, etc., the housing shortage would soon be over. They caught up with the Sunbeam outside the Pinewood film studios, then went on a long winding road which was looking lovely in the winter twilight. But the bare branches outlined against the pale sky and the smell of the gasworks which they afterwards encountered were all one to Sandy.

Duds did not know what she was expecting, but she had great faith in Lupin and felt that she must have had some reason for advising them to embark on this wild-goose chase. She realized that though her friend had never been remarkable for her brain, she seemed to have been endowed with an extra portion of intuition to make up for it. "There he is!" she cried aloud, as they approached Denham crossroads.

"Yes, that is it," agreed Tommy. "No, it isn't," he added.

"They have turned to the right," exclaimed Duds.

"It must be another car," said Tommy. "They would have gone straight on."

Sandy reached the crossroads. He could see the rear of a car having turned right for Slough instead of making for London. He was sure it was Gordon's car. He was not near enough to see the number, but he determined to take the risk. Where was Gordon taking Flo? Was this what Lupin had suspected, that he was not taking her home at all? He turned to the right.

"What on earth are you doing?" demanded Tommy.

Sandy did not answer. He drove desperately down the road, passed a lorry in defiance of all good driving and nearly collided with an ancient Austin, whose owner cursed him loudly and justifiably.

"It *is* their car," exclaimed Tommy, as they approached the saloon and were able to read the number. "They must have taken the wrong turning."

"I'll drop you at the next pub," said Sandy. "Duds had better come with me."

"You don't think . . ." said Tommy.

"I have thought all along that he murdered Jo and that he will murder Flo too, unless we stop him in time."

"Rot!" muttered Tommy.

"Lupin practically convinced me that it was rot last night, but something or other has made her change her mind since then. Ring her up at her club and tell her what they are doing." He slowed down as they passed a public house. "It looks as if they were making for the south, doesn't it? He may be hoping to get her abroad, away from her friends. After all, why did he say that they were going back to London? If he were just taking her for a little holiday somewhere he would have said so. You must admit it looks a bit fishy." He stopped the car and pushed Lupin's card into Tommy's unwilling hand.

CHAPTER 20

MR. BORDEN read Lupin's letter over his breakfast that morning and he smiled as he read. I suppose she had a good deal of money spent on her education, he said to himself, but it is no use pretending that she can express herself in a lucid manner. All the same, she has a brain— or is it mere intuition? She jumps to things that it would take the rest of us, even those of us who imagine we've trained minds, a long time, if ever, to reach. I suppose it is her tremendous interest in her fellow creatures that helps her to see things that are dark to others. A publisher named Veazey! Veazey and Dalrymple, I suppose. What does she expect me to do about it, hurry to the publishing office and ask Mr.

Veazey if his secretary were blackmailing him? Besides, it said definitely in the paper that the girl committed suicide by taking an overdose of diamorphine. Lupin must be chasing a mare's nest this time.

He read through the rest of his letters, which were dull, and picked up his paper. He was having a holiday for a few weeks over Christmas and the New Year, and it was very pleasant to sit by the fire with his pipe and newspaper. Mr. Borden was a private detective of some repute. He was popular with Scotland Yard and he could afford to take a holiday when he was in the mood. He had decided to stay in England this winter, partly for patriotic reasons, partly because there is something very restful about holiday-making in one's own home. There was really nothing that he need do today and he spread out his paper comfortably.

Thoughts of Lupin came between him and the news. They had been through some very interesting times together. He admired her very much in a perfectly platonic manner, although at times she exasperated him. He supposed he would have to answer her letter. He struggled through it once again. Why should anyone send anybody else an unexpected tin of weed-killer in the middle of the winter? It really was rather peculiar, but a doctor could hardly mistake arsenic for diamorphine. Was the weed-killer tin camouflaging something else? What had the publisher and his secretary been discussing when he said, 'Five hundred is my last word,' and she had replied 'We'll see?' The news in the paper was very dull. It was rather boring sitting about all the morning, and he wished he had gone away somewhere for his holiday.

After all, he decided, there would be no harm in going to see this Veazey and asking him point blank why he had sent a tin of weed-killer to Mr. Lethbridge. The thing was probably perfectly simple and natural if one only knew. He wrote a note to be sent up by the office boy.

Dear Sir,

I hope you will forgive me calling on you, but I have just heard from Lady Lupin Hastings, who is staying with her friends, Mr. and Mrs. Lethbridge, at Pickering, near Fordham, in Buckinghamshire. It seems that Mr. Lethbridge received a tin of weed-killer from the local chemist yesterday morning, and on investigation finds that it was ordered and signed for by you. I am sure there is some simple explanation of this transaction, but as I am on the spot they thought it would save

time if I asked you about it straight away. I will not keep
you many minutes.

Yours faithfully,
P. Borden.

On arriving at the offices of Veazey and Dalrymple, Borden sent
the note up with his official card and after quite a short interval was
informed that the publisher would see him. Within a few minutes he
found himself in his presence.

"It is very good indeed of you to see me," said Mr. Borden, "but
there are one or two little matters that Mr. Lethbridge thought you
might clear up for us."

"One or two! You just mentioned the tin of weed-killer that I sent to
Mr. Lethbridge and which I can easily explain. Is anything the matter?
I did not think that there was any doubt that Miss Harnet had commit-
ted suicide." He was very pale and he did not seem at all at his ease.

"No, it seems a pretty clear case," agreed Borden. "But just as a
matter of interest, why did you send Mr. Lethbridge a tin of weed-killer?"

"I thought it was diamorphine that killed her," persisted the publisher. "It said so in the papers."

"I am not suggesting that the weed-killer had anything to do
with the death of Miss Harnet," said Mr. Borden. "But Mr. Lethbridge was naturally surprised at receiving the tin and I gather he went
to the shop, at which it had been bought, to find out in whose name it
had been ordered."

"There is really no mystery about it," said Mr. Veazey. "My wife
asked me to get a tin of weed-killer in the village and to send it to Mr.
Lethbridge. I don't know why she wished to send him a tin of weed-
killer, but it must have had something to do with the conversation they
had had the day before at teatime. She took a great fancy to the young
man and to his house and grounds. I suppose it was something to do
with the garden. My wife is very interested in gardens. She said she
had tried to get a tin at Fordham but had been unable to do so and would
I be sure to try in the village of Pickering. That is all I can tell you,
but it is a most natural explanation, is it not? My wife is a very good-
natured woman, always trying to do things for others."

"Thank you very much, Mr. Veazey. There is just one thing more.
Mrs. Lethbridge quite inadvertently heard you say to Miss Harnet on the
Sunday preceding her death, 'Five hundred is my last word'. To which

she replied, 'We shall see.' Have you anything to say about that?"

"We were discussing a novel that had just come up for publication and she wanted to give a bigger advance on royalties than I deemed expedient."

"I see," said Mr. Borden. "Five hundred certainly sounds a generous advance, not that I know much about such matters. I do not think I need detain you any longer," and he rose to go.

As he held out his hand Mr. Veazey made no attempt to take it. He looked at him in a puzzled way, then said, "Sit down, if you don't mind, Mr. Borden. I had better explain everything to you," he added, as his guest sat down once more in his chair, "though it is rather difficult."

"I will do my best to understand," replied the detective.

"The fact is that my wife is a very brilliant woman, a remarkable woman." Veazey shuffled a little in his seat and said in an embarrassed way, "I think the world of my wife."

Mr. Borden was convinced that he was speaking the truth. "I have always heard what a great writer she is," he replied, and as the advertisements he had read of her novels always gave this impression he was not altogether guilty of an untruth.

"The trouble," said Mr. Veazey, "is that for some extraordinary reason her books don't sell."

Mr. Borden was startled. He had not realized this and a sudden feeling of sympathy with the publisher arose within him. He obviously loved and admired his wife and it must be a terrible grief to him that he should sell the books of other authors while hers were a failure. "But," he said, "surely they go very well. After all, you, who deal with novels all the time, find yourself comparing them with those of somebody else perhaps, and you allow yourself to be disheartened."

"We lost on her first book," said Mr. Veazey simply. "Since then I have paid for their publication myself. My partner was very decent but I felt it was the only thing to do. She has no idea. I have managed the advertisements and even some of the reviews to a certain extent, but she thinks . . ." and his face clouded.

"Of course I expect it is only a question of time," said Mr. Borden.

"I suppose in a way she is a little old-fashioned," said Veazey, thoughtfully. "It is difficult to keep abreast and what would have been considered very exciting twenty years ago cuts no ice with this generation. Then she tries to bring them up to date, which loses her the older readers. However it is, I try to make her think that they are a great success, and no one but my partner, so far as I knew, had guessed my secret. Then my secretary, Miss Harnet, found out. I was a fool, but she was a very capable girl and I trusted her. I sent her to get something out of my private safe and she looked through the papers that she found there, and—well, she discovered my secret."

"It was very clever of her. She must have pieced things together pretty cunningly."

"Yes, she must. She was a very clever woman. She came to me and told me that she had discovered that my wife was not a literary success and that people would be interested to know that I paid for the publication of her books. Like a fool, I blurted out that she did not know herself and of course Josephine fastened on that and said that unless I gave her a thousand pounds she would go to my wife and tell her. It would have broken her heart."

"Nasty," commented Borden shortly.

"Very nasty, but wait until I tell you the rest. This happened just before Christmas. I was nearly off my head with worry. A publisher's life is not an easy one these days. I . . . had heavy expenses connected with my wife's books, because apart from the ordinary expenses and the advertisements, I had to send her large royalties as from the firm to make her think she was doing well. I was really put to it to lay my hands on a thousand pounds. I told Miss Harnet that I would let her know when we came back after the Christmas holidays and she agreed to wait until then. To my surprise I ran into her while we were staying with my wife's cousins in the country. We met Miss Harnet and her relations at the Hunt Ball. They all seemed such nice simple people, I could hardly credit that one of them could be a blackmailer. I tried to appeal to her better feelings then and there, but a dance does not give much opportunity, so I took my wife to call on the cousin, with whom I had danced and I found very friendly. I saw Josephine alone but she was adamant, and I, like a fool, offered her five hundred pounds. She laughed at me."

"And then?"

"Well, this is the extraordinary thing. The next night she was quite different. I couldn't have believed it. Something must have happened in between—I suppose the thing that made her decide to take her own life, poor girl. But of course I knew nothing of that then. Well, anyway, she came and she said that she was sorry that she had been so horrible- —those were her own words. She hadn't ever really meant it but she had been feeling spiteful about everything and everybody. Anyway, she asked me to forgive her and assured me that she would never breathe a word of my secret to a living soul. I am glad we parted friends as things turned out, poor girl! We shall never know what was at the back of it all."

"Yes, you must be glad your last recollections are pleasant ones. Thank you very much for telling me all this. I think it is very kind of you. The only thing is, I wonder why your wife wanted to send a tin of weed-killer to Mr. Lethbridge. I am not for a moment suggesting that there was anything questionable in the action, but you must agree that as a matter of interest it would be nice to clear up the matter."

"Yes," agreed Mr. Veazey. "Come home with me and have a drink. If my wife is available we will ask her about it. She may have forgotten. On the other hand she may have some perfectly natural explanation. Like all really brilliant people she is very erratic. It may have something to do with the plot of a novel."

They walked back to the Veazeys' house together and sat in the publisher's library. Sherry was produced. After a few minutes Veazey said he would go in search of his wife.

Mr. Borden sipped his sherry and reflected on what a wonderful man this was. He thought it was refreshing to find a man so much in love with his wife. He was probably typical of the majority of his fellow creatures. Unfortunately it is the minority that get publicity and give the impression that love and devotion are things of the past.

After some minutes had elapsed the Veazeys returned together. The famous novelist greeted Mr. Borden with a dazzling smile. "How lovely to see you again," she said. "We haven't met for ages."

"No, we haven't, have we?" replied Borden, rather feebly, never having set eyes on the lady before.

"I am afraid when I am immersed in my work I am shockingly unsociable," explained Olivia. "I lose touch with the tangible world and get lost in a world of my own creation."

"It must be very interesting," hazarded Borden.

"Interesting," said Olivia intensely. "Yes, sometimes it is interesting but sometimes it is heartbreaking. I have to follow as I am led and sometimes the way is hard and thorny."

"Yes," agreed Borden, sympathetically. "A writer who really gets inside her characters as you do must often suffer with them."

She looked at him with respect. "How well you understand,"

she said. "Some people think that you can write with your brain and with your hand. They do not realize that it takes your whole soul."

"The sort of people who say they wish they had time to write a novel," suggested Borden.

Olivia laughed. "You have said it," she replied, feeling very *en rapport* with this delightful young friend of her husband.

"By the way," said Borden, "I think you met some friends of mine this Christmas, a Mr. and Mrs. Lethbridge."

"Lethbridge." She put her hand to her head.

"You know, darling, that nice young fellow at Old Place, Pickering. You liked the house."

"Wait!" she cried. "It is coming back. A house with a marvelous atmosphere and a nice unpretentious young man. He did not bother me for autographs or anything of that sort. Of course, I remember now, he told me that that lovely house was overrun with rats. What a tragedy. I meant to send him some rat poison. Did I send him some rat poison? It seemed so sad that such a lovely house should be destroyed by vermin. Besides, I should like to stay there and write my next novel, but I could not stay in the same house as rats. Wait, it is all coming back. I asked at Fordham. I am almost sure that I went into a chemist's shop there and asked for rat poison—or did I ask for weed-killer?"

"You asked me to try to get you a tin of weed-killer at Pickering," replied her husband, "because you could not get any at Fordham and you asked me to have it sent straight to Lethbridge."

"Did I?" She laughed merrily. "It was rat poison that I meant to send. He must have wondered why I sent him weed-killer."

CHAPTER 21

TOMMY FOUND himself standing in the road, clutching Lupin's card and wondering what he was supposed to be doing. Why on earth should he ring up Lupin to tell her that Gordon and Flo had decided to turn to the right at Denham crossroads instead of going straight on to London? What business was it of his or Lupin's or of anyone's, except the two people concerned? He was fond of Lupin. She was a very old friend and he knew that she was devoted to Duds, but she really had grown rather interfering, he thought. Of course, he supposed clergymen's wives had to be a bit interfering, what with getting the children to come to Sunday school and all that, but it was a bit hard when they carried it into weekday life.

First of all there had been that business about the weed-killer. Admittedly it was a bit queer that Veazey, a man whom he hardly knew, should suddenly send him a tin of it, but then, if Lupin had not busied herself in the matter, he would never have known that it was Veazey. He would have just returned the tin to the shop from which it had been sent and there would have been an end of the matter. After all, Jo had not been killed by weed-killer, so why bother about it? Then, of course, inspired by Lupin, Duds had to remember that ridiculous story about Jo and the publisher and five hundred pounds or editions or whatever they were. Surely a man could speak to his own secretary about business affairs without everyone weaving detective stories round them. Sandy had egged them on because he had never liked Jo. But he oughtn't to have remembered that he hadn't liked her now that she was dead. Anyway, here they were chasing the Pinhorns all over the countryside. After all, it really was in rather doubtful taste, considering that poor Flo was in trouble. The fact that Sandy had once been in love with her, as Tommy had gathered from Duds, made the whole thing more awkward and embarrassing.

Why weren't they all comfortably at home? If only the Pinhorns had been allowed to depart in the normal manner, he was sure he would not have asked them any impertinent questions as to their destination. And if Lupin had gone straight back to her husband, as a good wife should, instead of lurking about at her club expecting people to ring her up, and if Sandy could have gone to wherever he did go, if he ever went anywhere, life might be quite pleasant again. They might even forget all about this ghastly Christmas houseparty.

After all, if he did ring Lupin up, he could not tell her where the Pinhorns were going, because he did not know himself. They might have taken the wrong turning at the crossroads or they might have decided to go away for a little holiday together without telling anyone. What more natural? Tommy was fond of Flo. She had been so nice in helping Duds with the housework during that dreadful week. He had not cared much for Gordon, but he really had nothing against him. He was evidently a good husband and Flo seemed devoted to him. As for his wanting to murder her, the idea was ridiculous. People one knew did not go about murdering each other.

He knocked on the door of the public house. A drink was what he wanted. He could think better after a drink and decide whether to ring up or not. Bother. There was no answer. Of course it could not be six o'clock yet. They had left home soon after four and though it seemed ages ago, it could not possibly be more than an hour, if that. They had only driven about twenty miles or so. Probably it was barely five. What was he going to do between now and six o'clock? He might stand in the road for an hour or he might fill in the time walking to the next local, then he would probably be put off with a glass of bottled beer. How was he to get home? No one seemed to have thought of that. They had just left him stranded and driven on.

Sandy and Duds had not given him a thought. They had just parked him in a dark road and gone on with their mad career. Tommy began to feel desperately ill-used, browned off, as he would have expressed it. After all, he had made it up with Duds. He had magnanimously forgiven her for suspecting him of having had an affair with Jo in the box room. Surely in return she might have been a little more thoughtful for his comfort. His mind switched suddenly to the Dumbletons. He had not cared for Henry. Even if Duds had not rather liked him in her early youth, he would never have fancied the man. Yet he had a wife who devoted herself to his interests.

He thought of Irene as he had last seen her after the funeral, calm and poised to the end. "No, thank you very much," she had said, "we must get back. I don't want Henry to drive in the dark if we can help it. He is not thoroughly over his attack of asthma," and she had smiled protectively at her husband. Yes, she was a wife in a thousand. She had not turned a hair at finding her husband in another woman's room in the middle of the night. She had, in fact, helped him out of a very difficult situation. She was a fine woman and he admired her very much. Still, he would rather have Duds, his own Duds, with all her faults. His heart warmed at the thought of her. He would not really like a protective wife. He remembered the awful days of their estrangement. No, they must never quarrel again. What did she want him to do, bless her heart, ring up Lupin and tell her where the Pinhorns had gone? Oh well, if it were going to please Duds, of course he would do it at once, not that he knew where they had gone, nor did he know where to ring up from, but he would not let those little obstacles stand in his way.

He strode along the road. Though when he had been in Sandy's car the whole place had been black with traffic, there seemed to be nothing of any sort in sight at the moment. A vast emptiness surrounded him. After a bit he came to a turning and thought he saw some buildings in the distance. He made his way towards them—yes, he was in a village street. Here was another public house, shut alas! He passed a cottage or two and a couple of shops when to his joy he came to the post office. But it appeared also to be closed. He felt that a post office ought to be open at any rate until six o'clock. If it were too early for the public houses to be open, surely it was too early for the post offices to be shut. That was sound reasoning enough. After all, it might have been some one wanting to ring up about something important, a matter of life and death perhaps.

How did one ring up from a strange village when everything was shut? He poked about, knocking on doors and windows and eventually gave it up as a bad job. There were not many houses in the street and he did not think that those there were would be on the telephone. He was now anxious to effect the call. He felt that he would be serving Duds by so doing, but he was thwarted at every turn. He saw the church tower outlined against the pale sky. The church—Lupin—vicarage! Of course, he must try the vicarage. It would be sure to be on the telephone and perhaps if he explained that he wanted to ring up a vicar's wife, they would not think it peculiar of him to burst in on them like a bolt from the blue.

Not that he liked the idea of calling at a strange house and encountering clergymen and their wives and daughters. He was not the sort of person who cared for intruding himself on strangers and to obtrude himself on a strange clergyman's family would be worse than anything else. No. Nothing could be worse than standing alone in this cold village street.

He approached the vicarage. It was a large, rambling house, built when the clergy of the Church of England looked on having at least twelve children apiece as important as believing the Thirty-Nine Articles. There was one light in a far window. Tommy groped his way to the front door and found a bell pull. He pulled it gingerly, then, resolving that if " 'twere done when 'tis done, then it were well it were done thoroughly," he gave a vigorous pull. The bell reverberated throughout the big house. Tommy was a matter-of-fact sort of person, but even he began to feel a bit eerie. The fading light, the big ramshackle house, the empty street, the jangling bell, on the top, too, of suicide, tins of weed-killer, and stories of blackmail interspersed with inquests and funerals, made him wish that he were standing once again on the bridge of his minesweeper. Give him a westerly gale blowing, the gear fouling a wreck and five turns of sweep wire round his screw—at least he would have known what he was up against, whereas now . . .

The door opened and an oblong of pale light showed a thin clerical figure with ruffled hair and crooked pince-nez, but the welcoming smile made up for all other shortcomings. "My dear fellow," he said, "I am glad you have come!"

Tommy was surprised but pleased at this warm welcome. "Oh, thanks awfully," he said. "I wonder if I might use your telephone?"

"But of course. Perhaps you would like to do that straight away and then we'll have tea and a nice long talk." He led the way down a lengthy corridor and eventually introduced Tommy to an old-fashioned telephone receiver.

Tommy found that he was still clasping the card with Lupin's number on it, which was just as well, as he had forgotten both that and the name of the club. He managed to decipher it by the light of a pale electric bulb and lifted the receiver. It took a long time to get through and he began to wonder whether he ever would and whether there was such a number or such a club or such a person as Lupin. Everything was happening in a very strange way this afternoon. Here he was standing in a strange vicarage, and whatever had the old man meant about a long talk? It was very kind of him to allow him to use his telephone and there had been some mention of tea, unless Tommy had imagined it, and that would be very welcome. In return he would have to listen to the long talk. So long as he was not expected to contribute to it, he didn't mind. He was one of the few people who preferred listening to talking.

"What?" He had heard the welcome words "You are through," and after a pause a male voice said "Hullo."

"May I speak to Lady Lupin Hastings?" inquired Tommy.

"What name?"

"Lady Lupin Hastings."

"Might I have your name?"

"Oh, Mr. Lethbridge."

"Mr. Lemon?"

There was another long pause during which time Tommy feared he would be disconnected and have to start all over again. At last a feminine voice which actually sounded like Lupin's said "Hullo".

"Is that you, Lupin?"

"Yes, is it Tommy?"

"Yes."

"I thought it must be. I knew I didn't know anyone else called Lemon."

"Do be quiet. I just rang up to say that Sandy thought you might like to know that Gordon turned right at Denham crossroads."

"Oh, he did, did he?"

"I am just telling you he did."

"Yes, I know, but where do you think he is going?"

"How on earth should I know? I suppose he has decided to take Flo for a holiday—and a jolly good idea too."

"Yes, absolutely. But would they be making for the coast? I mean, suppose they decided to take a holiday abroad, could they go that way?"

"I suppose so, if they went from Southampton. I shouldn't think they are going abroad. They would hardly have had their passports and so on with them—not that it is any business of ours, anyway."

"No, of course not, but they have taken the Southampton route? That is all I wanted to know. Thanks awfully," and she rang off before Tommy had time to explain that there was no reason to suppose they were going to Southampton just because they had turned to the right. There were plenty of other places they could be making for. Not that he cared whether they went to Southampton or Timbuktu. Slamming down the receiver rather angrily, he started off down the corridor, only to realize that he had taken the wrong turning and had not the least idea where he was.

A light shone from under a door in the distance and in desperation he walked to it, knocked without any result, and opened it to find himself in a large, well-lit kitchen. An elderly woman sat at the head of the table drinking tea. On one side of her was a very pretty girl and on the other a rather sheepish youth. The reason that his knock had been ignored was they were in the middle of a loud and animated conversation and had not heard him.

"I am frightfully sorry," said Tommy, turning to go out and blundering into the dresser.

"That is all right, sir. I expect you are the gentleman the vicar was expecting. This is my niece, Gladys, what works at the post office, come to tea with me and brought her young gentleman with her."

"Oh Auntie, aren't you awful," giggled Gladys.

Tommy wondered whether that was why he had found the post office shut up so early, but charitably, and taking Gladys's prettiness into account, supposed it was early closing day in this village. "I am afraid I lost my way," he said aloud. "I was using the telephone and I must have taken the wrong turning."

"It is easy enough in this house," replied the elderly woman, "though I don't mean what you mean, saucy," she said to Gladys's young man in a loud aside. He went rather red and looked at his plate, while Tommy, judging by his chin, wondered if he had ever meant anything in his life and thought what a pity it was that Gladys should be throwing herself away on him.

"I'll just take you along to the vicar's study," went on the house-keeper, as Tommy rightly concluded her to be.

"Oh, Auntie, remember your legs," remonstrated Gladys.

"That is what the vicar always says, 'Remember your legs, Mrs. Colbron,' and there he goes, clearing his own table and making his bed and doing all manner of things that a gentleman shouldn't, let alone a clergyman."

"He is a nice gentleman," replied Gladys warmly. Even her young man brought himself to mutter, "That's right."

Tommy was beginning to wonder how he was ever going to disentangle himself from this pleasant gathering, when, urged by her aunt, Gladys offered to escort him once again into the vicar's presence. He seized gratefully on this offer, though he wished that Gladys had not given him such a provocative look, nor her young man quite such a murderous one. If he did not kiss her in the dark passage Gladys might consider him remiss, whereas if he did the young man might not like it. To his great relief at this moment the vicar walked in and everything seemed perfectly natural at once.

"Oh, you have found your way to Mrs. Colbron, have you? That's right. How do you do, Gladys? How do you do, Alfred? I am so glad to see you. No, don't get up, Mrs. Colbron. You look after your legs. Gladys and Alfred, I'll be seeing you again soon, I hope. Come in whenever you like," and he led Tommy back into the corridor and after what seemed many miles of walking they arrived at his study. "Alfred is a quiet boy," he observed, "but I think he will make Gladys a good husband. Ah, here we are," and he opened the door for Tommy to precede him.

It was a pleasant room in which Tommy at last found himself. There was a bright wood fire and before it stood a tea table spread with such a tea as Tommy could not remember having seen since his boyhood. Three of the walls were lined with books, while the fourth consisted of windows, on the broad sills of which were bowls of bulbs.

"I got the tea myself," remarked the vicar. "Mrs. Colbron suffers from her legs," and he looked proudly at his handiwork while Tommy sat in the comfortable chair indicated to him, drank a hot sip of tea and took a large bite of hot buttered toast, on which the vicar had obviously lavished the whole of his week's butter ration. He realized that this was one of the pleasantest moments he had spent for a long time.

The vicar rambled on in an interesting manner all through tea, and Tommy occasionally answered, usually with his mouth full, but he appeared to give satisfaction to his listener.

It wasn't until the last crumb had disappeared and both men had lit their pipes that the vicar said, "Well, now for it, William. What exactly is the difficulty?"

CHAPTER 22

SANDY AND Duds kept on their way. It was not easy to keep the Sunbeam in sight without being seen themselves. Luckily, Gordon was too intent on his driving to look behind. He seemed in a hurry. Sandy crossed the Bath Road at Slough and they soon found themselves in the environs of Eton. There was Agar's Plough and there was Upper Club on their left. Against his will, Sandy's mind went back to a certain Fourth of June when Flo had worn a frock with poppies on it. He accelerated fiercely but had to pull up in the High Street, which, though empty of boys, was full of traffic.

By the time they reached the bridge there was no sign of Gordon. They went past the castle and were soon out on the Ascot Road. At last they thought they saw their quarry but were held up by a long excursion coach. It was evidently filled by some outing, as everyone in it was singing and several had changed hats. Duds envied them. It would be nice to be among cheerful and lighthearted people once more. Sandy was grim and purposeful. She wished Tommy were still with them. She would have liked one moderately cheerful companion.

Sandy kept carefully behind the coach. He felt pretty sure that the Sunbeam was just ahead of it. Now they were held up by traffic lights—that would give Gordon a good start of them again. Still, they could not miss him on the open road. As soon as they were allowed to proceed, they shot past the coach, the inhabitants of which waved to them in friendly fashion. Duds waved back but Sandy never noticed. He drove hell for leather until he came to a caution sign and found German prisoners working on the road. He crawled past them. Still, the Sunbeam must have been held up, too, with all this nonsense, he told himself.

"There it is!" he exclaimed at length, as they caught sight of the familiar number.

"You know," said Duds, "I can't see that there is anything very peculiar in their coming this way. Gordon may think it better not to take Flo straight back to London. I expect they decided to take a little holiday somewhere and didn't tell us about it in case we started trying to make suggestions. You know how maddening people can be. I have often suffered from telling people where I was going and them saying, 'Why don't you go somewhere else?' And of course if one were in trouble one simply wouldn't be able to take it."

Sandy grunted. He was busy driving and did not seem interested in Duds' remarks but she went on. "I think it is a very good idea to go for a holiday. Perhaps they are going abroad. That would make a complete change for Flo and would do her good. Traveling is bound to take one's mind off for a bit. What with passports and customs and trying to understand someone else's language, one has plenty of trouble all the time without brooding on anything, and that is just what Flo would have done if they had gone back to London. Everything would have reminded her of Jo, but now with any luck Gordon is taking her somewhere quite new. I expect he has been making his plans quietly the last few days. He is very kind and efficient. I am sorry, Sandy, but it is no good pretending that he isn't." Sandy did not answer. "All the same," she went on, undeterred by her companion's taciturnity, "I wonder what bee Lupin had in her bonnet. She must have had some reason for telling us to come out on this game of follow my leader."

Sandy had been lurking behind a charabanc, but this now elected to draw up outside a public house. Duds could not help rather envying the passengers. She looked at Sandy. He did not seem to be noticing them; his face was set and stern. He might have been a total abstainer for all the effect the words 'Fully Licensed' had on him. Having speeded past the charabanc he drew up rather abruptly, as he was nearer the Sunbeam than he wished. The small car skidded and Duds hoped that they would not soon be taking the principal parts in another inquest. However, she did not express her hopes, as she knew men did not welcome anything that seemed to throw criticism on their driving.

Conversation not being encouraged, Duds devoted herself to her own thoughts. First among these was the desire for a drink. Something cool and long, she thought; beer would be very refreshing. On the other hand, she felt something a little stronger might be helpful at the moment, something to support her spirits during this nightmare drive. Thinking of spirits it struck her that a whisky and soda would be rather nice, the sort of whisky and soda one could have had in pre-war days when one wasn't having to eke out one's half-bottle among all one's friends and neighbors for several months.

The thought of drink led on to the thought of food. Duds had not felt hungry at luncheon just before the funeral and afterwards, what with worrying about Flo and seeing that Lupin caught her train, she had forgotten to eat anything with her cup of tea. A light dinner would be pleasant, a really good soup, followed perhaps by a Dover sole, then roast chicken and bread sauce or a slice or two of saddle of lamb with some red currant jelly, a cream ice with hot chocolate sauce to follow, or would something a little more substantial be better, such as roly-poly pudding with treacle, though one did not usually have that at dinner? Then a nice savory to finish the meal, angels on horseback or soft roes on toast, or what about a Welsh rarebit? Oh dear, she would be lucky if she got a bit of cold liver sausage.

They were now passing through Andover and it was getting quite dark. Duds' thoughts wandered to Tommy and she wondered why she had ever been such a fool as to think that he had cared for Jo. She must have been quite off her head. There had been something queer about this houseparty. From the beginning it had gone badly and it had got on her mind and made her imagine things. Tommy had been just as bad. He had really thought that she was having an affair with Henry— Henry, with whom she had finished fifteen years ago! One did not want one's love affairs served up again like minced mutton or, rather, minced fish.

Dear Tommy, she hoped he was not having an awful time. It was rather dreary for him being cast out on to the high road. Would he find a telephone? Even more important, would he find a local and would it be open? How would he find his way home again? They all seemed to be off their heads. What was the idea? How she wished that this ghastly drive were over and that she and Tommy were safe at home together once more. It was all very well for Sandy to drive as if he were tired of life. She wasn't. She wanted to go on living with Tommy.

She thought of Jo, poor Jo, who had been so unhappy and to whom she had not been frightfully sympathetic. She wished that she had been nicer to her. It was because she had been so sad that she had seemed so tiresome. Duds ought to have guessed that there was some such reason. She had always been fond of the twins as children and she ought not to have failed them now that they were grown up. Had she always liked Flo the better? She was not sure. Looking back, she rather thought she had, but she had been so accustomed to looking on them as two parts of a whole that she had taken it for granted that she liked them equally.

Sandy gave vent to a low exclamation of concern and Duds was recalled from her thoughts of past days. She looked in front of them. There was the blue Sunbeam, but the number was not the same as Gordon's car. Had he changed the number? She had read of such things being done, but she did not quite see when he could have done it. They had missed him coming through Eton and Windsor, but they had seen him again since then. In fact he had never been out of their sight for long enough in which to remove his number plates and attach others.

"It isn't him," she said ungrammatically and rather unnecessarily.

Sandy vouchsafed no answer. He passed the offending Sunbeam and tore on down the dark road. Duds managed to light a cigarette with a somewhat shaky hand and settled down once more to her own thoughts. Gordon and Flo had obviously turned off down some side road and had by now arrived at some quiet hotel where they could have a little holiday in peace. But it was no good imparting her belief to Sandy.

She reverted in her mind to Jo and the whole history of the disastrous houseparty. She remembered the first evening when she had accidentally seen her in the embrace of a man, whom she had taken to be Henry, not that she had seen him. It might have been someone else. Then she recalled her words to the publisher about money—if it were money—and she was pretty sure it was.

Could she have been blackmailing him? Then she had certainly said to someone, Duds did not know whom, "I can get hold of it all right." What had she been talking about? Had she been confiding to someone else her intention of taking an overdose of diamorphine? Surely not or they would have done something about it! Unless of course it were a suicide pact! If that were the case, the second party had not kept faith. Could it have been Henry? Had he gone to her room meaning to take poison with her and had his courage then failed him? On the other hand he might have taken it and being so used to it, it had failed to work.

But then if it had been Henry with whom Jo had entered into the pact, she would not have said, "I can get hold of it," because Henry had already got it and would have brought it with him to the tryst. No, it couldn't have been Henry, and Duds did not think it could be Flo. Why should she enter into a suicide pact? She was happily married. She had everything to induce her to want to live. Of course, Sandy might easily do something of the kind, but not with Jo. He detested Jo and he would not have entered into any pact with her. Besides, if he had decided to commit suicide he would not have muffed it, she thought.

At this moment they narrowly missed a head-on collision with a tram as they reached the outskirts of Southampton. As Sandy drew up sharply Duds was thrown violently forwards, then backwards. For a moment she wondered whether she and Sandy had entered into a suicide pact together. She could not remember doing so but it certainly seemed like it.

It took her a few minutes to collect herself, then she realized that her imagination was running away with her. Talk of Lupin getting bees in her bonnet. But this long, perilous drive on an empty stomach, especially on the top of a funeral, was rather trying to the nerves. Then what was it that Jo had been talking about to Mr. Veazey? Could it have been a secret document? Would Henry have been a party to a blackmailing scheme? No, definitely not. Sandy? No. Flo? No. Gordon? Of course not. He and Jo did not like each other. They certainly would not have been partners in anything, even if either of them would have descended to blackmail, which of course they wouldn't. It was horrible to think of Gordon in such a connection when he had been so kind and helpful all through the visit and especially at its terrible conclusion. And as for poor Jo, she was of course quite innocent of such a thing. The five hundred was something to do with a novelist's royalties and Jo was kindly trying to persuade Mr. Veazey to pay more. As for the "I can get hold of it, all right," she had been talking about a pot of glue with which to mend something that was broken or it might have been some interesting book that she wanted to lend someone.

"Hush," said Sandy unnecessarily, for Duds had not spoken. They drew up at the side of the road and Duds followed the direction of Sandy's eyes. There was the Sunbeam with its correct number just ahead of them, turning into a public parking place. They waited for a minute or two and were rewarded by the sight of Gordon and Flo emerging on foot, each carrying a suitcase and walking in the direction of the harbor.

Sandy jumped out of the car, and Duds followed him, feeling rather cramped in the legs but trying to keep up with him. She was sure they would be had up for leaving their car in the road and she did hope that Sandy would not want her to accost her cousins when they obviously wished to avoid seeing her. Flo had made it quite clear that she did not wish to see anyone and it was not very nice to push oneself in where one was not wanted.

They followed the others in a surreptitious manner. Anyone watching them would have come to the conclusion that they were a couple of pickpockets, if not worse. Once Gordon stopped to light a cigarette and Sandy dragged Duds into a doorway. Eventually the little procession reached the dock gates. Flo paused, put down her suitcase, and Duds, who was only a few paces behind, heard to her great surprise, the words, "This bloody thing weighs a ton."

Duds stood stock still, unable to believe her ears, but Sandy bounded forward. "Let me carry it for you, Flo," he said.

Gordon turned round and faced the two intruders. His pleasant, good-looking face was a mask of fury, but his companion had collected herself and addressed them, "Hullo, Sandy, how nice to see you. And Duds too? Gordon and I are going abroad for a little while to try to forget."

Duds noticed a young man in a plain blue suit hovering near them and wonderedd what he wanted. Then she turned to her cousin and looked at her in a bewildered fashion. "Oh, I see," she said uncertainly.

Sandy, too, was looking intently at the face illuminated by the bright lights.

"Jo?" he exclaimed.

CHAPTER 23

"OH, GOOD!" said Lupin as she greeted Mr. Borden, who had met her by appointment at her club. "I am glad to see you as you will tidy up my mind for me. It is in the most ghastly mess."

"Well, I think I have got to the bottom of the weed-killer. Of course the people concerned may have been lying but their story rang true to me and, according to you, the weed-killer has not been used."

"No, not at all, at least I don't think so, unless of course they took it out and then sealed up the tin again. It would be difficult but then most murders are difficult, at least I should imagine so, not that I have ever done one myself, so far that is, though the Sunday school superintendent can be pretty maddening. Still, I know I should never have the brains to carry it through. But what about the blackmailing business? You know, 'Five hundred is my last word' or whatever it was, just like a story book."

When Mr. Borden was able to get in a word he described his visit to the publisher's office and subsequently to his home, also all that had passed between him and the Veazeys that morning.

"What a lamb the man must be!" exclaimed Lupin. "He must be devoted to his wife. Personally I should not like it. I mean I should rather Andrew had no secrets from me, like the time he told me my address to the Women's Institute hadn't been so hot. But still, it does show that he is fond of his wife and I do think husbands ought to be, don't you? Oh dear, you haven't got a wife, have you? Do get one. You would make such a nice husband. But I still don't quite see why the novelist wanted to send rat poison to Tommy. They never told me about any rats but then of course Jo committing suicide may have put it out of their heads. If it were suicide, that is. That is what I wanted to talk to you about. What?" as a page came up. "Telephone? Mr. Lemon? So sorry," she added to Mr. Borden, and left the room.

"Well," she said, as she returned. "They are off to the coast. I had a sort of premonition, if that is the word I mean, about it, I don't know why. Not that there is any earthly reason for it and in any case what more natural than for Gordon—that is Mr. Pinhorn, you know— to take Flo, his wife, to the seaside for a change after all that she has gone through, instead of going back to London. All the same, you are in with Scotland Yard, aren't you? Could you arrange for someone to look out for them if they do arrive at Southampton? I mean it would be funny for them to be going abroad, because it's not the sort of thing you can do on the spur of the moment, is it? Passports I mean, and so on, so it would be a little funny." She gave Borden the number of their car, which she found, after several attempts, inside her ration book. "I should like Duds and her cousin Sandy just to have an opportunity of speaking to them before they embark. If they do embark, I mean."

"From where do you expect them to embark?"

"I don't really expect they will, but Tommy, that is, Duds' husband, the one who has just rung me up, was ringing up from a little village off the Windsor Road. They had turned right at Denham crossroads instead of going straight on, as they would have done if they were going to London. They gave us all to understand they were going straight home. They live in London. Would it be Southampton they were making for, do you think, if they were making for anywhere?"

"It might be," replied Borden, and he got up and left the room. He felt that he would find a telephone more easily if he asked a porter than if he allowed Lupin to direct him. "Now do tell me," he said when he returned, "what exactly you have got on your mind."

"Well, it sounds too fantastic and mad for words, but Duds had a pair of twin cousins."

"So it said in the papers."

"As girls they were quite extraordinarily alike. I was a bridesmaid with them when they were fourteen and you could not tell one from the other. Duds said they weren't a bit alike now they were grown up, but it seems hard to believe. It may have just been that they did their hair differently and used different makeup and so on. These things make a lot of difference, you know."

"They must."

"Anyway, as I was saying, I knew them when they were children. It is awfully difficult to know where to begin, but it seems that Sandy—he is the one that is driving with Duds—he is her cousin too. Well, he has always been most frightfully in love with Flo ever since they were children, more or less, I gather. They were sort of half-engaged, at least he thought they were but she didn't, if you know what I mean. Then the war came along and poor old Sandy got captured by the Germans and stuck into prison. He says it wasn't too bad as prisons go but it can't have been very nice. Well, of course, when the war was over and he was released, he was rather thrilled about it all because of getting back to Flo. Then when he arrived in England he heard that she was married to Gordon."

"Pretty rotten," observed Borden.

"Yes," agreed Lupin. "And yet Flo doesn't seem to have been that sort of person, not that I know much about her. I don't think she had ever realized that she was engaged to Sandy. It was a boy and girl sort of thing and I daresay she never took it seriously. She could have barely left school at the beginning of the war. Well, Duds got all matriarchal and invited all her relations to spend Christmas with her. They didn't know they were going to meet each other and of course when Sandy suddenly found himself face to face with Flo and Gordon it shook him up pretty badly, as you may guess. He could hardly bring himself to speak to anyone during the Christmas festivities, which did not exactly add to the gaiety of the houseparty, which in any case was pretty grim from what I've heard. Well, anyway, everything seemed to come to a head on the last night when they had that fancy dress party. Sandy and Flo got together and had it all out. She confessed that she had made a mistake in marrying Gordon. She had had a girlish infatuation for him. He really is very good-looking in a sort of way, if you like that kind of thing, and chock full of charm, a thing I personally always suspect. But I daresay I should have liked it at Flo's age. Anyway, it soon wore off and she realized that she had slipped up badly and that they had nothing in common. Then Sandy reappeared and she realized at once that he was the person she ought to have married, but she had known him for so long and taken him so much for granted that she had never taken the idea of marrying him seriously, nor had she imagined that he had taken it seriously either. However, when she saw him again she knew what a fool she had been and that what she had felt for Gordon was all eyewash."

"Who told you all this?"

"Sandy. I know it sounds very queer his telling such a thing to anyone, let alone a complete stranger, and he would not have told me unless he had had a very good reason, but he had somehow got it into his head that Gordon had killed Jo because Flo was going to give her half her money. She has a lot of money, you know. It was left her by a grandfather who willed it to the eldest grandchild. As they were twins she thought they ought to share it. Gordon may not have agreed with her about this. Anyway, Sandy didn't think he would and he thought that was why he had got rid of poor Jo. Then it suddenly struck him that if he had killed one he might kill the other too and scoop the lot. Naturally Sandy was rather upset."

"And you believed him."

"No, I didn't believe that part. I thought he was just being a bit melodramatic and overwrought, quite natural in the circumstances, of course, not counting all he had gone through in the war. But I did believe what he told me about Flo. I am certain that he did not invent that, though of course I told it to you in my own words. And if Gordon had guessed and thought that there was any possibility of her leaving him and taking her money with her, he wouldn't have liked it. Still, I didn't think that he was a murderer and I told Sandy not to be an idiot, because after all it had all been a perfectly straightforward suicide. It was as plain as a pikestaff, whatever a pikestaff is, and if the coroner was satisfied it wasn't for us to wonder why. Then after I had got rid of Sandy I started thinking."

"Yes."

"Well, of course Flo had had the most frightful shock and she must have been terribly unhappy, but to whom would she naturally have turned? If it were Sandy that she really cared for, she might have turned to him or she might not. It would have caused rather a lot of complications and she might have had a sort of feeling about it. I mean she wouldn't think it was right to care for another man when she had a husband and she may have regretted what she had said to Sandy the night before.

"But why not Duds? Duds had been a sort of elder sister to them all their lives and was absolutely devoted to them both, especially to Flo. Surely the natural thing would have been for her to have hurled herself on Duds and clung to her. But no, she refused to see anyone except Gordon. She shut herself up in her room and he took up all her meals. After telling Sandy that her marriage was a mistake, would she have clung to her husband like that? She might, probably would, refuse to go away with Sandy, she might even refuse to see him. She might be determined to stick to Gordon and be a good wife to him. But in a time of trouble would she have wanted to be alone with him all the time? Would he have been any comfort to her?

"No wonder Sandy thought it a bit sinister. I told him that I thought she was driven by remorse because she had been thinking of herself and Sandy at the time when Jo was preparing to take her own life. But though remorse might cut out Sandy, why should it cut out Duds?"

"Didn't she see her at all?"

"Once after lunch for five minutes with the blinds down. As soon as Duds went in Flo started to cry, so of course she tried to comfort her. But Flo said it brought back the old days too vividly and Duds felt that she wanted her to go. I think she was really a bit hurt about it, though she said she understood."

"Didn't anyone else see her?"

"Yes, I did. The very next morning at breakfast Gordon suddenly said that she would very much like to see me and would I stay with her during the inquest. Why on earth me? I hardly knew her. It seemed so peculiar and I felt rather uncomfortable. Then Gordon said that it was easier for her to see a stranger than one of the family, as it did not bring back remembrances. It all sounded very plausible and Duds did not seem to mind. I was quite taken in at the time. It was only afterwards that I began to wonder."

"Did Sandy, as you call him, think that Pinhorn was exercising some authority over his wife to prevent her seeing members of her own family?"

"Yes, I think he had some mad idea like that. Still, my idea is much madder. Well, anyway, I went to see her while the others were at the inquest, and you know I've seen a good many people in sorrow. One does when one is a clergyman's wife, and, though I didn't notice much at the time, looking back on it I had a feeling that something was wrong. She was sad and rather self-reproachful, but she was not heartbroken. She was perfectly poised. I haven't got a sister, but if my brother, or even if Duds for that matter, committed suicide I don't believe I should be poised."

"I see your point. I have had a good deal to do with people in trouble too, especially those suffering from shock. It is very difficult to make any hard and fast rule and of course some people have remarkable self-control. But I have an idea you would penetrate an assumed composure."

"I don't know about that. It was only afterwards that it struck me that Flo had been a little too consistent. I mean sometimes people in trouble talk the whole time without ceasing, and sometimes they go into a queer vacant silence. Sometimes they laugh and sometimes they cry. Sometimes, as you say, they are obviously controlling themselves and trying to sound natural. But Flo was sweet and sad and collected the whole time."

"It was not till afterwards that it struck you."

"No, I don't think so. I was feeling so sad about it that I didn't really begin to think at all for some time. I was trying not to cry. I think it was after I had left her that I had a sort of feeling that I had been to a play, a very sad play, and that the heroine had acted frightfully well.

"But the really queer thing about it all was her attitude to Gordon. I didn't notice it at the time. It was not till after my talk with Sandy that I began to worry about it. I had been chattering a bit, you know how one does, like a dentist when he is stopping a tooth, just about nothing on earth, and I happened to say that I didn't mind being a clergyman's wife so long as the clergyman was Andrew. And she said she was just the same and that she wouldn't mind what Gordon was so long as they could always be together. Nothing in the world really mattered to her so long as she had him. I was thankful to hear it because, of course, I know all about that sort of thing—well you know how silly I am about Andrew and I was so glad to think that she was silly too, because it is so lovely.

"But then that night Sandy came in with his story and I could not think why Flo had gone to all that trouble to put on an act with me because, as I said, I am quite certain Sandy was speaking the truth, though I suppose you will say that I have no evidence or something stuffy like that."

"What exactly are you driving at?"

"Well, I am rather putting off telling you, because you will probably have me certified and that will be bad for Andrew and the children, but there is just one other thing," and she told him the story of the pearl brooch. "She said that it had never turned up," she concluded.

"You had forgotten yourself what had happened for the moment."

"Yes, that is true, though something seemed to be nagging at my mind while I was talking. But don't you think she would have remembered finding it and sending it to me? I mean at fourteen the whole episode would have made rather an impression."

"Are you trying to tell me that it is Flo who is dead, and that it is her sister with whom you talked?"

"How quick you are!" exclaimed Lupin admiringly. "It only came to me in church during the funeral. Two or three things were worrying me and then suddenly for no reason at all the whole thing flashed on me. It was rather funny that if it were Flo she did not know that it was Sandy she loved, not Gordon, also that she did not know that she had returned my brooch. And why wouldn't she see Duds except with the blinds down?

"I looked at her sitting in the front pew with Gordon and I thought of the Macbeths, I can't imagine why, and then everything fell into place, but I daresay I am raving. Yes," she said to a page boy who approached her, "I am wanted on the telephone? You had better come too," she added to Borden.

They went together and Lupin picked up the receiver. "Hullo, yes, it is, Lupin. Are you Duds? You have? Well done. No, I don't think I shall be surprised. It isn't Flo, is it? It is Jo?"

CHAPTER 24

THEY WERE sitting in Andrew's study at Glanville Vicarage, Lupin and Andrew, Tommy and Duds, and Mr. Borden. The second inquest had been held at Southampton the day before, and Lupin had invited them all to come home with her. She had asked Sandy too but she had understood his refusal. He wanted to go away somewhere by himself.

"I can't believe it even now," said Duds.

"Try not to think about it, darling," begged Tommy, putting an arm round her shoulders.

"I can't help thinking about it. It goes round and round in my head like a squirrel in a cage. If only we had not asked them for Christmas it might never have happened."

"You need not feel that," replied Borden. "It was not done on the spur of the moment. The whole thing had been planned for a very long time, probably before Pinhorn had even met your cousin Florence. It was very unfortunate for you that they should have chosen your house in which to carry out their plans."

"Poor little Flo! And poor, poor Sandy!"

"His firm is being awfully decent," said Tommy. "They are sending him out to Canada almost at once. It will make all the difference to him, a new place, new people."

"He will never forget," said Duds.

"No," agreed Lupin. "He will never forget Flo and he would not want to. She will always be a lovely memory in his life. And you see he knows that she really did love him and that her marrying Gordon was a mistake. He will always have that satisfaction. If she had lived I don't see what they could have done. From what you tell about Flo, I don't think she would have gone against her conscience and broken the promises that she made at her wedding. She would have stuck to Gordon and that would have been very hard on Sandy, harder even than it is now. And as Tommy says, the new life will help him."

"What on earth made her marry Gordon to start with?" demanded Tommy.

"It certainly was a queer choice," agreed Borden. "I suppose he had a sort of fascination for women, but he was a nasty bit of work. He went to pieces at once. If he had not tried to bolt when you spoke to Miss Harnet," he went on to Duds, "I think she might have brazened it out. After all, there was not much our man could have done. He could not have arrested them without a warrant."

"I said that she was like Lady Macbeth," murmured Lupin. But no one took any notice of her.

"It was awful," said Duds. "I thought that Sandy had gone stark staring mad, then of course I saw it for myself. I saw at once that Flo was looking different and I had heard her speaking quite differently too. But I just thought it was the shock of Jo's death that had changed her. I never thought of her being Jo until Sandy spoke. And even then I couldn't believe it. But then Gordon started to bolt and your man, whoever he was, blew a whistle. I didn't really see what was happening. I was in a daze. Then I began to realize it, that it was Jo, I mean. Hairdressing and makeup does alter people a lot, but there had always been something different about their mouths, even as children. I must have noticed it subconsciously, though I had never thought about it before."

"It is the feature that gives away the character more than any other," put in Borden.

"She bent down," went on Duds, "but of course it never struck me what she was doing. I thought that she was fastening her suspender. It is funny how one's mind works at the most awful times. I found myself thinking, 'Fancy Jo having a broken suspender.' She was always so perfectly turned out, you see. Still, even if I had known what she was doing. I don't think I should have stopped her. I couldn't have borne . . ." she shuddered.

"No, of course not," agreed Lupin. "But she must have got an awful lot of diamorphine from somewhere, I mean to give herself an injection as well as Flo. I shouldn't have thought Henry Dumbleton would have carried enough about with him to kill two people."

"I wondered about that," replied Borden. "She became unconscious before they reached the police station. She never came round and died within a few hours. She must have taken a very big dose. Did she know Dumbleton before she came to stay with you?" he asked Duds.

"Yes, they had met. I don't know if she knew him well or whether she had started an affair with him before or not. I had never thought about it."

"Of course she had," explained Lupin. "That is why Henry suddenly invited himself to you for Christmas. I wonder what excuse he gave to Irene!"

"You may be right," replied Duds. "I wondered rather why they suddenly wanted to come."

"My theory," said Borden, "is that Miss Harnet had found out that Dumbleton took diamorphine, so set about enslaving him. Probably a fairly easy job."

"Quite easy," agreed Duds.

"You ought to know," murmured Lupin.

Borden did not catch this interchange. "She probably got some from him before she went down to your house," he continued. "She could extract it from his bottle by means of a hypodermic syringe. He would probably keep a bottle of it at his office. A woman with her ingenuity would find some way of helping herself. Very likely she took a little each time she visited him there. I believe that she had everything planned out and was determined to poison herself if the worst came to the worst. She had to have enough diamorphine to kill two people. She managed to collect enough to kill one before the house-party and relied on getting the rest while there. She very likely suggested to Dumbleton that he should invite himself for Christmas."

"Why did I let them come?"

"As Mr. Borden said," put in Lupin, "if you had not had the party it would all have happened somewhere else. Jo had made up her mind to get rid of Flo and there was nothing anyone could do to stop her. I suppose she had Gordon absolutely under her thumb."

"That, I gather, will be his defense, for what it is worth. He blurted out everything at the police station that evening, how it had all been her doing. I think he was probably speaking the truth. His counsel may try to get him off as being under undue influence, but I should not think it will be much good. After all, he is a man."

"If he is a man I hope that I am a rabbit," declared Tommy. "His story is that he fell madly in love with Miss Harnet and that she hypnotized him. She persuaded him to marry her sister and persuaded him to aid and abet her in killing her. She, of course, was to slip into her sister's place, taking her husband and her money and no one was to be any the wiser."

"But she could have had the husband anyway," objected Lupin. "I mean it was she whom he wanted to marry originally, and as for the money, Duds said that Flo was only too anxious to go halves."

"It seems," said Borden, with an apologetic glance towards Duds, "that Miss Harnet was always inordinately fond of money. In fact she was almost unbalanced on the subject. She would not have been content with half her sister's fortune when she saw the chance of getting the whole."

"You know," said Duds, "I keep on remembering things now when I look back, things which I never noticed at the time. You see, I always looked on Flo and Jo as the twins and thought of them together. I was quite young myself in the days when I used to stay there, so I didn't bother much one way or the other. I just thought 'There are the darling twins.' But I realize now that it was Flo of whom I was really fond. I took for granted that Jo was another Flo, though even then, if I had taken the trouble to think, I must have known that they were quite different, except as regards looks. Jo was always on the lookout for what you were going to give her. She used to wangle half-crowns out of one. I am afraid it rather amused me at the time. She would offer to get things for me at the village shop and keep the change and that sort of thing. I suppose she really was rather a horrid little girl, but Flo was so sweet it never occurred to me that Jo wasn't too. They were just the twins to me. I will never forget how lovely they looked the night of that Hunt Ball just before the war. I simply can't believe it. I must wake up and find that it is all a dream," and she began to cry.

"Don't let us talk about it any more," said Lupin, getting up and leading Duds from the room. "Poor Jo's mind was diseased, that is the only way to look at it. Perhaps she will be given another chance. We cannot tell."

The three men sat in silence for a few minutes, then Tommy said, "I can't think why she bothered about that blackmail business, if she were so soon to lay her hands on the whole of Flo's fortune."

"That was one of her slips," replied Borden. "I suppose her love of money was so great that she could not bear to miss any opportunity of making even a little. As a matter of fact, she pulled herself out of that rather well, pretending to repent at the last moment and so giving color to the theory that she had already decided to take her own life and wanted to leave the world on good terms with everybody. But of course Mrs. Lethbridge heard that snatch of conversation between her and Mr. Veazey on the Sunday evening and it made her think a bit. The less people think on these occasions, the better it is for the criminal."

"Her business with me was rather well done," admitted Tommy thoughtfully. "She had already done some spadework with Duds. They went for a walk together on Boxing Day and she told her how terribly unhappy she was. She did not go into any details but just left Duds with the impression that she had been very badly hurt and that was why she seemed so bitter. Duds said something about it to me that evening, Boxing Day evening, I mean, so I wasn't really so frightfully surprised when Jo let herself go, as she did that last night, though I felt rather awkward about it all, and frightfully sorry for the kid. Oh, and then Gordon had confided a bit to Duds at the Hunt Ball, how he and Flo were worried because Jo seemed so unhappy and how they couldn't think why she wouldn't take the money they had offered her. It was very clever, because when she told me that it was Gordon she was in love with, everything fell into place, and I saw why she was bitter with Flo and would not accept anything from her. Anyway, I fell for it! But if only I had gone straight to Duds we might have done something, and anyway . . ." he hesitated and looked rather embarrassed. He was thinking that even if they had not been able to save poor Flo, their own misunderstanding might have been prevented.

Borden mistook his embarrassment. "You have nothing to blame yourself for," he said. "People often do threaten to take their own lives when they are unhappy, but they very seldom carry out their threats."

"I suppose it was my evidence at the inquest that made them bring it in as suicide," said Tommy. "It did seem pretty conclusive, her scene with me, her making it up with Flo and with old Veazey and then the note that she left. And of course there were the hints of her sorrow that she and Gordon had both dropped to Duds. I was absolutely convinced myself at the time. Talking about the inquest, how did she get out of going to it? I mean I know the doctor gave her a certificate to say that she was suffering from shock, but how did she diddle him? Or do you think she really was suffering from shock? I suppose one would feel pretty wonky if one had just murdered one's sister. On the other hand, she must have been a pretty cold-blooded piece."

"There is no doubt that she was a superb actress," replied Borden, "but on the other hand I should be ready to bet that she took a pretty big dose of aspirin or something of that sort to slow down her pulse. She left nothing to chance. Of course the doctor would be expecting to find her pretty well knocked out at the presumed suicide of her twin sister but he would no doubt feel her pulse, in which case he would have been surprised to find it normal. I think I must have a word with him some time, just as a matter of interest."

"She was a clever woman," said Andrew, "but she made a big mistake when she agreed to see Lupin that morning."

"Yes, that was her chief blunder," agreed Borden.

"I suppose she did not realize that Lupin is not such a fool as she looks," said Tommy. Then, realizing that this might have been put better, he went rather red and murmured, "Sorry, Andrew, but you know what I mean."

Andrew burst out laughing. "Yes, I know what you mean," he replied. "No offense taken."

"I suppose," went on Tommy, "that Jo thought she was being rather clever and that she would easily put it across Lupin, and that she would lull any possible suspicions on the part of anyone else."

"She evidently had no idea of her sister's affection for Mr. Ferguson," said Borden. "She took for granted that she was in love with Pinhorn. It was unfortunate for her that she should have dwelt so much on her devotion for him and on their happiness together, because when later on Lady Lupin heard Ferguson's story it was difficult for her to reconcile the two versions. That, and the story of the pearl brooch, put very definite suspicions into her head."

"I remember those pearl brooches," said Tommy reminiscently. "Duds and I went together to choose them."

"The scheme was almost foolproof," remarked Andrew. "It seemed obvious to everyone that Jo had committed suicide owing to being disappointed in her love for Gordon Pinhorn. I suppose they would have gone abroad for several years and by the time that they returned it would never have entered into anyone's head that she was not Florence. But what about signatures? Was Jo's writing enough like Flo's to pass muster?"

"She had made sure of that. When the police went through her things they found a letter of Flo's with several copies attached. Jo had been practicing copying her handwriting for some time and was pretty well perfect at it. Of course the letter that she wrote to Mrs. Lethbridge at the time of her supposed suicide was in her own original hand, which was quite different."

"It was silly of her not to burn the copies."

"Yes. When I said she thought of everything, I was wrong. She made three bad mistakes—no, four. One, the blackmailing, which first put the idea of murder into your heads; two, the interview with Lady Lupin; three, leaving the evidence that she had been trying to imitate her sister's handwriting; and four, putting the note in the bedroom too soon. I suppose it never entered into her or Pinhorn's head when they arranged the letter and the bottle so carefully that anyone would go into the room that night. Miss Harnet might have realized that in encouraging Dumbleton as she had done, of course for the purpose of obtaining the diamorphine, she had raised in him certain hopes, and that he might have been expected to act in just the way he did. If only he had not been attacked by asthma at the critical moment, things might have been cleared up much sooner. However, I do not think anything could have saved Mrs. Pinhorn. When her grandfather left his fortune to her, he was signing her death warrant."

"I suppose so," agreed Tommy. "But you know all this does go to show that however clever you are, it is a pretty hopeless job trying to commit a crime. I mean you are bound to slip up somewhere and get found out, so it is hardly worth while trying. All right, Andrew, I know what you are going to say."

"Then you can take it as said."

"Of course," admitted Tommy, grudgingly, "Gordon was clever up to a point. I never cared for him but I should not have put him down as a criminal."

"He must have been a good actor," agreed Borden. "But he had not got the nerve for crime. He lost his head entirely at the critical moment. Of course, according to his story he took no part in the actual murder, but he was undoubtedly an accessory after the fact and connived at it in every way from the time he married Mrs. Pinhorn, Or rather from the time Miss Harnet first introduced him to her or arranged for them to meet as she undoubtedly did."

"He encouraged the woman he loved to commit a murder," said Andrew. "I should be inclined to say that he was guilty of a double murder."

"According to him, Miss Harnet gave her sister a drugged drink while they were talking together in Mrs. Pinhorn's room that night. Then, while she was unconscious, she injected more diamorphine by means of a hypodermic syringe. After which she undressed her and dressed her up again in her own clothes, a Spanish fancy dress I understand, doing her hair and even painting her face." Hardened detective as he was, Borden gave a shudder. "That woman must have had nerves of steel," he declared.

"Of course it was the hair and the makeup that made them look so different," reflected Tommy. "I mean Jo had her hair done high on her head and it made her look taller and her face longer and she used more makeup and stuff. And Flo had her hair parted in the middle and brushed very smooth, so that her face looked rounder. All the same, if I had seen Jo I don't think I would have mistaken her for Flo, whatever she had done to herself."

"That was why she was so careful not to see you or your wife," explained Borden.

"Yes, of course. But what about the hypodermic? Why didn't they find a mark at the post mortem?"

"It would be a very tiny mark and they would not be looking for anything of the sort," replied Borden. "They found diamorphine in the stomach. She had taken some by mouth, you remember. It all seemed straightforward enough without looking for marks."

"I was afraid they would have an exhumation or something grim," remarked Tommy.

"It wasn't necessary. The body at Southampton was identified beyond doubt as Miss Harnet's. Apart from Mrs. Lethbridge and Mr. Ferguson, you remember they called the dentist who had attended both the sisters since they were children. There was also Mr. Pinhorn's confession that the body at Fordham was his wife's."

"I suppose he watched Jo during the whole performance and handed her the things as she wanted them," said Tommy. "One would not have believed there could have been a creature like that in the world. Then he carried her back to her room—Jo's room rather—and arranged her on the bed. That was when Sandy saw him coming out. I think I am going to be sick. Sorry."

Andrew produced half a bottle of whisky that he had been keeping in case of need. This seemed to be the moment for it. The thought of that cold-blooded murder, the object mere gain of money, with no excuse of passion or revenge, made all three men feel definitely ill.

"Well," remarked Tommy, at length, "one good thing is, I don't think Henry will go about visiting any more girls' bedrooms in the middle of the night. This ought to have learned him for good and all."

"If it hadn't been for you ringing up from Denham or wherever it was," said Borden, "we would never have caught them. It would have been very difficult for Mrs. Lethbridge or Mr. Ferguson to have done anything, even after Pinhorn bolted, if I hadn't managed to got a plain-clothes man put on to watch out for them."

"I as near as anything didn't ring you up," confessed Tommy. "I was pretty fed up with the whole thing. They dropped me at a village close to Denham crossroads and it was as dark as hell—sorry, Andrew—and the pubs were shut. So was the post office. I found the girl from there having her tea with her young man and her aunt at the vicar-age. That was a queer do if you like," he went on, forgetting the trag-edy for a moment. "The vicar welcomed me like a long lost son, and I was so thankful to be warm and to have something to eat and drink that I didn't realize till too late that he had mistaken me for a fellow with religious doubts. I had just grasped it, and was trying to think up a doubt, when the real fellow burst in, and of course I had eaten all his toast."

"Did he mind?"

"No, I must say he took it awfully well. We all laughed quite a lot and the parson produced some beer. We had rather an amusing time. You must meet him some day, Andrew."

"The one with the doubts?" asked Andrew, apprehensively.

"No, the parson," replied Tommy. "You really would like him a lot. As a matter of fact 'Doubts' wasn't so bad as you would expect. He took me to the station on the back of his motor bicycle."

Lupin came back into the room. "I have settled Duds down with some aspirin," she said. "Poor darling. I am afraid it will be some time before she is herself again."

"I don't think she will ever get over it," said Tommy, gloomily. "She thought the world of those two. She was so fond of them as kids.

Of course she has always been frightfully keen on kids."

"Do you know, Tommy, not that it is any business of mine, and I expect you will think it is the most awful nerve, my suggesting it, but if I were you, I mean her feeling as she does about children, well I can't help feeling that if I hadn't got Peter and Jill, I should have adopted some. There is something about children in a house that stops one brooding. I say, what is that ghastly noise?"

"Our offspring, darling," replied Andrew. "As you so rightly observe, children do stop one from brooding."

"I say, that is rather an idea, Loops. I wonder whether Duds would like it. The place rather calls out for children in a way."

"Blow!" exclaimed Lupin, as she picked up the telephone receiver. "Hullo. Yes, it is Lady Lupin speaking. What? Oh, Mrs. Stuart can't address the Mothers' Union on Monday. Oh dear, I suppose I shall have to find someone else. As a matter of fact I have a friend staying with me who would be very good if only I can persuade her to do it, a Mrs. Lethbridge. Yes, I will do my best. Well, that's that," she remarked, putting back the receiver.

THE END

This is the fourth book in the Lady Lupin quartet. The other three—*Who Killed the Curate?* (0-915230-44-5, $14.00), *The Mystery at Orchard House* (0-915230-54-2, $14.95) and *Penelope Passes or Why Did She Die?* (0-915230-61.5, $14.95)—are all available and may be purchased from the same bookseller who sold you *Dancing With Death*. A catalog of other Rue Morgue Press vintage mysteries follows.

About The Rue Morgue Press

The Rue Morgue vintage mystery line is designed to bring back into print those books that were favorites of readers between the turn of the century and the 1960s. The editors welcome suggests for reprints. To receive our catalog or make suggestions, write The Rue Morgue Press, P.O. Box 4119, Boulder, Colorado (1-800-699-6214).

Catalog of Rue Morgue Press titles
as of January 2004

Titles are listed by author. All books are quality trade paperbacks measuring 9 by 6 inches, usually with full-color covers and printed on paper designed not to yellow or deteriorate. These are permanent books.

Joanna Cannan. The books by this English writer are among our most popular titles. Modern reviewers favorably compared our two Cannan reprints with the best books of the Golden Age of detective fiction. "Worthy of being discussed in the same breath with an Agatha Christie or a Josephine Tey."—Sally Fellows, *Mystery News.* "First-rate Golden Age detection with a likeable detective, a complex and believable murderer, and a level of style and craft that bears comparison with Sayers, Allingham, and Marsh."—Jon L. Breen, *Ellery Queen's Mystery Magazine.* Set in the late 1930s in a village that was a fictionalized version of Oxfordshire, both titles feature young Scotland Yard inspector Guy Northeast. *They Rang Up the Police* (0-915230-27-5, $14.00) and *Death at The Dog* (0-915230-23-2, $14.00).

Glyn Carr. The author is really Showell Styles, one of the foremost English mountain climbers of his era as well as one of that sport's most celebrated historians. Carr turned to crime fiction when he realized that mountains provided a ideal setting for committing murders. The 15 books featuring Shakespearean actor Abercrombie "Filthy" Lewker are set on peaks scattered around the globe, although the author returned again and again to his favorite climbs in Wales, where his first mystery, published in 1951, *Death on Milestone Buttress* (0-915230-

29-1, $14.00), is set. Lewker is a marvelous Falstaffian character whose exploits have been praised by such discerning critics as Jacques Barzun and Wendell Hertig Taylor in *A Catalogue of Crime*.

Torrey Chanslor. *Our First Murder* (0-915230-50-X, $14.95). When a headless corpse is discovered in a Manhattan theatrical lodging house, who better to call in than the Beagle sisters? Sixty-five-year-old Amanda employs good old East Biddicut common sense to run the agency, while her younger sister Lutie prowls the streets and nightclubs of 1940 Manhattan looking for clues. It's their first murder case since inheriting the Beagle Private Detective Agency from their older brother, but you'd never know the sisters had spent all of their lives knitting and tending to their garden in a small, sleepy upstate New York town. Lutie is a real charmer, who learned her craft by reading scores of lurid detective novels borrowed from the East Biddicut Circulating Library. With her younger cousin Marthy in tow, Lutie is totally at ease as she questions suspects and orders vintage champagne. Of course, if trouble pops up, there's always that pearl-handled revolver tucked away in her purse. *Our First Murder* is a charming hybrid of the private eye, traditional, and cozy mystery, written in 1940 by a woman who earned two Caldecott nominations for her illustrations of children's books. *Our Second Murder* will be published early in 2004.

Clyde B. Clason. Clason has been praised not only for his elaborate plots and skillful use of the locked room gambit but also for his scholarship. He may be one of the few mystery authors—and no doubt the first—to provide a full bibliography of his sources. *The Man from Tibet* (0-915230-17-8, $14.00) is one of his best (selected in 2001 in *The History of Mystery* as one of the 25 great amateur detective novels of all time) and highly recommended by the dean of locked room mystery scholars, Robert Adey, as "highly original." It's also one of the first popular novels to make use of Tibetan culture. *Murder Gone Minoan* (0-915230-60-7, $14.95) is set on a channel island off the coast of Southern California where a Greek department store magnate has recreated a Minoan palace.

Joan Coggin. *Who Killed the Curate?* Meet Lady Lupin Lorrimer Hastings, the young, lovely, scatterbrained and kindhearted daughter of an earl, now the newlywed wife of the vicar of St. Marks Parish in Glanville, Sussex. When it comes to matters clerical, she literally doesn't know Jews from Jesuits and she's hopelessly at sea at meetings of the Mothers' Union, Girl Guides, or Temperance Society, but she's determined to make husband Andrew proud of her—or, at least, not to embarrass him too badly. So when Andrew's curate is poisoned, Lady Lupin enlists the help of her old society pals, Duds and Tommy Lethbridge, as well as Andrew's nephew, a British secret service agent, to get at the truth. Lupin refuses to believe Diana Lloyd, the 38-year-old author of children's and detective stories, could have done the deed, and casts her net out over the other parishioners. All the suspects seem so nice, much more so than the victim, and Lupin announces she'll help the killer escape if only he or she confesses. Set at Christmas 1937 and first published in England in 1944, this is the first American appearance of *Who Killed the Curate?* "Marvelous."—*Deadly Pleasures.* "A complete delight."—*Reviewing the Evidence.* (0-915230-44-5, $14.00). The comic antics continue unabated in *The Mystery at Orchard House* (0-915230-54-2, $14.95), *Penelope Passes or Why Did She Die?* (0-915230-61-5, $14.95), and *Dancing with Death* (0-915230-62-3, $14.95).

Manning Coles. The two English writers who collaborated as Coles are best known for those witty spy novels featuring Tommy Hambledon, but they also wrote four delightful—and funny—ghost novels. *The Far Traveller* (0-915230-35-6, $14.00) is a stand-alone novel in which a film company unknowingly hires the ghost of a long-dead German graf to play himself in a movie. "I laughed until I hurt. I liked it so much, I went back to page 1 and read it a second time."—Peggy Itzen, *Cozies, Capers & Crimes.* The other three books feature two cousins, one English, one American, and their spectral pet monkey who got a little drunk and tried to stop—futilely and fatally—a German advance outside a small French village during the 1870 Franco-Prussian War. Flash forward to the 1950s where this comic trio of friendly ghosts rematerialize to aid relatives in danger in *Brief Candles* (0-915230-24-0, 156 pages, $14.00), *Happy Returns* (0-915230-

31-3, $14.00) and *Come and Go* (0-915230-34-8, $14.00).

Norbert Davis. There have been a lot of dogs in mystery fiction, from Baynard Kendrick's guide dog to Virginia Lanier's bloodhounds, but there's never been one quite like Carstairs. Doan, a short, chubby Los Angeles private eye, won Carstairs in a crap game, but there never is any question as to who the boss is in this relationship. Carstairs isn't just any Great Dane. He is so big that Doan figures he really ought to be considered another species. He scorns baby talk and belly rubs—unless administered by a pretty girl—and growls whenever Doan has a drink. His full name is Dougal's Laird Carstairs and as a sleuth he rarely barks up the wrong tree. He's down in Mexico with Doan, ostensibly to convince a missing fugitive that he would do well to stay put, in *The Mouse in the Mountain* (0-915230-41-0, $14.00), first published in 1943 and followed by two other Doan and Carstairs novels. A staff pick at The Sleuth of Baker Street in Toronto, Murder by the Book in Houston and The Poisoned Pen in Scottsdale. Four star review in *Romantic Times*. "A laugh a minute romp…hilarious dialogue and descriptions…utterly engaging, downright fun read…fetch this one! Highly recommended."—Michele A. Reed, *I Love a Mystery*. "Deft, charming…unique…one of my top ten all time favorite novels."—Ed Gorman, *Mystery Scene*. The second book, *Sally's in the Alley* (0-915230-46-1, $14.00), was equally well-received. *Publishers Weekly*: "Norbert Davis committed suicide in 1949, but his incomparable crime-fighting duo, Doan, the tippling private eye, and Carstairs, the huge and preternaturally clever Great Dane, march on in a re-release of the 1943 *Sally's in the Alley*. Doan's on a government-sponsored mission to find an ore deposit in the Mojave Desert…in an old-fashioned romp that matches its bloody crimes with belly laughs." The editor of *Mystery Scene* chimed in: "I love Craig Rice. Davis is her equal." "The funniest P.I. novel ever written."—*The Drood Review*. The raves continued for final book in the trilogy, *Oh, Murderer Mine* (0-915230-57-7, $14.00). "He touches the hardboiled markers but manages to run amok in a genre known for confinement…This book is just plain funny."—Ed Lin, *Forbes.com*.

Elizabeth Dean. In Emma Marsh Dean created one of the first independent female sleuths in the genre. Written in the screwball style of the 1930s, the Marsh books were described in a review in *Deadly Pleasures* by award-winning mystery writer Sujata Massey as a series that "froths over with the same effervescent humor as the best Hepburn-Grant films." *Murder is a Serious Business* (0-915230-28-3, $14.95), is set in a Boston antique store just as the Great Depression is drawing to a close. *Murder a Mile High* (0-915230-39-9, $14.00) moves to the Central City Opera House in the Colorado mountains, where Emma has been summoned by an old chum, the opera's reigning diva. Emma not only has to find a murderer, she may also have to catch a Nazi spy. "Fascinating."—*Romantic Times.*

Constance & Gwenyth Little. These two Australian-born sisters from New Jersey have developed almost a cult following among mystery readers. Critic Diane Plumley, writing in *Dastardly Deeds*, called their 21 mysteries "celluloid comedy written on paper." Each book, published between 1938 and 1953, was a stand-alone, but there was no mistaking a Little heroine. She hated housework, wasn't averse to a little gold-digging (so long as she called the shots), and couldn't help antagonizing cops and potential beaux. The Rue Morgue Press intends to reprint all of their books. Currently available: *The Black Thumb* (0-915230-48-8, $14.00), *The Black Coat* (0-915230-40-2, $14.00), *Black Corridors* (0-915230-33-X, $14.00), *The Black Gloves* (0-915230-20-8, $14.00), *Black-Headed Pins* (0-915230-25-9, $14.00), *The Black Honeymoon* (0-915230-21-6, $14.00), *The Black Paw* (0-915230-37-2, $14.00), *The Black Stocking* (0-915230-30-5, $14.00), *Great Black Kanba* (0-915230-22-4, $14.00), *The Grey Mist Murders* (0-915230-26-7, $14.00), *The Black Eye* (0-915230-45-3, $14.00), *The Black Shrouds* (0-915230-52-6, $14.00), and *The Black Rustle* (0-915230-58-5, $14.00).

Marlys Millhiser. Our only non-vintage mystery, *The Mirror* (0-915230-15-1, $17.95) is our all-time bestselling book, now in a seventh printing. How could you not be intrigued by a novel in which "you find the main character marrying her own grandfather and giving birth to her own mother," as one reviewer put it of this supernatural, time-travel (sort of) piece of wonderful make-believe set both in the mountains above Boulder, Colorado, at the turn of the century and in the city itself in 1978. Internet book services list scores of rave reviews from readers who often call it the "best book I've ever read."

James Norman. The marvelously titled *Murder, Chop Chop* (0-915230-16-X, $13.00) is a wonderful example of the eccentric detective novel. "The book has the butter-wouldn't-melt-in-his-mouth cool of Rick in *Casablanca.*"—*The Rocky Mountain News*. "Amuses the reader no end."—*Mystery News*. "This long out-of-print masterpiece is intricately plotted, full of eccentric characters and very humorous indeed. Highly recommended."—*Mysteries by Mail*. Meet Gimiendo Hernandez Quinto, a gigantic Mexican who once rode with Pancho Villa and who now trains *guerrilleros* for the Nationalist Chinese government when he isn't solving murders. At his side is a beautiful Eurasian known as Mountain of Virtue, a woman as dangerous to men as she is irresistible. First published in 1942.

Sheila Pim. *Ellery Queen's Mystery Magazine* said of these wonderful Irish village mysteries that Pim "depicts with style and humor everyday life." *Booklist* said they were in "the best tradition of Agatha Christie." Beekeeper Edward Gildea uses his knowledge of bees and plants to good use in *A Hive of Suspects* (0-915230-38-0, $14.00). *Creeping Venom* (0-915230-42-9, $14.00) blends politics and religion into a deadly mixture. *A Brush with Death* (0-915230-49-6, $14.00) grafts a clever art scam onto the stem of a gardening mystery.

Craig Rice. *Home Sweet Homicide.* This marvelously funny and utterly charming tale (set in 1942 and first published in 1944) of three children who "help" their widowed mystery writer mother solve a real-life murder and nab a handsome cop boyfriend along the way made just about every list of the best mysteries for the first half of the 20th century, including the Haycraft-Queen Cornerstone list (probably the most prestigious honor roll in the history of crime fiction), James Sandoe's *Reader's Guide to Crime,* and Melvyn Barnes' *Murder in Print*. Rice was of course best known for her screwball mystery comedies featuring Chicago criminal attorney John J. Malone. *Home Sweet Homicide* is a delightful cozy mystery partially based on Rice's own home life. Rice, the first mystery writer to appear on the cover of *Time*, died in 1957 at the age of 49. 0-915230-53-4, $14.95

Charlotte Murray Russell. Spinster sleuth Jane Amanda Edwards tangles with a murderer and Nazi spies in *The Message of the Mute Dog* (0-915230-43-7, $14.00), a culinary cozy set just before Pearl Harbor. "Perhaps the mother of today's cozy."—*The Mystery Reader*.

Sarsfield, Maureen. These two mysteries featuring Inspector Lane Parry of Scotland Yard are among our most popular books. Both are set in Sussex. *Murder at Shots Hall* (0-915230-55-8, $14.95) features Flikka Ashley, a thirtyish sculptor with a past she would prefer remain hidden. It was originally published as *Green December Fills the Graveyard* in 1945. Parry is back in Sussex, trapped by a blizzard at a country hotel where a war hero has been pushed out of a window to his death in *Murder at Beechlands* (0-915230-56-9, $14.95). First published in 1948 in England as *A Party for None* and in the U.S. as *A Party for Lawty*. The owner of Houston's Murder by the Book called these two books the best publications from The Rue Morgue Press.

Juanita Sheridan. Sheridan was one of the most colorful figures in the history of detective fiction, as you can see from the introduction to *The Chinese Chop* (0-915230-32-1, 155 pages, $14.00). Her books are equally colorful, as well as examples of how mysteries with female protagonists began changing after World War II. The postwar housing crunch finds Janice Cameron, newly arrived in New York City from Hawaii, without a place to live until she answers an ad for a roommate. It turns out the advertiser is an acquaintance from Hawaii, Lily Wu. First published in 1949, this ground-breaking book was the first of four to feature Lily and be told by her Watson, Janice, a first-time novelist. "Highly recommended."—*I Love a Mystery*. "Puts to lie the common misconception that strong, self-reliant, non-spinster-or-comic sleuths didn't appear on the scene until the 1970s."—*Ellery Queen's Mystery Magazine*. The first book in the series to be set in Hawaii is *The Kahuna Killer* (0-915230-47-X, $14.00). " Originally published five decades ago (though it doesn't feel like it), this detective story featuring charming Chinese sleuth Lily Wu has the friends and foster sisters investigating mysterious events—blood on an ancient altar, pagan rites, and the appearance of a kahuna (a witch doctor)—and the death of a sultry hula girl in 1950s Oahu."—*Publishers Weekly*. Third in the series is *The Mamo Murders* (0915230-51-8, $14.00), set on a Maui cattle ranch. The final book in the quartet, *The Waikiki Widow* (0-915230-59-3, $14.00) is set in Honolulu tea industry.